The Huntrodds Coincidences

JP Major

Published by JP Major, 2021.

THE HUNTRODDS COINCIDENCES

First edition. April 20, 2021.

Written by JP Major.

Table of Contents

The Huntrodds Coincidences...1

Note from the author...3

Chapter 1 | Cars: 0; The Police: 1 5

Chapter 2 | The caravan.. 13

Chapter 3 | The Groom and his Best Man 15

Chapter 4 | One golf course/two collections 33

Chapter 5 | Bad Karma and Screaming shouldn't mix 37

Chapter 6 | Mr and Mrs Huntrodds................................. 41

Chapter 7 | Heaven can wait 63

Chapter 8 | Blue hats and Brown coats 65

Chapter 9 | All roads lead everyone to Whitby..............73

Chapter 10 | More blue hats and brown coats................ 75

Chapter 11 | Soccer and Stones in Shropshire 87

Chapter 12 | Two trains; Two houses; Two orphans 103

Chapter 13 | Two pagers/One aroma 109

Chapter 14 | Spike's box set and Sue's book club 115

Chapter 15 | Magpies always come in pairs 127

Chapter 16 | A big yellow taxi nearly took this girl away........129

Chapter 17 | Accountants and Goffers: hiding in the Bushes, with another Loraine 133

Chapter 18 | A young addict dies when budgets are tight 147

Chapter 19 | My first yellow taxi.................................... 161

Chapter 20 | The Rookie and crate of salmon............. 169

Chapter 21 | The Agent in the High Street 177

Chapter 22 | Titan on line meets Agent in the High Street... 185

Chapter 23 | My third secret venue 191

Chapter 24 | Why was his caravan there today? 195

Chapter 25 | What can you see out of a friend's bedroom window... 199

Chapter 26 | Two tartan bags..215

Chapter 27 | Lucky that caravan's here............................223

Chapter 28 | The driving gloves were no coincidence..............239
Chapter 29 | One blue hat, one brown coat, one green hat, one red car..243
THE END...249

For Jean. During the course of creating this opus, I often felt I was overcomplicating the story. But then I figured that together we have been *losing the plot* for over thirty years – and that hasn't worked out so bad, so just kept on going. I wouldn't have had it any other way. Here's to our next three decades.

And to James, without whom this lockdown effort would have remained little more than a bland 156 page *Word* document. I only hope that people don't think too unkindly of him for it.

Note from the author

I started work on these lockdown ramblings on 17 May 2020. The Covid virus had reached the UK a few months earlier and I, like most right minded citizens, was dutifully following the government's instructions and keeping my front door closed to the world outside. I'd organised the delivery of a daily newspaper and had tried to settle into a routine which centred on reading it from cover to cover – something I was fortunate enough to be able to do in our back garden. But there are just so many times one can fail to complete the *Guardian* crossword without looking for different distractions and one day I found myself drawn to an article on how to write a book; or more specifically, how a number of published authors and one whose efforts had yet to see the light of print advised approaching the task.

The person without a *Best Selling* tag to his name was Richard Osman. His *The Thursday Murder Club* has since become a huge hit, but at the time it was nothing more than words on a page that no one had seen. So, ignoring the pearls of wisdom offered by the likes of Margaret Atwood and Iain Rankin (even though I have drunk with the latter on a couple of occasions in Edinburgh's Oxford Bar and almost consider him as a mate) I thought - who better to listen to than the co-host of a programme called *Pointless*.

RO's advice was to sit down for two hours every day; try to get about 500 words down before you allow yourself to stand up; and don't edit as you go along. Within a month he said, the figure showing in the bottom left hand corner of your laptop's screen should be in the region of 20,000 – which, for him had proved to be a sort of springboard.

True to Xander's sidekick's formula, I reached 20,011 on 18 June. My work rate/output halved over the following months in line with the changes in lockdown procedures, but I stayed with it and by November I had topped 60,000 (which apparently is the minimum number of words you need to legitimately be able to call your book, *a book*).

Three thorough read throughs prompted a great number of edits and by March 2021 I had just under 75,000 words on 150 pages in a *Word* document – and what I considered to be a completed story.

In what can only be described as total self-indulgence, I paid £59 for a professional designer to put some colour and spice onto the cover and, within grasp of a year to the day since first reading Mr Osman's guidance, *The Huntrodds Coincidences* was finished and in the form of something I could stroke, put onto my book shelf and be able to flick through with a touch of achievement and pride.

JP Major

14 May 2021

Chapter 1
Cars: 0; The Police: 1

MAN

If there isn't a parking space out front, or I can't see my car from the window, we're eating somewhere else (Jay Leno)

Arrival Day started out a bit shitty.

I'd spent most of the night staring out of the bedroom window, willing my car to appear. It had been left at the golf course the day before as planned and now, sweating on its safe return, it seemed the only productive thing I could think of doing was to scan up and down the quiet and deserted road hoping to spot some familiar approaching headlights. I'd also hoped to catch sight of the driver. We had carried out all our previous transactions, for want of a better word, from a distance: the only contact we'd ever had was by phone. This time though the stakes were a great deal higher, and I felt that any downside our paths crossing might bring were worth the risks.

My wife had gone to London to check on her two rented properties leaving me alone for the night. I had tried to stay awake and upright, setting up camp sitting on her sewing chair with my chin in my hands and my elbows resting on the sill. I realised that plan must have failed quite early on when I was jolted into consciousness by the front doorbell.

I swayed downstairs, rubbing my raw elbows and wondering who on earth might visit at such an early hour. The opaque sheet of flying bees with which my wife had covered the door's dull frosted glass distorted the caller's face, but the iconic Custodian helmet, long since worn by English Bobbies on the beat, gave the game away. The police, or rather, a single policeman, had come to call. I opened the door and standing on the mat was Police Constable 42: the number both on his warrant card and lapels. Now I had no idea what he was about to ask me, although I'd have thought if anyone could come up with the answer to any question in the universe, it would have been a police officer whose number was 42. However, it seemed he needed to speak with me anyway, so I let him into the hallway.

As he entered the house, my view onto the drive that he'd been blocking cleared. There was still no car, but this was not the time to be sharing that information with PC 42.

He started speaking, but I was barely listening. I think he was apologising for the early hour. The clock on the wall showed it was a quarter past six but, he explained, as he was about to come off shift from night duty it was not quite so crack of dawn for him and he'd hoped to speak with me before returning to the station.

He jolted me back from the thoughts of my carless drive with reports of a peeping Tom in one of the houses overlooking the rear gardens in my street. Had I seen anything? I told him, no. He asked if it was possible for me to see into the bedrooms of these buildings from my house. "Only when I stand on top of the wardrobe with a pair of binoculars", I offered. He didn't find that quite as funny as I'd hoped, but it seemed to be the moment that led him to decide I was unlikely to be the best source to help him crack this particular case, whatever case it was, as he half saluted, said, "'Evenin' all" (if only he really had) and left.

THE HUNTRODDS COINCIDENCES

My absent car created problems on so many levels, and I don't just mean it scuppered the planned shopping trip (although I had run out of milk and black tea is never the right way to start a day). There were goods to check, payments to be made, and merchandise to be dispersed. The lack of my vehicle threw all of that up into the air.

This would take some thinking about. There were obviously some calls I'd need to make, but first I rang Seckie to get her onto the case. I started, ever so calmly, outlining what had happened over the past 24 hours, but became aware, as the timeline of my tale approached the present moment, that my voice had crept up a semitone or two and my measured summarisation had segued into a babbling of random words: car, golf clubs, bobby's hats, binoculars. I seemed to recover from this temporary departure from reality and mumbled something along the lines that this needed to be managed carefully.

Until then, she had met my ramblings with silence, but on this first pause for breath she chipped in saying, with, I sensed, more than a modicum of exasperation, "I don't need *you* to tell me that. Of course it will have to be dealt with delicately. I know the score. Anyway", she said before putting down the phone, "this is unlike you to panic".

Now I didn't need *her* to tell *me* that, but this was the first time in over 18 months that this latest venture of mine had caused so much as a loss of appetite, let alone valuable goods AND a whole bloody car.

Having put her on notice, I left her to wait by her phone while I made the call that would set the hares (or whatever the equivalent on the continent is) running.

There were four numbers to choose from. Number one was for a problem with the setup. Number two came into play if there was a dispute with the delivery. The third was for issues with the merchandise and the fourth for anything relating to payment.

First things first. One and three were for my exclusive use. If, for any reason, I couldn't get the container to the required point at the required time, I'd call the first number. The third option would come into play if, following a successful delivery, there was anything wrong with the merchandise that might affect my payment. Given the container for my package (in this instance, my car) was not where it should have been (my driveway), by the required time (now), I was thinking something has gone pretty wrong. Now for sure, that's a huge issue and one that's never happened before, but while this was, indeed, very uncharted territory, right then that wasn't the thing most worrying me.

My secretary had confirmed she'd left the car at the designated location last night, so there was no need for *phone number one* from my end. Of course, had something occurred preventing them from being able to make the drop my telephone would have rung off its cradle long ago. The phone had remained silent so clearly no one had felt the need to dial the second number.

Moments after punching the final digit of option three on the face of my phone, my call connected and my suspicions were confirmed. There was no preamble, no passwords or mother's maiden names to give. The security systems that had been put in place when we first started this liaison negated the need for such basic measures. The connection was as secure as if the two of us had been in the same hermetically sealed room as each other.

For added (or, as I felt, dramatic and over the top) insurance, there were only certain phrases either party were permitted to use and any deviation would, at the very least, trigger alarm and caution. Each possible scenario for each stage of the process had been considered and reduced down to the bare basics, designed to ascertain, first, foremost and with the minimum amount of debate or discussion, what problem had occurred and where in the chain that problem was currently sitting. Was the issue at their end, on my doorstep or somewhere in the middle? The only possible reasons I would make this particular call was either that I didn't have the goods, or I had them and didn't like what I had. Anything outside of this binary choice would fall into the purview of telephone numbers one, two or four.

The voice at the other end of the line simply said, "Goods delivered as planned. Confirm receipt."

Bugger. I had clearly hoped to bat the ball well and truly into someone else's court, but it seems that someone was ahead of me and had already hit the damn thing back past me.

"No receipt" were the only two words the script permitted me to say. Any expansion or explanation would have resulted in disconnection. As it happened, as soon as I'd mentioned the second of these two words, that's exactly what did happen. The line just went dead. I knew wheels were now being put in motion and that my role in all this was just to wait.

Half an hour later, Seckie called back. The meet was to be tomorrow, in Whitby.

Whitby.

What on earth was their fixation with the eastern section of our coastline? Perhaps they could see its outline with a powerful telescope and felt comforted by being able, albeit only theoretically, to keep an eye on things? Anyway, while this little seaside town on the North Sea of England's largest county had been their location of choice once before, there had been so many others, (Skegness, Sunderland and a number of God forsaken stuck in the 19th century places along this bleak edge of the country), that predicting the next venue was always impossible.

Anyway, why the delay? I was already on the point of freaking out and now I had another 24 hours in which to freak further. Had I been thinking clearly, I probably might have guessed this is how they would play things. They would want to make absolutely sure what had taken place, who was saying what, or even who might be saying one thing, but meaning something totally different. In short, there were facts to be assessed, stories to be checked, stories to be reassessed and facts to be rechecked before they started on the serious issue of what the hell had happened.

Of course this meant that I too had this modicum of space to mull things over but, try as I might to make my own sense of it all, I couldn't seem to get off first base. The only thing I had to go on was that my car was missing, which was slightly ironic, as its absence sort of meant I didn't actually have anything to go anywhere on. In any event, I needed to hear The Postman's side of the story before I'd be able to work anything out.

Despite having literally just spoken with him, any practical details relating to our relationship were always dealt with through a third party; in this case, my secretary. She would also have to deal with the more fundamental problem of how I was going to get to my remote destination without a vehicle. Hiring a car would leave too many traces, so we'd need to suss out the convoluted route of public transport the on-going effects of Beaching's past efforts would force me to take.

For the second time this morning the doorbell took me by surprise and made me realise I'd not really been listening to what my Secretary had been saying down the other end of the phone.

I could see through the bees that PC 42 had returned. What on earth could he want this time? And were these appearances really only being prompted by an unrelated issue – or was this all something more than just a coincidence. I slammed the phone down, cutting Seckie off mid flow, and opened the door to see what Her Majesty's finest had forgotten. "Just one thing", he said. "I meant to leave you with my direct line and contact details, just in case anything relevant springs to mind". I took his card and bade him farewell, completely failing to stop myself motioning a half salute as he plodded down the empty drive.

"If anything springs to mind". The only thing that had sprung to my mind was that I didn't have all the details of the meeting that Seckie had been wittering on about. I tried to ring her back, but there was no reply. I couldn't imagine where on earth she might have disappeared to, but I couldn't waste any more time on that now. There was much to prepare, and I'd call her later. Things certainly weren't panning out quite as they should have done. I didn't really have a clue what had happened; nor what was going to happen. In fact, at that moment, the only thing I had any certainty about was what I'd be having for lunch tomorrow.

Chapter 2
The caravan

SEVEN
Be patient with your neighbour: he may move or, better still, face
misfortune (Egyptian proverb)

I'd hardly slept a wink the night before last, and this evening was
panning out to be pretty similar. Tonight, however, instead of just
tossing, turning and annoying my wife, I thought I'd try a more
traditional remedy: whisky and hot milk.

Last night's exploits had seen me relegated to the spare room at
the front of the house so, with my tumbler and mug in hand I sat
at the window watching the world go by and willing myself some
kip. Of course, at three o'clock in the morning, very little of the
world is opting to wander by in any noticeable form, so I was reduced
to staring out into, pretty much nothingness. However, as my eyes
adjusted to the late night light it seemed I was not the only one
struggling to snooze.

It took a moment of two until I was sure who it was: of course,
it was *him*. It was bound to be him. He'd plagued me in one way or
another from the day we'd moved into Number 7: take down that
bright green lamp on your porch – it shines across the street into

our lounge; are you really going to paint your front door *that* colour; if you must play *Andre Rieu's* music, keep it down; do you have to leave your bins out for so long after the rubbish has been collected; isn't it about time you fixed that dreadful grinding sound the garage door makes when opening and closing it; the grass strips outside our houses are for *everyone* – not for parking on, etc. etc. etc.

There was one time when I thought he was about to be neighbourly when he brought me over a cup of tea. I was having trouble manoeuvring our new caravan onto our drive, trying to avoid - amongst other things - his precious verges. I really was ready for a break and a bit of refreshment, but it was soon clear his offering was meant with heavy sarcasm rather than kindness and love.

How like him now, not even allowing me to suffer insomnia without taunting me from across the street.

I've been keeping the caravan around the corner at a friend's who has acres of land. I've a good mind to drive it back here – and churn up the damn grass while I'd doing it.

Chapter 3

The Groom and his Best Man

SECKIE

Stuck in the middle, with you (Gerry Rafferty)

The day started a little earlier than expected.

I'd arrived at the office at 6:00am. Ungodly, unearthly, un-anything else you could possibly think of, but it was Arrival Day and this is what I did on Arrival Day.

As far as I was concerned, yesterday had worked as planned. My job now was to wait for the call from my man that would trigger the next stage. When the phone rang it was immediately clear that things had gone some distance away from how he'd expected them to go. A next stage would still be triggered: just not the one he'd anticipated.

Looking back and thinking about how slick the operation has become of late, makes my early concerns about getting involved unfounded. I'd been with him for about a year. It started with me being a Person Friday (at least that was the term used in the politically correctly worded job description I'd applied for): making coffee, running errands, that kind of thing. But I was (still am!) pretty smart and within a matter of weeks I'd moved on to typing letters, and keeping the books, and accompanying him on a trip to

Belgium, and oh, yes - sleeping with him. I was (still am!) young, trim and bendy (which he liked). He was distinguished, funny, well off and unavailable (all of which, especially the last bit, I liked). His wife didn't understand him (which ones ever do?). Not that I cared, particularly at the outset. He was pretty bendy too.

We made sure the job and our flexible exploits were kept completely apart. And I mean, absolutely separate. When I woke up in that hotel room in Whitby after our first night together, my instinct was that this – whatever this was going to be - had to be kept away from the office. Without such a division, nothing could possibly be made to work. But I couldn't immediately see how we'd achieve that. He'd barely allowed so much as a cigarette paper to come between us from the moment we'd met in the bar the previous evening, to the moment on the bed a few seconds ago.

But it was soon clear he understood that too. All we both had to do was sort out the practical side of things.

I don't recall us consciously setting out to put together a plan of action, or our *Protocol* as we would playfully entitle it, to ensure the longevity of, well.......whatever it was we had suddenly found ourselves talking about developing. But the discussion over that first breakfast soon became just that. It was all a little exciting, very daring and extremely sexy – in a different, unbendy sort of way - as we began plotting where we would go from here. How would we contact each other: would there be coded messages on the end of a dictated letter? Where would we meet: surely it would not be an endless list of grotty motels? And how do we manage quality time together: there were only so many overnight business meetings we could go on without arousing suspicion from either his wife or our fellow workers.

We ruled out making using text or in fact any such means by phone or on a mobile straight away. There were just too many films of cheating husbands and wives (yes, OK and secretaries), where the entire plot is brought crumbling down to the ground by the wronged partner stumbling across an errant or unwise message. We settled on a pager system. There were probably more sophisticated alternatives we might have come up with, but with sophistication comes complexity. This way we could leave our prime method of communications lying around in plain sight, yet their detail could only be accessed by our own code and confirmatory PIN. And we restricted their use purely to us. There was no business, or even casual, "get me a pint of milk" allowed.

There would be some grotty motels involved while the passions were high, though, to be frank, during the opening stages of our liaison anywhere would do. But there were measures we could take to make things more pleasurable. The way the chocolate market had been developing easily justified an increase in the frequency of his quarterly European business trips. Making the solitary bag carrying journey I'd been on a couple of weeks ago a regular event seemed a pretty good idea too.

Of course what had started out as just sex (albeit quite contorted sex) would soon explode with passion and intensity into something far greater and with absolutely no warning what so ever. There was no nudge, nudge or wink that might have offered so much as a modest head's up: within a matter of weeks, we'd fallen in love. I knew he was smitten before he'd had even an inkling, but by the time it had dawned on him, it had become as clear as glass to us both.

During that initial breakfast though, any thoughts of love, or anything else that might have wandered in or out of my head were flushed away the moment I discovered that the man I'd just spent the night with, and with whom I seemed to have spent the last hour across the table from planning the next stage of my life, was a diamond smuggler.

Not that he came out with it quite like that. Looking back, there was much more of a gradual reveal to the revelation he was leading up to. I can't recall exactly what prompted it, but at some point between him puncturing the yoke on his poached egg and adding a blob of tomato ketchup to his plate, I became aware that he had started chatting about jewellery: necklaces, brooches and rings, that sort of thing. For my own part, I think I more or less packed up listening to what he was saying as I began imagining these things being draped all over me. Glinting images of these baubles merged in my head with pictures of our previous night's exploits. It would be fair to say, in that split moment, I was in a really great place. Suddenly I realised he had stopped talking and so attempted to refocus. Seemingly unaware of my brief reverie, he lent across the table, stroked my arm and asked if I wanted to add even more spice to the red hot chilli pepper situation we seemed to have just embarked on. My knee jerk reaction was to gag at such a cheesy culinary line but, I suppose, relieved he hadn't tried to guild that lily with talk of his etchings I instead played along and told him he should have worked out by now that my tastes were much more Madras than Biryani and so what a ridiculous question to ask. And that's how I became engaged, actually, maybe entangled is a more appropriate word, in *the business.*

He told me it was all about moving uncut Diamonds from A to B: from Botswana to Belgium. I resisted the urge to chip in and suggest that, given the geography, it might be better to think of moving the gems from B to B and let him continue.

The transport vehicle of choice was the STOL aircraft, able to Take-Off and Land, on Short runways, often on grassy plains well away from commercial airports. Once the diamonds were outside the confines of the mine, getting them to the Mediterranean coast was fairly easy. Of course, the perimeter security in Gaborone was extraordinary: the pit owners were funny that way and had invested hard earned (by the local miners) cash (pocketed by the proprietors) in state-of-the-art detection equipment. They also paid men and women to work undercover to sneak out people trying to sneak out the goods and bribed police chiefs to make sure they'd divert all possible resources to provide added protection for their merchandise. This force field certainly protected the immediate site and the immediate surroundings. But, as they say in NFL football, it's the first ten yards that are the hardest. If you can get a ball into safe hands over the top of the opposing defence line, then – not wishing to confuse two of America's national games but, the home run's a breeze.

I began to sense that the plot of an early Ian Fleming novel and lyric from one of Paul Simon's songs were about to be revealed as the inspiration for the unconventional diamond extractions. I only hoped they'd got the dialogue and lyrics the right way round because Simon's main literary dalliance was an unimaginative children's book called, *At The Zoo* and Fleming famously couldn't sing a note. Anyway, it seems that the actual ruse they eventually settled on was to play the odds.

There are only so many literal cracks and crevices that all the money and precautions in the world can cement over, and while their success rate thwarted around 95% of attempted thefts, a very juicy 5% of the proceeds of the continent's richest diamond mine was still getting through and the firm my man was now working with (for?) had somehow found a way to get hold of it.

Once the stones were over the top and outside the compound, the 4,000 miles between there and Mediterranean coast in Libya was an uncontested stroll in the desert. The chaos in this northern African country and in its mirror nation across the sea, Greece, whose border patrols were swamped trying to manage the continuous wave of economic and political migrants, if anything, aided the mission. As long as the boat, ship, submarine, canoe, surfboard or any other ocean faring means that wandered into

Hellenic waters weren't overloaded with people desperate to flee their homelands, you could pretty much sail onto their terra firma unmolested and offload whatever gear you'd brought with you.

There are several little, mainly UK, tourist locations on the Peloponnese region ideal for such landings. Most were sea side Shirley Valentine spots where daily sightings of strangers were commonplace. These were places where people one didn't know were expected rather than suspected. Renee and Costa's taverna in Stoupa is a perfect example: you could walk the fifty odd yards from the water's edge up the steps straight onto their patio, though there were many other choices equally good. All were close enough to Kalamata; a major city in the area with busy streets, great transport connections and confused authorities. In short, an ideal place for someone who has both goods, and business, to keep hidden.

So, Out of Africa: a fine title for a mundane film, but also the prime aim with regards to smuggling diamonds. Into Greece: still cinematically acceptable, but also, so far as the trade in stolen gems was concerned, no sweat. It was the journey from there that the problems were most likely to occur. The free trade arrangement operated within the European Union certainly made things easier than they might have been – and we [for I was soon to become one of the merry band] smugglers knew that. But the authorities aren't stupid, and they know that we know that. Their checks and balances were far more sophisticated than the tin pot resistance in Africa and getting past, or through, or over them had, of late, been getting more and more difficult.

Of course, we know that they know that we know that. The usual path for this sort of contraband was up through one of the Balkan countries and along some convoluted route before arriving in Belgium, or, more specifically, Antwerp. Or even more specifically, The Diamond Quarter. Once the goods had been delivered into the sanctity of the *Diamantkwartier*, all was well. But of late, the authorities had massively ramped up their interest in these later stages of our north-westerly journey with a view to clamp down hard on any valuables they found where they shouldn't have been. And they were becoming ever more successful in their efforts.

In this business, one expects to lose a few, but win quite a lot. When the Customs guys' success rates started to swap those expectation levels around – to their favour – it was time to look at options. And this, apparently, was where my guy had come in.

His legitimate business is very niche, very select, and really very profitable. I'm not sure how it was described on the paperwork in Companies House but, in short he imported fancy chocolates and pastries into the UK. Not that these were items you'd find on a pick and mix counter in *Poundland* or the high street shops. No, these were sweetmeats and confection for the gentry. His market was the posh hotels, the chic boutiques and the exclusive retail outlets. These businesses all had high value clients who would be wowed by the opulence of the goods on display and seemed keen to pay up irrespective of the price on the tag. And while his mark-up was big, his customers' mark-ups were even bigger. Everyone was happy, and he did his best to keep things that way.

He would regularly visit his buyers to make sure he kept them sweet and show off the latest extravagant (and overpriced) product that their clients "…..would have to see to believe". In the interests of maintaining equilibrium, he would balance those calls with trips to the Belgium suppliers (so they could keep him sweet!). His favoured method of travel to the continent was by train. He was actually on the first Eurostar, Waterloo to Paris, in 1994, and was immediately smitten. If a Eurostar service went within 150 miles of his destination, then no other options would even be considered. I knew from experience – and him constantly reminding me or anyone else who'd listen - the furthest you can travel north to south in Belgium is less than that so, whenever I was tasked with arranging a trip, the first ticket purchased would be for the six and a half-hour ride (he did all his paperwork on the train) from St Pancras to Antwerp. He worked with a select few businesses, some in the centre of the country in Braine-l'Alleud, some a little further west around Liege, but distance in such a small land, and one with a Grade A transport system to virtually anywhere from Antwerp, getting where he wanted to go was never a problem.

And nor was there any second thoughts from his hosts that they might do anything other than take him to Belgium's second city where they would wine, dine, entertain and keep him really sweet.

There was one occasion he was with his favourite supplier, a man he called Cup Cake. My face must have given away exactly what rushed through my mind the moment he told me this, because I remember how perfuse he was in stressing, many many times, that their relationship was purely business. Honestly. You can trust me.

Hmmmm.

Anyway, as usual, he was doing his best to be a fine *schmoozee* (no one who is trying to give you a good experience at their expense wants to feel anything other than that you've had the best time of your life) and it was no surprise that the afternoon business lunch had long since turned into an evening drinking session. Spirits were high and gibberish was being spoken. Cup Cake's brother had joined them. He was something to do with rough diamonds, not that my guy had the faintest idea what they were. Anyway, I'm guessing it was while CCs brother was explaining what he actually did that the notion of a "blingy" present for his wife cropped up.

I have no idea if she ever got the sparkly gift spoken of that night, but much of the rest of the talk started the aforementioned hares running. The next two trips to Antwerp came somewhat quicker and closer together than was the norm. Neither caused him to leave the city's centre and while both involved the long business lunches and

Cup Cake's sibling, Cup Cake's sibling's sibling was no longer in attendance.

During these visits he learnt that Antwerp's once flowing place in the diamond market was slowly ebbing away. The modern diamond centres no longer had the need for polished "trading centres" that no longer added any actual value. New York's strong retail market remained key, but polishing, sorting and jewellery manufacturing could be done almost as well, and certainly much cheaper, elsewhere. But Antwerp's infrastructure, expertise of workforce and geographically central location enabled it to maintain an active involvement in the market, albeit one that focused on rough diamonds. It was at this stage I learned that this was literally the "rough" rock prior to it being cut or processed into something his wife would want to wear on her [bony] little finger. This was what Choc Drop, as he had by now been named, was involved in. In fact, it was the core of the business he effectively ran on behalf of his father-in-law.

From what I gathered, CD's work exploits had always been above board. But that changed two or three years ago.

Times had suddenly gotten a little harder, margins a little tighter and money in extraordinarily short supply. With his business on the brink he'd gone to Brussels, spending the best part of a week trawling around the various banks, large and small, hoping for a miracle. Instead, he found an old friend. He'd sort of grown up with Jimmy Forsythe; the two of them having met *pre-teens* the day their parents had dumped them both at a boarding school just outside Hamilton in Scotland. Contact remained until they went their separate ways a decade or so later, though not before Jimmy had acted as the groom's right hand man at his young Belgium chum's nuptials.

Fast forward ten years and our man is on the Rue de Chene, heading for a last ditch bail out effort and a loan from *Argenta Bank*. He's a few minutes early so pauses to look up at the Manneken Pis, probably the least impressive land mark in the world. Feeling like a man directly in line of MP's aim, he turns and bang: bumps, literally, into his ex-Best Man.

The poor bank clerk at Argenta left waiting for an 11:00am appointment that will never show is immediately forgotten. Instead, over coffee, cake and much reminiscing, old acquaintances are renewed.

He tells Jim about his wife, "......yes, of course we're still together, what a shame she's not here today..."; his children, "....straight A students: they couldn't be any more perfect..."; and his business, "With the financial state my company is in, I'm performing more at the other end of the alphabet: things could hardly be any worse! Anyway," he asks, "what about you?"

"Well," his long lost pal says, "I import diamonds. Perhaps we could find a way to work together."

And, in the aftermath of hearing the ins and outs of his chum's rather dodgy activities, find a way, they did.

He was hesitant first. Up until that moment his whole life had been spent well and truly above board, but he found the chance of rescuing his business by buying the occasional, small, slightly below board but very profitable package from Botswana, too much to resist. The untaxed gains from this contraband were manna from heaven, or, at least, Africa and helped get him back on an even keel; but soon, he needed more.

His friend however, was hesitant to up the ante for fear of taking unreasonable risks. There had already been too many shipments caught and lost en route: the well-trodden path up through the Balkans seems to have become easy prey for the authorities. Forsythe told him that if he wanted to increase the stakes he'd need to sort out a new system himself.

And apparently that's exactly what the man from Antwerp did.

The nub of his idea was to ditch James's failing *Plan A* and instead use a couple of trusty old contacts who would bring the gems the long way round, so to speak. Instead of coming up through mainland Europe, they would ship the stones into Ireland, through any of the hundreds of sleepy coastal towns and fishing villages. Here the contraband would be passed into the hands of one of his trustees, he'd quaintly named, presumably in some sort of homage to Quentin Tarantino, *The Postman*. This guy's task would be to get the goods to the second contact, *The Receiver* (we'd obviously stuck with the Pulp Fiction theme), in England, who would skip across the channel and pop the goodies into Chop Drop's very own fair Belgium hands.

And for a while, his little plan had worked a charm.

Who knows whether its success was because the authorities didn't even contemplate such a convoluted trip might be tried. But, whatever the reason, delivery after delivery of profitable merchandise, successfully made its way to Antwerp, along this new found route. Everyone was happy: the structure of this fresh approach had been given the thumbs up and it remained unaltered for about a year. Or to be more precise, right up until the day *The Receiver* was caught.

It would appear that such was the success of this alternative means of getting from A (or B!) to B that everyone had become a tad complacent. In short, they had given the rookie two prong team, in charge of these ultimate stages of the transfer, too much freedom in how they managed their bit of the process. The former, experienced runners of Plan A had found a steady pace at which to navigate the loot along the track largely unsupervised. Alas, those now running the last leg of Plan B hadn't controlled the baton they'd been handed as well as they might.

It was at this stage in Choc Drop's story that my man held up his hand and confessed he really didn't have a clue where this entire Diamonds Are Forever tale was heading. In his defence, I guess, there are only so many different Belgium beers in different shaped glasses that one can consume without losing the ability to see the bleeding obvious staring you in the face. But as gormless as his lack of comprehension must have seemed, he asked his continental chum why on earth he was being told all this.

I suppose the storyteller could quite understandably have decided the slowness in uptake of the man opposite him meant he was not, after all, the man for him and that now would be the appropriate point to close his book and move on. But he didn't.

Why did he continue? Who knows. Possibly it was because he had matched his listener stein for stein. Or perhaps he felt the tale he was telling had come somewhat out of left field, and such lack of comprehension needed some understanding on his part. Or maybe his parents were biblical and had called him Job. Whatever the reason, he simply said there was a serious backlog of parcels that were currently stuck in transit – and he was desperately looking for a plunger.

He ploughed on, thankfully with no further plumbing metaphors, to explain that in addition to the re-routing of the diamonds, he had added an extra layer to his squad. This took the form of a new team member through whom the payments would now flow, rather than directly to the Postman, as was currently the case. It would be a sort of accountant role.

To complete his setup, he just needed to find a replacement for the Receiver. Someone who could be slotted in between the mailman and the new bean counter. Possibly, he suggested, a well-established entrepreneur, who already conducted regular trips to the Low Countries and, perhaps, would be up for visiting his suppliers' brother a little more often?

Hard to believe, but it was at this stage that the penny – finally - dropped.

The fallout from the erstwhile Receiver's demise prompted one further rethink, and it was decided, from hereon in, that contact between all three protagonists should be kept to a minimum. In fact, there was no need for the new man to even know the identities of the two either side of him in the process.

All parties were wary of each other at first, but by the time the number of successful collections, payments and profits had wandered into double figures, everyone had gotten delighted about trusting everyone else. Indeed, during the six or seven months before I showed up, the relationship between my guy, the Postman and the Accountant had, as best as I could tell, exceeded everyone's expectations.

The one wrinkle in this otherwise smooth operation had been the rather clunky coordination between the three of them. The no contact edict was quite difficult to manage without, well, contact. Doing things at arm's length had proved somewhat challenging.

The general idea was simple enough. The entire process would be kick started with my man receiving a payment from Choc Drop's brother's confectionary bank account. A totally normal transaction, easily hidden in plain sight amongst the many other legitimate movements of monies between the two business colleagues. Apparently, it often related to phantom orders for Ice Diamond petit fours (it seems the Belgians do have a sense of humour).

The Postman, having sneaked the goods into England, would then find a way to pass them on to him. Payment for the merchandise would be made the next day to a third party (The Accountant), the Postman's contact. Admittedly, this added an extra layer of complexity, but it meant he would never be the one actually receiving any money direct. Making things as difficult for potential watchers was a key consideration. Once the account had been settled, Postie and his abacus handler would drop out of the equation, leaving my hero to cross the channel and deliver the rocks to a fourth party (a chum of Choc Drop's) in Antwerp.

So far, nothing had actually gone wrong, but it had come close a few times. On one occasion the Accountant was waiting to receive payment in the Stamford Bridge Inn, Chester rather than a hostelry in the capital's Fulham Road. Then there were the uncertainties. An overly vigilant Greek guard, an alert Irish customs officer, or an unexpected check on the Northern Ireland border would sometimes delay proceedings, so the timings of each stage when diamonds changed hands could never be fixed in advance. And it was deemed prudent to keep selecting different locations for the Postman to make his deliveries; ditto to the manner in which my Collector effected the payments.

All in all, these elaborate arrangements reduced the risks of being found out, but they came at a price. Just keeping the three key personnel aware of what was happening, where and by when, had become a strain. As much as everyone wanted to increase the level of business activity, everyone was equally fearful that such greed might just burst the seams. The operation needed some additional oversight and management. Anyway, these concerns had prompted *The Choc* to consider adding yet another body into the mix: a sort of general coordinator.

So, one day, not long before I began working for him, my chap was asked if he could find someone who might take on such a role. And a short while after I'd started my new job, and an ever shorter while after I'd shared his bed for the first time, that's exactly what he did.

Returning to Arrival Day, when the gems were supposed to have......arrived, I would normally be in the office by 6:00am putting the pieces in place so that payment could be made. I then just had to wait for the clock to tick onto 6:30 when his call would come through, triggering my springing into action. To be honest, there was very little springing, or action involved, but when all you're doing is waiting for a phone to ring and listening to the sports report on the Today programme, a girl has to dream a bit. That fleeting reverie was shattered, not so much by the piercing sound of the telephone, though it is a somewhat loud contraption, but by looking up at the clock seeing it was 6:15. This wasn't the right time for the call. Things had not gone to his plan.

I picked up the receiver and had barely said, "Hi", but he brushed past any pleasantries and started blurting out what seemed like random phrases: no car; no call; police hats; oh no, the bloody police and Douglas Adams; the car, the CAR gone; Lady Godiva; binoculars............

Actually, Douglas Adams and Lady Godiva aside, random is perhaps not totally fair. It was a little more like what happens when you listen to a David Bowie song – just in reverse.

You're absorbed in the music, perhaps only half listening to the lyrics, and everything seems to make total sense. After the 37th time of hearing it - because when you're young and you've just bought a new record the law dictates that you must listen to it at least 37 times without a break - you try to give it a go on your guitar. You print off the music and words and see, for the first time, that he, you, all your mates and everyone in the world who has ever sung the song, have been singing gibberish.

I'm an alligator; I'm a mama-papa coming for you
I'm the space invader; I'll be a rock 'n' rollin' bitch for you
Keep your mouth shut, you're squawking like a pink monkey bird
And I'm busting up my brains for the words......

He was still babbling, pink monkey birdesque: "binoculars and wardrobes....". If I didn't stop this daydream, there'd be a ray gun put to his head the next time I saw him.

I started trying to piece his lyrics together by hurling questions at him.

I told you I'd taken the car to the golf course yesterday as we'd agreed, didn't I? Yes. No one's phoned to say there had been a change of plan, have they? No. But your car's not where it should be now? Another: No. So how are the police are involved? About now he seemed to get back some of the control that had been missing. Apparently the police presence was some sort of absurd coincidence, but without immediate access to Adams' babel fish I wasn't going to solve that particular puzzle anytime soon, so I returned to the moment. "Of course it will have to be dealt with delicately" I said. Who on earth does he think has been managing this for these past ten or eleven months? "I know the score. Anyway, this is unlike you to panic".

He rang off to make the necessary call from his end. The outcome from that conversation would dictate how things would proceed, so I sat back and waited for the Postman to call and tell me just what direction that would be.

The phone seemed to ring almost immediately, but looking up I saw that the hands on the clock had wandered past 6:35. My man was to meet the Accountant in Whitby, North Yorkshire, tomorrow at eleven. He gave me an address on the eastern half of the town. I made the point that the two people in the meeting we were arranging had never laid eyes on one another before. That was about to change, so we needed to give them a confirmatory code or sign. My first thought was very James Bond. Opening comment: My aubergine has gone soft. Reply: Then you'll have to find somewhere else to stick it.

Perhaps not.

My second was a little more dramatic, two red roses.

Perhaps too obvious. No one wanted to take any chances, but I still felt something visual was the right way to go. I suggested a Shrewsbury Town FC baseball cap. Someone wearing a cap in

Whitby – pretty common. One with the emblem of a football team from the English third division based well over 100 miles away – not so much.

I rang off and punched in my guy's number on the keypad. He answered immediately and I started detailing the next steps. I let his deep sigh pass without comment when I told him he'd be going to Whitby. (Get over it, I thought – at least you'll be having a decent lunch). I was about to tell him to make sure he packed his STFC cap with him when I heard his doorbell chime. He blurted, "Police. Gotta go" and hung up. I stared down at the silent receiver. This all seemed somewhat bizarre but any chance to mull things over further were put on hold when the phone rang. This could be tricky. It was probably him, but if the police were somehow at the other end of this call, perhaps better not to answer. Not just yet. Let's see what happens.

The ringing stopped. I left it for a quarter of an hour and tried to call him back. No reply. Maybe he was already making plans for tomorrow's meeting. If so, all's well and good, just so long as the local constabulary weren't involved, nor were the ones arranging it.

I'd catch up with him later and anyway, he was bound to have his beloved cap with him. The more I thought of it the more I warmed to my choice.

Two people meeting for the first time. Her waiting, looking, almost longing. Will he be the next person to come into view? Suddenly she catches sight of a well-toned body turning the corner and approaching the point of the rendezvous. He looks down at the ground. She glances away from him, teasing. A tress of hair manages to break free and flies across her face. He lifts his head. The atmosphere is electric. Their eyes meet for a flash of a second before both of them raise their sights and stare in wonder at the blue caps both of them are wearing. Each hat is stitched with three leopards' heads, all six beasts apparently poking their tongues out provocatively in what appears the opposite of a friendly welcome.

If only Lorraine Chase or the PG Tips monkeys could have been on hand to add some gravitas.

Caps aside, I realised I hadn't had time to give him the actual coordinates for his meeting, so I rattled them off in a quick text. No need to be too specific: he'd know what the words meant.

I thought I'd earned myself a coffee, but I had one more call to make before reaching for the kettle. I wanted to be totally sure there were no slip-ups.

Chapter 4
One golf course/two collections

POSTMAN

Things go better with Coke (1960s advert)

The day started at 6:14, in a way it never had before.

The phone that never, ever rang – rang. There were only two reasons he would be making a call on this "special reserved for no other reason" number: either he couldn't find them or he didn't like them.

I recalled my movements during the wee small hours of last night. The three relevant words in the coded location message I'd been sent: *Should Toby open the door, he would reveal Graham's focal point aimed at Colin. Simple,* were those following the male names in the text and would guide me to the pick-up point. Punching *open.focal.simple* into the *what3words app* I was moderately taken aback to find I was being directed to the Royal Blackheath Golf Club in south east London. I'd never had any time for the game and, indeed had only previously driven through the gates of a golf course once in my whole life - and this was it. That time it had been to collect a second hand beer engine I'd bought from the Steward on eBay. How strange my return to the oldest golf club in England would again see me tread no further afield than the red asphalt car park that encircled the 16th century clubhouse. At least I'd look the part carrying a golf bag.

I'd found the car parked on a track alongside the 9th fairway and the writing on the back of a crumpled Tesco till receipt left on the passenger seat: *Gary washed Brian's food before John wins everything* gave me what I needed to reveal my next stop.

To begin with I thought there must have been some mistake. I actually double, no triple checked the message because the result of my first attempt, in which I had typed *washed, foods* and *wins* into the app had suggested I should drive some 3,500 miles due west to the first-floor bedroom of a house in Beech Grove, Indiana, USA. Mental note to self: be more careful typing with the sausage fingers.

Once I'd deleted the *S* from *foods* it became clear that I'd not been meant to raise an unsuspecting snoozer from a pleasant slumber in their sleepy suburban area of a city in Midwest America, and I should instead head for a village in Kent.

I had driven the car to within a few metres of the exact spot I'd been instructed and left it there. The gems, in the false bottom of the golf bag had been safely tucked up in the boot, so I couldn't for the life of me fathom what might have gone wrong.

Returning to the phone call, I dutifully followed the script and said, "Goods delivered as planned. Confirm receipt." Any remote semblance of confidence I'd been feeling vanished when I heard the reply, "No receipt".

Bugger. The Accountant would take the next step as far as the business was concerned, so my first call was to her. She would be in charge of finding out what on earth had happened. Belying her normal demeanour, she sounded more than just nervous and far from confident when I outlined the situation, but she soon got things together. I think. She said they might as well go with where she'd intended to take receipt of the money and gave me an address to pass on to my contact. I called his secretary and told her what was planned.

With the new arrangements we'd put in place over these past months having gone without so much as even a half hitch, there had been no need to break the no contact rule. The voice at the other end of the phone had clearly latched on to this and was pointing out that as the two people we were trying to put together had never actually met, they'd need some means of being capable of recognising one another. While I knew my gal was more than able to pick her man out of a line-up, that wasn't common knowledge, so I played along. At the very least, it might have the effect of placating the chap who was going to meet her.

Personally I'd have balked at the prospect of wandering around anywhere in a Shrewsbury Town FC baseball cap, especially after what they'd done to my team a few years back, but, these were games other people would have to play. In any event, she'd always looked great in every sort of hat I'd ever seen her wear so I agreed to the head covering stipulation.

She sounded slightly unsure once I'd called her back to relay details of the required headwear. "Of course you are aware of what he looks like," I said, "but he doesn't know that, does he? And anyway, he couldn't pick you out from Adam, sorry, Eve." She seemed to be mulling that over, but before she could come back and raise any real objection – unlikely, or make an alternative suggestion, I certainly would have, I just told her to get back to me on how the meeting turned out and replaced the handset into its docking station.

Now, with the ball volleyed firmly over the net and into at least two other courts, I could get down to the more serious predicament – mine.

Any question on delivery was well and truly in my own backyard, and I needed to act fast to find out what had happened. Others would also be put onto the case, but it would be much better all round – and easier to make absolutely sure I would be in no way implicated – if I got to the bottom of things first.

And, of course, this wasn't my only problem. What about the other goods? If he didn't have the gems – and the jury was still out on why on earth that should be - was that all he was short of?

I pressed 6 on the speed dial and prayed that I'd hear a lucid and sober voice at the other end. Why I wished that I've no idea. I wasn't usually able to tell whether he'd had a skin full or not over the phone and, once my call was answered, I realised I couldn't tell this time either. But despite being a man who has never seemed too troubled by the notion of thinking before he speaks, he did at least sound compos, which was a relief. I explained what had happened, where he had to go and when he had to be there. I tried to stay calm while explaining that Whitby was in Yorkshire, that Yorkshire was not in Scotland and that he had to find out what my courier was doing, where he was going and who he was meeting.

I wasn't as totally reassured that he had everything quite as under control as he'd just suggested, but at 6:35 in the morning it was probably as good as I could hope for.

Chapter 5

Bad Karma and Screaming shouldn't mix

SECKIE

> Of all the gin joints in all the towns in all the world,
> she walks into mine (Rick Blaine)

It was on my third trip to the Chocolate Factory (whether they involved hard stones or soft centres it seemed sensible and safest to always think and refer to our continental sojourns in that way), that I first met The Postman.

There were many reasons this shouldn't have happened, not least because the business arrangements under which we operated had been designed to keep all the separate bits of the network – separate.

Of course we'd spoken numerous times on the telephone, but never face to face. I guess the rationale was that identifying someone to the authorities when all you had to go on was the tone of their voice, or the way they rolled their R's was less than straightforward. I'm not sure what leeway the architects of this cunning plan had thought they might allow, but I'm guessing a face-to-face encounter with one of the links either side of my position in the bracelet was somewhat more intimate than they would have hoped for.

My guy had had a meeting and, left kicking my heels, I pointed them, somewhat aimlessly, towards the banks of the Scheldt. I'd meandered off piste into Korte Koepoorstraat, when a man appeared at my side. Actually, I'd become aware of him a fraction of a second earlier. To all intents and purposes he was just another pedestrian, walking along this popular thoroughfare, albeit at a slightly quicker pace than I'd settled into. As he approached my shoulder, I heard my name mentioned, but it was spoken so softly that, at first, I didn't register it was really me who was being addressed. He pulled alongside and, maintaining his piano tone, said, "Meet the Postman in *The Bad Karma* bar. 20 minutes." He nodded left down the street we were crossing and, quickening his step, vanished into the crowd ahead.

I appreciate that at this stage in a film, cinema goers might feel the story was losing credibility if I gullibly followed this man's lead and joined him as instructed. But, despite the location of the rendezvous sounding slightly suspicious as well as being the name of the lead song on the soundtrack of Scream 4: this man clearly knew who I was and if indeed he was the Postman, I thought I should at least get onto a level footing with him.

I spotted him sitting in one of the dark wooden cosy looking (though seldom all that comfortable when you actually sit down) booths that you find in Irish bars around the world. He was facing out with his back to the wall which was probably just as well otherwise I may not have picked him.

As I sat down opposite him, I was feeling cautious and apprehensive, obviously, but also a tad excited. These senses were somewhat deflated when I spotted two pints of Guinness on the table, one of which he was pushing my way. I wondered momentarily if he'd asked for it to be shaken or stirred, but replaced that thought with one slightly more pressing: how he was going to explain he knew who I was and how to contact me. And anyway, what on earth could be so important that made him prepared to risk the wrath of the Chocolate Factory by revealing our secret identities to each another?

There was to be no preamble. He just dived straight in.

Somehow, (the "some" was never actually explained) he had obtained a photograph of me. He said that when my involvement in the process was first suggested he wasn't going to jeopardise this neat little earner – or risk going the way of his previous, and now incarcerated, partner – by accepting me at face value and putting himself at the mercy of someone he didn't know from Adam. Or Eve, for that matter. He'd done his due diligence on my guy when he was first touted as a replacement for his Receiver chum and, when my name had popped up some seven or eight months later, he'd simply followed a similar path, and checked me out too.

He did admit that since my arrival things had gone well. "Really well", he said. "Far better than everyone could have expected". He let that hang in the air a moment.

My arrival on the scene, and inclusion into the mix, had coincided with the launch of several fresh ranges of chocolate delights, which demanded a serious increase in the trips my boss (or, as things had become, *we*) needed to make. This provided the perfect cover to up the ante and put the new system – and me – on trial to test it all to the limit.

Over a four-week period I was central to making sure everyone and everything was in the right place, at the right time. I was Ground Control and everyone else was Major Tom. Every move came through me. Each new assignment, I co-ordinated. All timings and transfers happened only with my say so.

During my months' probation, we achieved a fifteen per cent jump in confectionary sales and a fivefold increase in the amount of stolen gems transported. This seemed to delight everyone, and a nice slice of the kudos came my way. I assumed it was this new found star status that had attracted the Postman's interest, enticed him out of the shadows and into a dimly lit bar looking across a table at two pints of stout and me. However, as he took a sip out of the glass nearest to him, what he was about to hit me with came from what I can only describe as several galaxies past wherever *way out of the blue* is.

"In short," he said, "I want to expand the relationship."

It wasn't immediately clear what he could possibly be leading up to so, other than crossing my fingers in the hope that he wasn't inferring anything sexual, I kept schtum and tried not to react.

I had a reasonable understanding of his end of the process. As far as I could tell, apart from his primary role, he did nothing other than a great deal of hanging around in bars on the south coast of Ireland, so I couldn't even begin to guess what he could possibly have available to expand.

But I hadn't been thinking out of the box. He wasn't the only man in the vicinity not totally on the up and up – and like-minded men can easily, even subconsciously, be drawn together, especially if there's money to be made.

He spared me the details but said he had established contact with someone who needed help *relocating* some wares into the Netherlands. He continued, making the case that the journey we were currently taking the diamonds on was: across the channel and turn right. Amsterdam, he reasoned, simply required us to veer in the other direction once we'd arrived on the continent.

He concluded by saying this would be a nice little additional earner that was virtually risk free. And if you're happy to get involved, then the money to be made in narcotics will make what you skim off the smuggled gem trade look as dull as the rough diamonds you're carrying themselves.

Chapter 6
Mr and Mrs Huntrodds

MAN
    Coincidence: The universe is rarely so lazy (Sherlock Holmes)

The journey to Whitby was not all that far, but it was certainly long enough to ensure that by half way I was sort of panicking. Funnily enough, the absent diamonds were hardly troubling me at all. They had been doing this a darn sight longer than the 18 months or so I'd been involved and had well-established ways to sort out issues and minor problems as they arose. There would be nothing to worry about just so long as I was in no way responsible for creating whatever it was they were trying to get to the bottom of. Given all I'd done this morning was wake up and open the door to a policeman, I felt pretty confident I was in the clear. No, my real concern related to the missing rocks of another kind.

Seckie's off piste meeting with the Postman had been as far away from the compacted snow as one could get without falling off the actual mountain. It ran contrary to the well-established structure we were supposed to be working within and risked many wraths from many people. Compounding that risk with the idea of doing a bit of business on the side and selecting processed cocaine as the base commodity for that enterprise just seemed to increase the number of potential wrath makers way beyond anything I even wanted to imagine. But then the money takes over and suddenly things begin to look, not only different but, you convince yourself, favourable.

She said she believed Postie's story that what we would be doing was small time. To the big boys and girls in this game the profits to be had were, in their terms, somewhat less than beer money. It was not worth their while risking their operations by getting out of bed for anything less than a sustainable six figure profit. Little League smuggling opportunities like these, that yielded them little more than the odd ten or twenty grand bungsy, would not prompt a mass setting of early morning alarm calls.

She seemed convinced that this would be more than a one off opportunity, and the door looked well and truly open for us to try our luck and get really rich, really quick. I told her I didn't doubt what she was saying but surely the jails (and hospitals?) are full of those who have tried walking through said door. In short, I was extremely wary. I was an ordinary, respectable, white, middle-aged, successful businessman, so why would I risk that?

Answering my own question, I suppose the reason was the money. I was doing OK, and our little diamond caper was working well, but it wasn't exactly bringing in piles of Euros. And I was some way off being anywhere close to being as cash rich as I needed, or wanted to be in the very near future.

I kept going back and forth between should I, or shouldn't I. The tipping factor came while watching an episode of The West Wing a few days after Seckie had first broached the subject. The underlying message from the programme was that the mandatory minimum sentencing policy for drug-related offences in America was racist. And, with ethnic minorities accounting for over 60% of narcotic arrests, there was no denying that. But the stat that really caught my eye was further down the scale. You had to scroll to the bottom of the page before finding the figure of 1% and the category that my facial colouring, age and squeaky clean persona would fall into. I liked the odds of 99 to 1 on being in my favour – the risk, such as it was, appeared worth it.

Of course, that was then. Right now that long shot seemed to be coming up hard on the rails. There had been one scare early on when I thought a sniffer dog was being led through the train just after pulling out of St Pancras on route to Amsterdam. This was a much greater degree of commotion than I usually encountered on the Eurostar, with a couple of burly dark-suited men with wires sticking out of their ears, barging along the aisle clearing the way for the sniffing mongrel. As it happened, it was the Home Secretary, his entourage and his guide dog on their way to Brussels. Other than that, it had been whatever the rail equivalent of plain sailing is. And as long as the skims; £4k here, £7k there, kept on coming – so did I.

But, as they apparently say on the streets, losing one's candy is a serious blow.

Had the hitherto bored Drug Kings and Queens suddenly woken up and taken an interest in our little side-line? Was someone further up or down the chain trying to pull a fast one? Were the police involved? Was PC 42 really only investigating a peeping Tom?

Whatever had happened, the prospect of becoming entangled with drug barons, deranged junkies or the law was starting to freak me out. If I'd have had three shoulders, I would be looking over them all simultaneously. I seriously had no idea how this was going to get resolved so, trying to throw my fear out of the window and into the passing, empty fields bordering the train track, I picked up the paperback I'd brought with me and tried to distract myself from the situation I was fretting about.

By the time we'd passed Ruswarp station my book, *The Jewel of Seven Stars*, by Bram Stoker was finished. This wasn't my usual genre, or at least it hadn't been until I received a letter from English

Heritage three or four months ago. I say it wasn't the sort of thing I'd naturally pick up from a bookshelf, but to be honest, I'm really not the greatest of readers, so plucking any publication from its natural resting place would be unusual. I started wading through the early Harry Potters when they first came out and, having quite liked the Philosopher's Stone, had every intension of running straight through all seven books. I gave up on that idea, however, when I got The Order of The Phoenix home from *Waterstones*. The book was so thick my thumb ached after about twenty minutes just holding it open. I suppose having sneaked it into my briefcase and slipping past the pay counter without stopping to lighten my wallet meant there was no real drive or financial commitment to continue reading and so made tossing the tome to one side to concentrate on massaging my hand a little less of a challenge.

My pollex remained unchallenged on any book for some time after that until an envelope with what looks like a square red wheel cog in the top left corner dropped onto my mat. The contents were informative, although not necessarily in a particularly interesting way.

Apparently English Heritage manages the Blue Plaques scheme which highlights buildings where notable women and men have lived (I didn't know that). Said scheme has been running since the 1860s (didn't know that either) but is restricted to locations in London (had been blissfully unaware of that fact too). Continuing with my education, I read that, although a recent trial to broaden it into a national programme had been discontinued after a few years (it sounded like a half-hearted effort), the desire remained to in some way stop it being viewed as so London centric. While fresh applications for plaques outside of the capital were not being considered, there was a plan to recognise locations north of Watford that had a historical connection to the discs that already existed inside the M25 ring. This, as I then found out, is where I, or rather my house, came in.

It seems that Bram Stoker, the author of *Dracula* (this was becoming a very informative morning for me) used my property as a sort of country retreat in the late 18th/early 19th century. Much of his work at the time was theatre based and, indeed, his residence in Chelsea is marked with the official English Heritage blue plaque. But, the letter continued, many, certainly the majority of his books were written around the time he'd rented/owned my humble abode and, considered opinion was that many, if not the majority had been penned, not in some bolthole in SW3, but in my living room. The long and short of it was that they wanted to recognise this (the new scheme was to use orange rather than blue plaques) and were seeking my permission to plaster a suitably worded, amberish circle of metal on my front wall.

There may be stronger reasons to start reading a book: a personal recommendation by someone who knows you and what you might like is probably one of the better ones. Stoker's work would not have been on a list of suggestions my nearest and dearest would have considered, for a moment, to have passed on to me. But I felt English Heritage had driven me to at least give his stuff a go and, providing myself with the added incentive of actually purchasing one of his novels, I clicked into my Amazon account and pressed the *Buy now* button next to Dracula.

I don't think it was just because I found Stoker's Dracula literally easier to handle than Rowling's Phoenix, although weighing in at 418 pages, over half the number JK had written, certainly helped. No, I actually enjoyed it. The language was painful, but the story fanciful. It didn't tax the brain all that much and, indeed, some of his works (Carmilla at 108 pages) could even slip into one's pocket without causing an unsightly bulge. Seven Stars weighed in at triple that, but I decided, nevertheless to have a stab at it, mainly because

I'd literally stumbled across it on our bookshelf at home. That piece of furniture was not one I visited with any great regularity so, while I have no idea from where the book came, nor when it got there, finding it in my home just seemed too much of a coincidence to let it pass.

Anyway, with the last of the 337 pages of my latest forage into his work turned, I had barely a few moments to dwell any further on the mystery before arriving in Whitby. As we pulled into the very Victorian looking station, I scanned the skies and wondered how suitably attired I was to match the elements I was about to be subjected to.

As I walked off the platform and through the station's huge archway, I saw a sky bereft of clouds (phew) but a taxi rank equally empty (bugger). The meet was taking place less than a mile from the station, and the individual titanic struggles the passing pedestrians were having with the wind (bugger again) made my shoulders drop. Stepping out from the shelter, the bitterest of north-east winds hit me. We "southern softies" – even though I live in the centre of England anyone from south of Yorkshire is usually considered thus – are often accused of being slightly wimpish about our weather tolerance levels, but, in defence of my people, today I felt like I was being blasted by everything Aeolus had in (his?) armoury.

While the area, somewhere in or around Whitby, or bloody Whitby as the wind and rain was prompting me to rename it was always the same, the actual meeting place was always different; so I needed GPS assistance.

With the wind still blowing and the taxi rank still empty, there was nothing I could do other than shrink my head down into the upturned lapels of my Burberry and rue the fact that, following an extraordinary game by the Shrews a few days earlier when we'd come back from two nil down against Colchester to win four/two, I'd thrown my cap high into the air in delight. The last time I saw that

hat it was being picked up by a young lad half a dozen rows below me who, glancing around and finding no one claiming ownership, plopped it on his bonce and disappeared smiling into the crowd. I only hoped that Seckie's slightly odd message, reminding me to pack the cap along with my toothbrush, was neither important nor going to cause a problem.

The best I could do was brace the elements without follicle protection so, like a [cold] donkey being tantalised with a [frozen] carrot on the end of an [icy] stick, I started walking in the direction the iPhone I was holding in front of me was pointing.

I never cease to be amused seeing myself pictured as a little blue dot on my phone, moving along in such a jerky way. There's always a bit of a delay in the time it takes the signal to bounce up to wherever it bounces before pinging back down and being translated into movement onto the screen. Sometimes, if I was sure no one was watching, I'd try to run on ahead quickly to watch me overtake myself. Yes, I know, the long winter nights must just fly by in my household, but I was attempting to traverse Whitby Bridge and the wind off the River Esk had trebled in intensity. What else was I to do to try and negate the pain of the crossing and keep my mind off the cold?

Reaching the other side of the bridge, it comforted me to be directed past Hadleys Fish Restaurant. Seckie and I had eaten there the day we'd started getting to know one another. She knows I am a sucker for this traditional English fare, and Hadleys was the best I'd tried in the area. I knew there'd be a reservation for a table in my name to facilitate my post rendezvous lunch.

As I turned into Church Street, I returned to my little beat the blue blob game.

Despite the road being made of large uneven brick sized stones, I managed the first hundred yards without too much difficulty. However, as I approached the end of the lane, the severity of my task was about to be ramped up a few notches. The direction Steve Jobs' contraption was pushing me in was a steep flight of 199 steps up the side of what I swear should technically be classed as a mountain. Nevertheless I somehow managed to wheeze towards the summit, pausing a few treads from the top to check progress.

I will say that yesterday, after I'd decoded the address for this meeting, my first reaction was to declare out loud, though to nobody in particular, you must be taking the piss!

Seckie's text had read, *I saw Brian balancing Abraham's thrillers and watched Trevor march towards Whitby Abbey*. Neat and well coded, I thought. But when I popped *balancing, thrillers* and *march* into the what3words app, and discovering I needed to find a property called Mad Monk Cottage, I actually looked over my shoulder to check if Seckie was nearby watching me and having some sort of laugh at my expense. Even Ben Elton would have avoided incorporating a venue with as clichéd a name as Mad Monk Cottage into either Blackadder or Upstart Crow, but the *what3words* app seemed very clear on that point.

As I climbed the last few steps, I could see St Mary's church standing large and high on my left. The shell of the larger and higher Abbey, now little more than a monument to Henry VIII's vengeance, stood a hundred additional paces diagonally right. The *towards Whitby Abbey* Seckie had tacked on the end of her message, which I'd initially considered superfluous, now served to confirm I was in the correct part of town.

It looked like I was being directed on a path between the two religious houses and across their cemetery. Without the benefit of a map you may think this sounds, at the very best, a slightly odd if not unlikely route, even for a sat nav to point one towards. But with precious little in the way of alternative roads or pathways to the left or right, and given that straight ahead I was staring out onto the North Sea, actual land was at a premium so I followed my blue master as instructed.

That was when the first coincidence of the day occurred. There were only a couple of other (live) souls in the graveyard: one in particular was scrabbling around the stones. He seemed to be reading the various epitaphs of souls (not alive), but in a slightly more measured and determined fashion than the absent minded way one normally does in such places. He was some way away but clearly dressed far more appropriately than I was for the gale like condition currently in play, although I remember thinking that deep dog shit brown was never a colour I would have gone for when buying an overcoat.

Perhaps at this point I should mention that it was the 19th of September. Now I appreciate that to anyone other than the immediate neighbours of St Mary's that might mean nothing at all, but the locals here call the 19th of September National Coincidence Day: and from the epitaph etched into one of the granite slabs stuck on an outside wall of the church I could see why.

The old tombstone that had caught my eye told about Mr and Mrs Huntrodds who, in 1600, were both born on the same day, 19th of September; who, years later, married each other on the same day (also the 19th of September); and, yet more years later, in 1680, both died, within five hours of each other....on the same day (I was getting the idea), the 19th September.

Anyway, perhaps the coincidence that I had stumbled across the Huntrodds' final resting place on the same date that meant so much to them, played with my subconscious because throughout the day and wherever I seemed to look, something slightly odd was occurring. Now I'm not talking, "What!? Not in a million years could that happen!" odd, but certainly enough to solicit a bit of a knitted brow and slight pursing of the lips.

Earlier, across the road at the train station, I'd seen a young woman in a car, sporting a familiar blue baseball cap. It was a very distinctive hue, and I immediately recognised it as the colour of the football team I had supported since my childhood. Of course, it was also identical to the one I'd lost just a few days previously.

It had been many years since I'd first seen the Shrews play at the Gay Meadow, and while my thoughts flitted back to the times on the terraces with my father, I was briefly struck by just how far this hat was from its home. Now these hats aren't the greatest of sellers in Shropshire's county town, let alone some 200 miles northwest of there. Shrewsbury FC has a fine pedigree going back to 1886 – few of England's many football clubs can boast that – though our longevity is not matched by our success: getting somewhere near the top of the third tier of English football gives us supporters a fair chance of a nosebleed. Given I was in England's largest county, which hosts 10 professional teams of their own (most of them well above Town's usual league position) you'd have thought the locals are spoiled enough for choice that they'd never have the inclination to wander so far westward for their football fix. But a supporter usually only ever sees the upside of their team so with a passing smile I just concluded here was one fair Yorkshire Maid who had either seen the light where all her fellow county colleagues had not, or (more likely) found the cap lying in the gutter and needed some hair protection.

But if that wasn't odd enough, the car she was driving, a metallic red PT Cruiser, was identical to the one my wife and I had purchased together, brand new, to mark our tin wedding anniversary (yes, I know – what an old romantic). I probably wouldn't have registered the fact about the car we'd bought so many years ago, had it not then crossed my path a further three times. I wondered whether there were road works and diversions all over town that day directing everything down a single thoroughfare and thanked my good luck not to have had the option of a taxi.

Other happenings were slightly weirder. Again, not knock your socks off weird, but perhaps the knitted furrowed brow might now be accompanied by a deep and softly breathed "Hmmmm". As I turned from Mr and Mrs H, a loose piece of paper swirled up in the wind and hit me flush in the face. I peeled it away, and saw it was some type of a flyer with the heading in large red gothic letters which read Bram Stoker's Dracula and Whitby.

At first sight I thought this was just going to be the usual sort blurb produced by most towns throughout the world who desperately try to find some tenuous link to a famous face in an effort to sex up their heritage and boost tourism.

Valdemosa in the Island of Majorca has created a whole industry based on the few weeks Chopin once spent in the area. Even the Lion Hotel in my hometown of Shrewsbury dines out extensively on rumours that Charles Dickens was once seen outside the pub waiting for a hackney carriage, and suggestions that Disraeli left politically correct feedback about his stay in the visitors' book. Even Madame Tussauds herself gets a name check as a past resident: no doubt she waxed lyrical about the place.

I've never been convinced these *revelations* really enhance the experience for those enticed by the rhetoric. For example, let's say you are lured to the tearoom where Diana, Princess of Wales, reputedly once visited. After you've walked in the shop and looked around for a moment, what on earth is there to comment on other than, Oh. That's nice. Two sugars please?"

The unsolicited advertising poster that had floated my way however, clearly promised a much more concrete connection between this seaside town and the Prince of Darkness's author – and not just with the settlement I could see sprawled out before me at the foot of the cliff. The ground, on which I was currently standing in the lee of this eerie church, is near as damn it the actual spot where Bram Stoker had been inspired to write Dracula all those years ago. Indeed,

I was as close as one could be to the slab marking the final resting place of local resident William Swales: the name of the vampire's first victim. And to compound the tale even further, this was the same author of the book I'd finished reading only a few hours earlier. Now I don't want to really overstretch this coincidence thing, but if all that wasn't enough for you: wait until you hear about the money.

I left Mr Swales and the Huntrodds in peace and scrambled across the cemetery in what I hoped was the general direction of the unstable Friar's old abode.

The meeting would at best be described as inconclusive. Our whole setup is managed so that no one person in the process knows anyone other than the contacts that sit either side of them. I say "knows" although it was more of a "knew of". I'd long known how to contact the Postman, who was one up the line from me, to arrange delivery and, similarly, Seckie would liaise direct with the Accountant who I would eventually pay. This way it was all but impossible for anyone trying to put all the links together to make, successfully at least, a whole bracelet. One further wrinkle for any budding jeweller was that no one in the chain, not even the adjacent links, had actually met each other. And we had all been made absolutely clear that, unless something went wrong – and here we are talking seven rather than two on the Richter scale –it was to remain that way. Well, we'd long since passed the tremors of 6.9 on the dial so I was anticipating being able to transform the mental image I had created of my mystery contact: giant Popeye figure with anchor tattoos and a gold tooth, into something more real life.

· At the edge of the graveyard are a few rows of buildings lined up at ninety degrees to the sea. I followed the only thoroughfare available: a dusty track running between the houses on my left and the dilapidated Abbey on my right. Within moments I came across a small stone lodge with the words *Mad Monk Cottage* carved into the lintel above a brown door with a stained glass centre panel depicting two horses standing in front of the Abbey's facade.

The door was slightly ajar. I tried to widen the gap further with my toe, but something was stopping that from happening. "Stay there", the voice said. It was soft, feminine yet forceful and, I may have imagined it, delivered with just a hint of breathlessness. Either way, the Popeye image I'd created in my head had obviously been about as wide of the mark as it is possible to have been.

So far, the only indication anybody had that something was wrong was in the phrase I had relayed yesterday to the Postman, "no receipt". I sensed my mystery partner had a whole script at the ready to follow but my negative response to the question at the top of her list, asking if the vehicle was at the designated point, seemed to bring any further enquiries to an abrupt halt. For what seemed like ages, she said nothing. I was beginning to wonder if our liaison was in fact over, but then she said, "That doesn't bring me joy, only sorrow. Go. And wait. You know where".

To be frank, I wasn't completely sure of anything of the kind. I had absolutely no immediate idea what on earth I might do with such opposing instructions. But before I could elicit any clarifications, the door slammed shut on both my toe and my face.

Somewhat confused, I turned and went back across the churchyard, down the steps and along the cobbled stones to the beginning of Church Street. I crossed the road and pushed open the door to the diner I had passed by barely 30 minutes earlier, fully expecting a much warmer welcome than I'd just been afforded by the temporary resident of Mad Monk's palace: the kind of reception restaurant owners around the world save for those who take the trouble to book a table in advance.

Of course, given how the last 24 hours had gone, I should have known better, because the only greeting I received on stepping onto the restaurant's coarse hair mat with a faded turbot staring up at me was, "No, sir – we've no record of any reservation in your name." Seckie's slipping.

I then waited for what seemed enough time to catch, scale and gut a freshly caught herring, as well as fry it while the waitress flicked through the entire diary looking for my name and, trying to assess whether they could accommodate a potential customer without prior notice. Why do restaurants throughout the universe follow this same script? There's hardly anybody else here: just let me sit down and serve me! I understand if they're booked out and will be full to the gunnels within the half hour, but the slight intake of breath through the teeth from the maitre de as (s)he stares at an empty order book before suggesting, with a bit of luck and, at a push, we might be able to squeeze you in somewhere always niggles me. Especially when you're still the only person to have come through the door by the time the cheese board arrives.

I was, eventually, shown to a table in the corner, but instead of sitting down in my newly allotted chair, I threw my coat over the back of it and returned with her to the counter. This was one of those places where you ordered and paid for your meal at the bar before taking your seat, so I started that process by asking for a large piece of freshly fried haddock. Nothing else. No, I didn't want any coffee, thank you – it detracts from the taste of the batter. No tartar sauce or ketchup either, thanks. I find it just smothers the sumptuousness of what my father-in-law always referred to as the King of the Sea.

I used to take a side dish of mushy peas with my haddock, but a visit I once made to a fish bar in Pudsey put paid to that. Pudsey was once an innocuous suburb of Leeds, one of Yorkshire's major cities. It was not particularly well known to anyone outside of the area but achieved fame and notoriety when a local resident designed an oversized teddy bear, put a patch over one of its eyes, called it Pudsey and convinced the BBC to use it as the mascot for an annual fund raising telethon. Anyway, an old friend, Stephen Barber, had taken me to this provincial restaurant on the pretext of showing me some superb Yorkshire fare. As we took our seats, the server placed a large pot of tea, two cups, two plates of white bread and two slabs of butter on the table. Now we'd not ordered any of this, but Steve told me that was how they did things here. In the gap between this northern amuse-bouche being served and the young girl returning for our order, I picked up a piece of card wedged in between the salt and pepper pots. There were just six words typed neatly in the centre: "Warning. Mushy peas may contain gunshot".

By the time the waitress had returned to our table I had mentally reduced my (then) usual order (and, following that moment, forever more) to nothing but a large piece of haddock, sans pois.

A (pleasant) unintended consequence of placing such a sparse order is that it's never a very expensive experience – and even more (or less?) so in the rural north of the country.

Back to the counter in Hadley's and in exchange for my order I was given a bill (well, a small piece of paper about 2" x 3" torn out of a little carbon papered booklet) confirming my meal, 1 x Had (L), alongside the rather odd [but beautifully cheap] amount of £4.99. I pulled out my Nationwide visa and absent-mindedly hovered it over the cashless card reader, before noticing a scrappy bit of cardboard attached to its side saying "nowt working". Bugger. I knew I had no notes – I'd used the last fiver in my wallet that morning on *The Guardian* - and with the price of papers these days I was not confident I'd have much more than the £2.80 change the tobacconist had placed in my hand. Leaving the typo on the card reader's note to one side, I fished in my pocket and grabbed its total contents. To my pleasant surprise and also slight amazement, I found myself holding exactly the right amount of change. And, a la Jeffrey Archer, I mean not a penny more/not a penny less than the 499 requested. OK, so perhaps that might not warrant the deeply breathed, "Hmmm", but you have to at least grant me a modest and disbelieving shake of the head?

In any event, there were other reasons that the 19th of September remained lodged in my brain, though I probably wouldn't categorise those – at least not at this stage - as coincidental.

I don't want to over inflate the importance of these coincidences and oddities, almost all of which I discounted with barely two moments' thought. The one exception was the Shrewsbury Town FC baseball cap.

Where was Oscar Wilde when you needed him? To see one baseball cap in a strange location once might be a coincidence. Seeing a second one within an hour could be considered unbelievable.

There was no mistaking the three leopard faces, proudly sewn and embossed into the cap, from the coat of arms of Shrewsbury, the county town of Shropshire in the West Midlands and home to the team I've supported since before the Coracle Man had started fishing wayward balls out of the river Severn. I had passed off my first sighting at the railway station as....coincidence. For it to be making a repeat appearance was, shall we just say, unexpected. But no question. There, across the street from the restaurant, I could see the vivid blue STFC cap, bobbing along the pavement; though the body beneath it was certainly not that of the young woman I'd seen wearing it earlier. It was now on top of what looked like a middle-aged man's head. I say, middle-aged man – his sex was indisputable, but he had pulled his lapels so high against the wind that there was barely a gap between the top of his coat and the bottom of his hat, so my age assessment was not conclusive. Also, I suppose the coat didn't strike me as one to which the younger generation might reach. For a start, it was that strange shade of what I'd call dog shit brown. Was this the only colour available in this part of the world? It also had what looked like a cape over the shoulders, though it was definitely part of the garment – I think they call them Inverness or frock coats? In any event, it was more Vera than Villanelle.

This whole scene prompted the return of a niggle that had been rattling around my brain, on and off, for the past few hours. Deciding now would be as good a time as any to do something about it I pressed the respond button to my Secretary's earlier text, and typed, *STFC cap?* She came back almost immediately with: For identification (wrong time of year for red roses).

So that's it. Someone is looking for me wearing a Shrews hat I no longer possess; whereas everyone in this godforsaken town seems to have one perched on their head. Good plan!

I watched, absentmindedly, as the back of the cap began to fade from view, though not before noticing its wearer had barged, perhaps with an equal lack of contemplation, into a young woman nearly knocking her off her feet.

My thoughts returned to the matter in hand. I had other fish to fry and, smiling at my own joke but without seeing how the clash on cobbled Church Street turned out, I pushed my empty plate to one side and started studying my fellow diners. Where was my blue hatted contact? How was I to go and wait? And where?

I was sure the meeting I'd bobbed along to earlier at the Monk house, even without my cap, must have at least progressed things to the next level: not that I was at all sure where or what that level was. Perhaps all I could do was be alert for the next move – whatever that turned out to be – and ready to bring things to a head.

Although the table to which I'd been squeezed by the accommodating waitress earlier could hardly be described as the best seat in the house, it was the perfect vantage point from which to monitor the comings and goings of subsequent diners – had there had been any. Indeed, there were only two other punters in the whole place (another small chuckle at my pun): I'm sure it was just coincidence(?) but the three of us had been seated almost as far apart from each other as was physically possible. With my back to the side wall I had a clear view of everyone inside - and an equally clear sight of the front door should anyone join our merry band. I made a mental note that it was a Mrs Bergman who was to my right in the corner of the restaurant while a Mr Dean Martin was the huge hulk of a man slouched at a table opposite. Neither of these fellow diners looked likely candidates for anything even remotely suspicious, but then when do they ever?

Allocating manufactured names was an old habit I'd picked up years ago at a Motivational conference. I remember it dragging on for hours and was the last place in the world I wanted to be, but my then boss had paid for it and forced me to go, so I went and there I remained. Anyway, although I discarded 95% of what Mr Motivator droned on about, two things stayed with me. One was a name remembering trick. Note the very first impression you get when you meet someone; and it had to be the very first, or this wouldn't work. Give that thought a name and link it to their actual name. On your next meeting you will instantly recall the false label and their name will flood to mind on the back of that.

This technique helped in my assessment of what I should look out for. I wouldn't actually know what I was looking for until I saw it, but I doubted the Mrs Bergman, frail and fidgety Swedish woman taking minuscule sips of tea and adjusting the teaspoon in her saucer at ten-second intervals, had anything more sinister than a lipstick and a hankie in her faux snakeskin handbag. Similarly, it was hard to imagine snoozy Dean Martin, a largish looking man with tufts of ginger hair sticking out from beneath a green beret of sorts (was he really asleep at this lunchtime hour?) as little more than just a little old wine drinker.

The other thing I took away from that dreary course was the MM Challenge: how to keep things fresh and people on their toes

He suggested to the audience that, when we went home that evening, just when the family (it was only my wife and me but as long as there was at least one other person involved, the ruse would work) was ready to decamp into the living room to watch the television, I should get into the room first, sit in the other person's usual chair and wait. He then prattled on for ages about the psychological effects of this experiment and, while I'd long since switched off by then, the general premise must have stuck with me because when I went home that evening I thought I'd give it a go.

I can still recall Wifie's face and the disruption it caused. When I say, disruption, I don't mean it with a capital "D", but suddenly the table she puts her wine glass on, and the pouffe where she rests her feet are both out of reach. It just disrupts (again, with a lowercase "d") things and puts one off one's guard.

A teenage boy walked in, nudging me out of my living room and back into the chip shop. He looked a tad Dickensian and I instinctively labelled him, Jim Lad. He bought some food and took a seat a couple of tables down from me, but again I saw no danger: this young cabin boy wouldn't have the power to swing a cosh in my direction even if he had one, which I was sure he didn't.

For a moment, my uninvited dining guests prompted a bizarre Las Vegas image in my mind involving a cabaret act crooning on the Orient Express en route to Treasure Island, but I was brought back to Whitby when the door opened and Frock Coat man, or, Vlad as I would now choose to call him sidled in. There was no blue cap in sight but the coat was unmistakable and caused me to take more than just a second look. Now it was up close I could see how well travelled it had been. Not quite *Michael over the Himalaya and round the Pacific Palin* travelled, but I had certainly seen it fluttering among the graveyard barely 60 minutes ago.

He placed the newspaper he was carrying onto a table a few down from me that the server had pointed him towards and, completely blanking Ingrid, Dean, Jim and myself, walked to the counter.

I watched as he scanned the menu, placed his order and fumbled around for the cash (he seemed to have come better equipped than me). As he turned to make his way back to his table he saw, not only the paper he'd left there a moment ago but also me, sitting by it, in his chair.

I couldn't have wished for a more perfect reaction. On the occasion I'd done this to my wife she was most definitely taken aback – but only momentarily. She soon regained her composure and shouted, "What on earth are you playing at?" By comparison, Vlad's reaction was less dramatic. He simply froze. His head stayed facing me, but his eyes darted over towards the table by the wall he was sure I'd actually been sitting at when he came in. I just stared straight at him and, had I not motioned him towards the seat opposite me with a slight nod, he might have remained rooted to his spot for some time.

He pulled back the chair and, as he bent into place, went to speak but I cut him off. "Just sit down and don't say a word" I whispered. At this stage I was aiming for politician calm rather than *East Enders* menace, though if that had to change, so be it.

"As things stand," I said, "I have no idea how you fit into all of this. I do know however I've seen you following me around the churchyard this morning and that, of all the restaurants in all the world, you've chosen today to walk into mine – and, despite this being 19th September, that's just a couple of coincidences too far for me at the moment. Now, I think there are two things we can probably both agree on. To begin with, the proprietors of Hadleys Fish Restaurant really don't deserve any trouble. Second, I'm sitting here thinking about a meeting I need to have with a woman and while she may or may not end up looking like a 1920s fictional muscular American cartoon character (if Vlad wasn't sure at this stage what was going on, this piece of news didn't seem to help clear the mists all that much) I reckon we both know that the bits resting, albeit I suspect somewhat uncomfortably between your legs at the moment, confirm that ain't you."

"But what only one of knows," I continued, "is that I've got a gun underneath this table pointing at those bits of yours so, put your hands where I can see them, keep both your mouth and that ridiculous Victorian coat you're wearing buttoned up, and listen."

"I know the score. Once the goods are delivered, I pay the money or I'm in trouble. Everything has always gone swimmingly so I haven't had cause before to play out this little charade – but I must say, now it's come about I didn't expect it to involve some drag queen in costume. If I'd have known I would have brought along my club scarf to match the cap I'm guessing is screwed up in your pocket."

He said nothing.

"Now," I told him, "I am going to get up slowly and you are going to keep your hands on the table in plain sight. You are going to wait until I've left, then you can contact your contact – or whoever is pulling your strings and tell her not to try to pull mine again. Tell her, I'm done waiting, now I'm going to go."

I got up, acknowledged the waitress at the counter and slid out of the door.

Chapter 7

Heaven can wait

PETE

I think, therefore I am... confused (Benjamin Hoff)

St Peter is sitting outside the Pearly Gates, checking in the new arrivals. He'd had to deal with a couple of administrate cock ups involving David Niven and Warren Beatty – neither of whom were due to have arrived for a number of years - but other than that it had been a slow day. He was just thinking about shutting up shop when a chap appears. He looks somewhat dazed and bewildered. St Peter is kind and welcoming, asks the man who he is and how he got here. The guy tells him his name, frowns and hesitates a few times before saying,

"I have really no idea what has happened. There I was, looking around, minding my own business, when a dirty great big wooden trunk lands on my head. The thing came completely out of the blue and the next thing I knew - I was here."

St Peter sympathised, thanked him for his tale, and shepherded him through the Gates.

A few moments passed – it's hard to be specific because time in those parts is such a relative concept – and then a second figure appeared. He was quite a large, well-built Charles Atlas sort of man, and he looked very mad. St Peter couldn't tell at once if he was about to explode or indeed had already done so, but he asked for some ID and the details of what had brought him here. The man, evidently agitated, spat out his name and proceeded to recount to the Apostle that he'd come home early from work one day to find his wife naked and breathless in bed. He said he'd scanned the room, ran to the open window and, looking out, saw a fellow in the street below attempting to walk away from the house in a nonchalant fashion. In a fit of uncontrollable rage he picked up the nearest thing to hand, a bedding trunk beneath the sill, and hurled it on top of the fleeing figure. "The strain of it all seems to have been too much for my heart," he said, which had obviously given out and resulted in him arriving here.

The Gates duly swung open, allowing the angry husband to walk through.

St Peter's mind turned briefly to an earlier pint and conversation he'd had with Gabriel in the Angel's Tavern when a third character came into view. He wasn't wearing a stitch of clothing and St P was eager to hear his story.

"Well", the naked man said, having been ticked off the register. "There I was, sitting in this trunk.........."

Chapter 8

Blue hats and Brown coats

VLAD

> Sometimes I'm confused by what I think is really obvious.
> But what I think is really obvious, obviously isn't obvious
> (Michael Stipe)

I have really no idea what has happened. There I was, looking around, minding my own business................

Everything had started so well. I'd come up to Whitby the day before, staying overnight in the Melrose Guest House. This part of the world doesn't have the greatest of transport connections, and if I'd tried to do the trip from home in one day I wouldn't have arrived before nightfall. I had actually considered whether arriving in town after dark was in fact a better choice: it would certainly have added to the experience, but after mulling things over I decided that my first recce of the cemetery (and this advice probably holds true for graveyards all over the world) was doubtless best done in sunlight.

I'd stumbled across the Irish poet, Abraham Stoker, while studying 19th Century American writers at Exeter University. I was actually searching for *The Lady, or the Tiger?* by Frank Richard

Stockton. He was a poet I'd learned of while doing some research on Mark Twain and quite liked his cheeky style. Similar to many writers of his day, his works are better recognised than Stockton is himself. He is probably best known today for a series of innovative children's fairy tales, in particular, the one I was aiming for. I remembered it well from my youth. It's the one about a man sentenced to an unusual punishment for having a romance with a king's beloved daughter. Taken to the public arena, he is faced with two doors. Behind one is a hungry tiger that, if let loose, will devour him. Behind the other is a beautiful lady-in-waiting, whom, if he opens her door, he will have to marry. While the crowd waits anxiously for his decision, he sees the princess among the spectators pointing him towards the door on the right. The lover starts to open the door and ... the story ends abruptly there. Did the princess save her love by pointing to the door leading to the lady-in-waiting, or did she prefer to see her lover die at the teeth of the tiger rather than see him marry someone else? That quandary has made the story a staple in English classes in many schools.

In aiming for Stockton's book, my fat fingers had failed to successfully navigate around the stupid little keyboard on my aging and minuscule iPhone SE and I'd ended up instead with *The Lady of the Shroud* by this chap Stoker. I had never been much interested in ghosts and ghouls and had not even heard of the term, Gothic Fiction, but while the stories were indeed someway away from the genre I'd previously sought, there was something here that felt intriguing.

I always felt authors from this era contributed little more than merely pushing the definition of the word *fiction* to the extreme. My brief dalliance with English Victorian writers, such as it had been, invariably left me whelmed, let alone underwhelmed. The tales were so twee, with the ends all covered in sugar and as neatly (and unbelievably) tied together as the conclusion of a Ricky Gervais sitcom. But this dark prose I'd stumbled across had unexpectedly gripped me. At first it all seems just too contrived. Early on in Chapter One, we learn that a man has inherited £1 million from a distant uncle. Well, of course he has. If only he'd looked down and seen the five winning lottery tickets suddenly stuck to his shoe, he could have saved himself the bother of going to the solicitor for such a paltry inheritance. No, I really didn't hold out much expectation. But soon I was drawn deeper into a darker, more intriguing place and I was hooked. I think I ploughed halfway through the book before I realised the author was the same chap who'd written Dracula. I know that sounds slightly unlikely, but it's the truth. I guess my mind sometimes blocks out obvious facts and leads me down a path away from common sense.

For example, it was, I lie to you not, three or four years after I'd spent a long weekend in Venice that I discovered this city was actually in Italy. I think I'd just assumed it was hovering off the coast of somewhere or other and just "out there on its own". Anyway, by the time I'd realised the identity of the writer of *Shroud Lady*, I was too far into its pages to turn back and pick up what would be the usual tome of choice for anyone stumbling across Abraham's (I deliberately refuse to think of him by his rather silly nickname) books a first time.

When I finished the story, I glanced over the inevitable column detailing other books by the author on the inside cover. Certainly *Dracula* was up there at the top of the alphabetical ranking, but my eye was drawn more to *The Watter's Mou'* at the foot of the list.

Sometimes, if you scan something quickly, your brain tells you what it thinks you've just read rather than what's actually on the paper - which is exactly what happened here. I suppose a combination of never having heard of a *watter's mou* and my ancient Scottish dialect being a tad rusty, that my sub conscious dismissed the actual letters I'd seen and replaced them with something I'd find easier to comprehend. This, I'm guessing, is how the name of Walter Matthau, a popular 20th century American comedy actor had popped into my head. In my defence, I had only recently watched on TV a film he did in the early 1960s, *The Cactus Flower*. It was a pretty typical movie of the times, instantly forgettable for many reasons other than it co stared an aspiring young actress, Goldie Hawn appearing in only her second film and winning an Oscar for it to boot. OK, so it is fair to say my fixation was a little more Hawn than Matthau, but either way, I think this was the reason I'd misread the title and my attention had wandered to the foot of the list rather than its apex.

Other than the vague similarity in name, the novel had nothing to do with anyone called Matthau. For that matter, it had nothing to do with anyone called Walter either. Nor Mou, come to that. But, whatever it was about, I'd been drawn to it and I think it was then that the notion – for it was little more than that, certainly nothing you'd describe as a rigid plan – that I might consume Stoker's work from bottom to top, saving his most notable effort for last.

And it was this notion I'd stuck with. Indeed, it wasn't until I had slid through *The Snake's Pass*; upped the ante with *Miss Betty*; followed the scent through *The Primrose Path* and consumed the other six books in BS's list, before I reached the Count. That milestone was passed a week ago last Saturday.

Alongside reading his works I'd also done a fair bit of background study on Abraham himself. I'd been to County Sligo in Ireland where he was raised; wandered around Dublin where he went to University (to be honest, this was more to try the Guinness than a serious attempt to broaden my knowledge about the man); spent time in London exploring the archives of The Lyceum Theatre, where he worked as a manager under Henry Irving; and visited his grave in north London's Golders Green cemetery. But I saved the trip to Whitby for last.

THE HUNTRODDS COINCIDENCES

I'd chosen my lodgings (as Abraham and every other Victorian author would surely have phrased it) to be relatively near to the plaque that commemorates his stay in the town in the twilight of the 19th Century while writing *Dracula*. It was also not that far to St Mary's church around which much of the local action in the story takes place.

By the time Abraham settled on the church as the location for the beginning of the English section of the book, it had been around for nearly 800 years, although its interior dates chiefly from around 100 years before the time the tale is set. It is situated on top of a cliff, overlooking the mouth of the River Esk and close to the ruins of Whitby Abbey.

While both my current and Stoker's old lodgings are on the west side of the river, the church is on the east; the easiest link between the two being the Whitby swing bridge. At this time of year the wind can hurl itself off the sea and along the estuary, making even the short crossing, shall we call it, bracing. It can most surely batter the hell out of you. I momentarily wondered if the local entrepreneurs who opened the restaurant that greets you on making it safely to the east side decided that fish and chips would be the suitably ironic choice of fare.

I turned left into Church Street and, walking parallel with the river and past the various tourist traps, arrived at the foot of the flight of 199 steps that lead up the hill to the cliff top.

On reaching the summit, the terrain struck me as dramatic. I had read that two significant land slips affecting the northern seaside edge of the church's grounds had caused the local residents considerable angst, especially when some human remains fell onto the street below, but I must say this only added to my own personal intrigue.

My first view of the site was extraordinary. It was so dark and overcast that there was very little I could actually see. Then the shadow of a cloud that had hitherto slightly obscured St. Mary's Church passed and I caught the ruins of the Abbey coming into view; and as the edge of a narrow band of light as sharp as a sword-cut moved along, the church and churchyard became gradually visible. I hoped I might suck in the flavour of the area on my own, and for a moment or two it seemed I would get my wish. Then I saw something dark stood behind a seat. What it was, whether man or beast, I could not tell.

I returned to the present with a modest jolt. Now was not the time to rehearse chunks of text from the book: I really just wanted to wander around and experience the setting.

There was no particular building or stone I was hunting for, although there is always something slightly mesmerising about graves that seem to compel one to pore over the ancient carvings and epitaphs despite having no genuine interest in them.

I could have spent days in that cemetery and as it was, I totally lost track of time. My earlier decision to skip breakfast was catching up on me, so I thought it as good an idea as any to grab a quick bite (not the first time I'd used that line since I'd began reading these novels) and then return for a second lap of the grounds.

That fish and chip restaurant I'd passed this side of the bridge seemed as fine a place as any for lunch so I strode back down the 199 steps, momentarily thinking that might have been an even better choice of title for John Buchan's novel: it would have made just as much sense as did settling on thirty-nine. Anyway, on reaching the bottom I turned left towards the chippy. A wee way down the street I saw a guy in a coat ridiculously similar to mine crash into a woman, nearly knocking her off her feet. I thought it best not to mess with him and, just to be on the safe side, crossed the road. Arriving at the restaurant I could see there were lots of spare tables and, plopping my newspaper down on one, went up to the counter to place an order.

THE HUNTRODDS COINCIDENCES

I had no idea at the time, but my day would have been much calmer if only I'd chosen *The Magpie* cafe on the other side of the bridge.

Chapter 9
All roads lead everyone to Whitby

DEAN MARTIN
I'm busy doing nothing working the whole day through (Bing
Crosby)

Well. There I was sitting in this trunk..............

The restaurant had barely been open a few minutes when I crossed the threshold, so I was first in, best dressed, and had a free range of tables to choose from. The waitress said she wasn't expecting a busy day, and they didn't have any reservations until the evening. That surprised and slightly worried me but I had little choice other than order, sit, eat, wait and mull over where things might go from here.

I'd not been able to contact or speak with anyone in the small envelope of time between the Postman's call and now. A text seemed my only option: for the moment, she'd just have to be happy with that. It was light on detail, but needed to include a warning: *Looks like I'm going to Whitby too – but not with you. Be careful, watch out for traps and make absolutely, totally, doubly sure you're talking to the right person. Talk later – at The Magpie* was as deep a message as I could muster.

It was an hour or so before another punter joined me in the café. A slight, pale (Swedish?) woman entered. She was followed almost immediately by the guy I was waiting for. The Postman's partner had changed little from the picture I was working from, so was easy to recognise. Of course, he didn't even know I existed, let alone what I looked like, so I had no need to hide away from him; not that he paid me any interest or attention. I think he must have been distracted by the lady who was taking the babiest of steps as she moved glacially in front of him because he didn't seem even to have registered there was anybody else around. I slouched downed in my seat, pulled my trusty green hat down as far as it would go and all but closed my eyes.

His meal arrived. I thought I'd hang on till he was halfway through before deciding if the situation called for me to make any sort of move. I wasn't sure I would get what we wanted by simply following him around for a bit, or if I needed to stir things up. A young lad walked in. No panic. No rush. I could wait.

Then some bloke out of a Victorian novel appeared. For a quiet day, this was turning into Piccadilly Circus. I let Dickensian Man settle down, but before I knew what was happening, my quarry had slid across to Charles' table and began talking to him.

Their conversation seemed pretty one sided and lasted less than a minute. I don't think CD had had the chance to emit as much as an, "Eh...?" before his uninvited guest simply stood up, acknowledged the waitress, turned and left.

When I first walked into the restaurant, I'm really not sure what I thought might happen but whatever it was, this wasn't quite it. At least, as far as my next steps were concerned, the decision had been made: I had to shift into track and tracing mode.

Chapter 10
More blue hats and brown coats

THE ACCOUNTANT

I'm prepared to meet my Maker. Whether my Maker is prepared to
meet me is another matter (Winston Churchill)

The day had started, as it always did, with me being woken by Sid.
The up side of not sleeping with him is a totally peaceful night. But
while throwing him out before going to bed usually achieves that,
the downside comes back to haunt me around five something with
his pitiful and piercing mews from the garden below. It's then a race
against time to get downstairs and let him in before he wakes up my
particularly easily niggled neighbour. We then start the pathetic daily
ritual: I fill his food bowl; he ignores it and zooms upstairs to my
room. I throw him off the bed; he waits for me to get back in and
then jumps on my head. I push him down between my legs; he sidles
up and starts 5 minutes of kneading my full bladder. I drift back to
sleep and wake up 20 minutes later when the radio alarm switches on
with him sleeping soundly at my feet as if he is the most the angelic
cat that has ever lived.

The change from this feline ritual occurred when the secure
phone rang. I looked at the radio just as the digital display clicked

over to thirty-eight minutes past six. This call from the Postman to ask for my settlement instructions was earlier than I'd expected, though I soon found out why.

Apparently, something was wrong with the delivery which meant the payment wouldn't be forthcoming. He said he couldn't fathom out what had happened and needed my help to get to the bottom of whatever it was that had gone awry. Bugger. This sort of distraction took me away from what I should be concentrating on.

I told him the only way to sort this out was for me to meet his courier face to face, and I gave him details of the meeting place I'd planned to use for the money transfer – it was as good and secure as any, so why not?

He called back a few minutes later and told me everything was set, but we both needed to wear Shrewsbury baseball caps so we could recognise one another. At first I misheard what he'd said because I replied that I was not putting any wild animal on my head for anyone, but he explained this was soccer rather than sorex related. I then mentioned I didn't need any headwear of any form because I already knew what the guy looked like. "Yes." he replied, somewhat annoyed, "Of course you know what he looks like, but he doesn't know that, does he?"

I suppose that was right. While I knew everything about this chap, he wouldn't have known me from Adam, or Eve. Before I had a chance to raise any further objections, or alternative suggestions regarding the means of mutual recognition foisted upon me, he just said that the hat I needed would be left in the car.

As the phone line went dead, it was clear that everything for tomorrow's meet was now in place and there was little or nothing I could do that would change anything. So, settling for kicking Sid off the bed, I moved towards the bathroom. My bladder was killing me and I needed to shower and GASO!

I arrived in Whitby well ahead of schedule, though in the course of my *Getting A Shift On*, I had failed to hear my phone ring sometime earlier (1 missed call/you have no voicemail messages). Still, at least there was a text.

It hadn't really crossed my mind that the person I'd actually be meeting later in the day might be some sort of ringer – nor that he could possibly be equally worried about my provenance, so I suppose the baseball cap equivalent of a red rose in the lapel and copy of the Financial Times under the arm made sense.

I was pretty certain I would be able to pick him out of a line-up, but what if the photo I'd been working from was not a great likeness, or he'd grown a beard or something? I needed to make absolutely, totally, doubly sure I was talking to the right guy. We didn't want anything to be mucked up by an undercover cop or a rookie mistake, so I should perhaps come up with some cunning plan for my back pocket, just in case.

While mulling over that little conundrum, I called into the hire car company to sign the paperwork and collect the keys.

The *DRAC 1* licence plate belonged to the only car parked in the reserved bays and was attached to a red Chrysler. I squeezed into the front seat and removed the Avis sticker hooked over the rear view mirror.

The rental was arranged some time ago when I'd originally settled on this location to collect the money. While it seemed I would be coming away empty-handed on that front, I needed to at least make sure I had a convincing tale to tell up the line. I had already advised them I wasn't expecting the payment to be made but, of course, at this moment they only had my word for that – and they would demand something slightly more concrete before there was any chance of them crossing me off their list of people to be suspicious about.

It can't be easy arranging for a blue baseball cap to be stuffed into the side pocket of a hired car in some obscure corner of the realm, but, I suppose I am working in a multi-million pound diamond smuggling business so such modest and minor transportation issues shouldn't really phase, trouble or concern me. And trying it on for size using the car's rear-view mirror I thought well, at least the colour matches my eyes.

I slid the seat as far forward as it would go, although as so often is the case for my diminutive frame, this was nowhere near far enough to enable my feet to reach the pedals. As I was trying to wedge my Louis Vuitton into place behind my back to provide some necessary support I started to familiarise myself with the car's controls. It was a relief to see this was a top of the range *PT Cruiser* with an integrated sat nav. Balancing a phone on the dashboard of an unfamiliar car in an unfamiliar town and with the metal corner of a designer handbag digging into your coccyx, is not only uncomfortable but, on a more practical level, is not the easiest way to navigate around town - particularly when there are so many diversions to negotiate.

Mad Monk Cottage was on the other side of the river. As anyone who has had the good fortune to visit this nape of the UK's neck will tell you, there are very few options when trying to drive from one end of the town to the other. The A171 seems to be the local's most popular road of choice and, luckily, the 75 yard wide Whitby Swing bridge, connecting the east part of town to the west, is on it. Unluckily, several sections of this main thoroughfare had suddenly all fallen into such a state of disrepair that it seemed every one of them was being rebuilt on the very day I was trying to travel along them. To add to my misfortune, it soon became apparent that the A171's exalted status amongst the indigenous population was due mainly to it being about the only road in town that either wasn't a cul-de-sac or didn't lead one straight into the sea. This left precious few alternatives for the sat nav to offer. I'd barely travelled 500 yards when I was forced to turn right onto Prospect Hill and the only advice my automated friend from the land of the free (I think Chrysler must make sure that only US voiced electronics are able to be heard in their vehicles) could proffer was, "Turn around and turn right onto the A171".

Eventually, my American car's systems met the challenge and I arrived at the cottage a mere 55 minutes after I'd set off on my circuitous 1.6 mile trip.

This was one of *their* safe houses. They seemed to be all over the place. Early on, I remember thinking what a coincidence that there was always a house or apartment on hand to accommodate these transactions. Of course, that thought soon passed. They were the ones feeding me the locations. There are no such things as coincidences.

The road up to the meeting place was the principal route travelled by tourist coaches to the Abbey, though there had been precious few sightings of those so far today. Towards the end of the street and on the right were several buildings, a sort of medieval estate, but I found Mad Monk's Cottage quite easily. Whoever had renovated these cottages - and you simply had to look at the dilapidated state of the consecrated ruin on my left to realise some serious money had been lashed out, at least on this side of the track - must have been a kind and thoughtful soul because instead of a line of meaningless numbers, each property had been given a quirky little name. The three words I was seeking had been chiselled into the stonework lintel, over a door with a rather bizarre stained glass window of two old nags in front of an crumbling church arch.

The customer's car park for the adjacent Whitby Brewery was deserted, so I thought that was as good a place as any to hide the PT Cruiser in plain sight. The entrance to the cottage was on the side of the house looking past the brewery and towards St Mary's Church. On crossing the threshold I could see immediately that the refurbishment had been carried out with at least some respect for the lifestyle of the previous monastic residents. The door led directly into the main living area revealing a room of simple design: any urge the modernisers had had to sex it up a bit, either by adding a bay window or making it lobbied off, had been resisted. I glanced around and, leaving the door slightly open, crossed the floor to a window facing the Abbey but with an excellent view left down the full length of road. I pulled up a chair, sat down and, resting an elbow on the sill and my chin in my hand, stared down the track waiting for my man to turn up.

And, for some time, waiting was all I did. For at least an hour I gazed down the road with not so much as the sight of man (specific or otherwise), beast (so long as you exclude seagulls) or even an anchorite (of any denomination) wandering into view. So little was happening that I found myself absent mindedly returning to a creative word game I used to play with my brother when we were holed up together in our bedrooms. The only rule was that your creation had to have a credible base. (As the eldest, I appointed myself the Sobiture (a neat little amalgam of *sole* and *arbiture*). Anyway, I had just got to the stage where I'd decided I must have been lulled into a state of stupdom, (a mix of stupor and boredom) when I was unexpectedly hurled into a condition of fenic (fear and panic). From over my shoulder, I heard footsteps crunching on the gravel leading up to the cottage. I quickly turned my attention up the path to the right, just in time to catch sight of a man leaving the track and heading directly towards me. This had caught me somewhat by surprise: I hadn't considered for a moment that he would appear on foot from across the churchyard on my right, the opposite direction from the way I had driven in.

THE HUNTRODDS COINCIDENCES

From the many photographs I'd seen, I knew the face of the the man I was expecting quite well. However, with the collar of his coat pulled up high against the wind and having only been able to grab the merest glimpse of this visitor, I was really far from certure (certain/sure) whether he was my intended or not. There wasn't even a cap of any colour or description on his head to assist in the identification process.

The gravel crunch outside stopped. I dashed the few steps from my window across the floor, arriving at the door just as he was beginning to nudge it open. Suddenly I realised I had no real idea how of how to play this. Quite late in the day for epiphanies, I know, but the tentative push he was making gave me a rush of unexpected courage and a moment to think. Until I could be absolutely sure I was talking to the right guy, keeping my identity secret (even in this tense stage I allowed myself a wry smile as I pictured myself with a mask and cape) could only have an upside for me, so I kicked a wodge of junk mail lying by my feet under the door preventing it being opened any further. I tried to add a bit a menace with a husky, "Stay there", a few semitones lower than normal and felt the pressure ease off.

The first thing I needed to find out was did he have the diamonds. Understanding that would dictate the next course of action.

There were several ways of doing this, I suppose, but I opted for the boringly conventional and, attempting to maintain my gravelly homage to Marlene Dietrich, whispered, "Do you have them?"

Learning that he didn't was a pain. At least if he'd had them and either wasn't happy with the quality, or worse and far more contentious, the quantity of the gems, it would have meant that this had become someone else's problem and I could bow out. As it was, I was still very much in the loop. It was only once everybody who mattered could be sure that he hadn't picked up the package that my involvement would be definitively ruled out, and I could return to my true purpose for being here.

Of course, the nagging question that kept flashing behind my very eyes was, why didn't he have them? The Postman had confirmed the drop, and I had no reason to disbelieve him, not that I would want to risk the bigger picture by challenging him too deeply. Anyway, until this was all resolved he wouldn't be paid, so if he was the one buggering about, he would also be the one being buggered. It had to be someone, or something else. Was this guy, barely six inches away from my nose, really who I thought he was. Sure, he was in the right place, here, at the right time, now, so he was certainly "involved", but there was only one of us wearing a damn blue baseball hat at the moment, and it certainly wasn't him. Why not? Did all this have any relationship to the other business we were looking at? Was this the sort of trap Dean wanted to warn me against? I needed to buy just a few moments to think things through and to make absolutely sure the person I'd be talking to face to face, was the same one I'd been dealing with all this time from afar. I had an idea and said, "That doesn't bring me joy, only sorrow. Go. And wait. You know where". Hoping to catch him off guard, I put my shoulder to the door and, with my full weight behind it, rammed the thing shut.

Although I could no longer see him, I sensed he had backed off a few feet. If he was who he should be, he'd know where to go and I'd meet him there. If he wasn't, I would just have to follow him until I found out who he really was.

I let his footsteps drift away. Following him in the car was going to be a nightmare and clearly not an option. In any event, he'd turned right at the top of the drive and was retracing his steps into what looked like a churchyard.

I gave him a few moments head start and took the opportunity of sending Dean a quick text before tentatively opening the door and peering round its corner. I spotted his beige coat disappearing

behind a gravestone so thought now was as good a time as any to set
out on his trail. If he was the right guy, I'd just be following him to
where I already knew he was going. The wrong guy would lead me
somewhere totally different - and if that was the case, I'd want to see
exactly where that was.

The open ground of the cemetery meant I'd had to hang back
somewhat further than I would have liked, and by the time I'd
reached the top of what seemed like a mountain of stairs, *The Coat*
was nowhere to be seen.

Pretty confident though that the only way he'd gone was down
– I went down. At the foot of the steps I found myself on Church
Street. I suppose, technically, I did have a choice to make, but as
veering right looked like a direct path into the North Sea, I turned
left. This had to be his route – didn't it? There was some sort of café
cum museum thing on my near side, but that was closed. Across the
street, Marie Antoinette's tea room was open, as was Hunters Sweet
shop a further few yards down, although both were devoid of clients.

The Black Horse Inn might have been a possibility, though as
I got closer I could see it was boarded up and undoubtedly long
closed. I was about to examine the White Horse & Griffin when
a man in a blue hat clattered into me. He clearly hadn't realised
that I was wandering aimlessly, not paying any attention at all to
exactly where I was going – he didn't even apologise for my lack of
awareness. As I was attempting to sway back into a more upright
and balanced position, I could see that the only other soul in this
otherwise deserted and unremarkable street was a young boy kicking
an old and worn tennis ball against the circular column in the market
square. He'd looked across momentarily but, I suppose seeing no real
carnage had occurred simply returned to his task. I did likewise.

I tried to look past him in case my quarry had darted off-road but
was brought back to Church Street by the flash of something from
a building at the end of the road. It was probably a metal plate or

letterbox reflecting the sun's rays my way, but whatever it was drew me to carry on beyond the 17th Century Guest House and stop on the pavement across from what I could now see was the glinting door of a fish and chip shop. To all intents and purposes, it appeared the man I had been following had stopped for lunch. This was not good. His selection of cuisine was fine, but his choice of restaurant: not so much.

Although my target did not have a clue what I looked like, I was sure two and two might quickly be put together if he spotted a strange woman hovering for too long on the empty road and gawping in through the shop's window. I turned back to the tennis footballer. He didn't seem overly wedded to his current activity and was intrigued by the notion of becoming my secret agent and finding out what he could about the mystery man I'd just pointed out. The deal was sealed with a £20 note and confirmed by my suggestion he use some of it to buy some chips to assist in his undercover activities - and the rest to purchase a proper football.

I remained on the other side of the main road and a little way up from the restaurant. The large panoramic window provided me with a good enough view of what was going on inside and, of course, now I also had a mole in place who could provide some first-hand detail that would, hopefully, fill in any blanks.

It looked like there were two other diners vying with my man for the waitress's attention, but the glint of the sun prevented me from getting a good look at either of them. As I watched my young talpid take up his position a couple of tables along from our target, a guy in a long shitty brown coat walked past me and, pausing only to glance at the menu card pinned on the notice board outside, entered the premises. He took the newspaper from under his arm and placed it on the empty table next to my mini spy, spun around and approached the counter. Behind him, I saw my prey slide across to the table where the tabloid had just been deposited.

My target now had his back to me and the window, and was looking directly at the hind quarters of the Shitty Coat guy. As the coat turned, I could see clearly the round of musical chairs that had gone on behind him was not something he had expected. The blood drained from his face and he just seemed frozen in time, though after a few moments he sat down and appeared to be listening intently to what his new dining partner had to say.

They'd not been together for more than a couple of minutes before my quarry stood up, exited the restaurant and turned left to cross the river back to the major part of town. After a few moments my small and super sleuth also appeared at the door and started making his way towards me. He had barely made it halfway across the road before the door opened again. Ashen faced man – his complexion was so dreadfully pale that all previous fixations on the hew of his apparel were totally forgotten – all but stumbled out onto the pavement. He looked left along Bridge Street and could see the fading shape of his erstwhile dining companion now on the bridge itself. He appeared to be wrestling with his thoughts and in a quandary as to which way to go. He briefly looked up Church Street, past (through?) me and James Bond junior, but seemed to settle instead on turning right and running away in the opposite direction from the river.

By now, my boy had reached my side and was giving me the gist of the conversation he'd overheard at the table next to him. Absolutely none of what he was relaying was making any sense. His debriefing was just throwing up more questions than answers. I needed a deeper understanding of what was going on, but I also needed to keep tabs on the disappearing figure on the bridge. I was still not certain that he'd understood my message. He was now moving in the correct general direction, but from this particular starting point his options were limited so that didn't really account for much. Another £20 note convinced *Nick Nack* to provide further details of what had just occurred and his agreement to accompany me on the trail of my rogue agent.

As we set out to follow in his wake, I kept the interrogation going and was so engrossed in his answers that I almost missed the chip shop door open for a fourth time in as many minutes. At first I was less than even moderately interested to see one of Hadley's two earlier diners appear. He started walking on the opposite side of the street from us, but in the same general direction. He seemed somewhat unstable on his feet, and I'd all but turned my attentions away from him and back to my questioning when he sort of tripped on the curb. It was while trying to regain his balance that the collar of his coat flapped down and I caught a flash of his face. I needed no more of a glimpse than that. How on earth did *he* get there?

Chapter 11
Soccer and Stones in Shropshire

THE POSTMAN
Nobody notices postmen, yet they have passions like other men
(G.K. Chesterton)

I began working for the Royal Mail many years ago. This was some time before it was privatised, though not that that made a great deal of difference to the job: at least, not at first. I was among the 50% not to be part of the 1997 New Labour government's target to get half of all school leavers into higher education. Instead, I wandered into the pot with the others and became an apprentice mechanic. I'd always been fairly handy around engines, but never thought I could earn a living at it. It took me under 18 months, during which I earned less in a day than the price of a litre of Duckhams 20w-50, to realise those early thoughts were bang on the money.

When I saw the Royal Mail advert suggesting I might bring in enough to buy two litres of oil and hour, or receive twice the amount my undergraduate friends were currently paying out in university fees every year well, the choice was simple. You do maths.

The organisation had a lot going for it. Losing the comfort and familiarity of your mates in the garage was soon replaced with the natural sense of camaraderie that came with being a Postie. And the 50:50 ratio I'd pondered on leaving school would also filter through to my new job: the early starts were more than balanced by the early finishes; and the rainy days were simply part of what you had to put up with for the outdoor life.

Of course, there were also the odd perks.

I developed the knack of spotting which envelopes contained birthday cards, and which of those were likely to have a wee note emblazoned with the Queen's face tucked inside. But I likewise became pretty good at selecting parcels likely to merit closer inspection.

Wayne Jalsh, an old family friend from Gdansk, played a quasi-uncle role during my early years. I can't recall how he was, or became involved in my life but, no matter: I never once questioned the back story to his existence because his presence, always involved........ presents. And not just on birthdays or Christmas. Every time he appeared at our door, so did a little something of wonder for me. Given some space and perhaps a quiet corner in a bar with a few pints of Pedigree, I bet I could remember each gift I was lucky enough to have received over the years; though such power of recall would not be down solely to the marvelousness of the prizes inside its wrappings. It would, at least in part, be related to the wrapping itself. I doubt it crossed Uncle Wayne's mind to ever use but a solitary rectangle of paper to hide his gift from me. And I often wondered if he'd had shares in Sellotape, because rarely would he pass me anything that had been bound together with less than half a roll of the stuff. It invariably took four times as long to get into any parcel of joy from Jalsh as it did a pressie from any rookie wrapper, and I suspect that heightened the anticipation for me to such a degree that I never forgot a single thing he gave me.

It also served me well in my latest line of endeavours. Unbeknown to Uncle W, I inherited one gift more than he had physically handed over: the ability to spot, at sixty paces, both items more secure than Fort Knox, and those more accessible and worthy of further exploration.

This skill made the selection process for suitable packages all the easier. I would then need only to make a subtle nick in the paper wrappings, or gently ease away a strip of poorly stuck tape, in order to decide if the risk of detouring the contents away from the intended recipient was worth taking.

I remember one such package in particular; it was the reason I turned in my blue tunic and hung up my satchel.

Just to be clear, this change of direction was entirely my decision. Actually, that's not quite true. In fact, thinking about it, it's not really even partially true. I had very little choice.

The parcel in question looked nothing special: it had come from somewhere overseas. I'd never seen the stamp before so couldn't place it, not that I was particularly interested, other than for professional reasons – in a train spotter kind of way - in doing so.

Had the brown paper wrapping not been torn, or I hadn't noticed that the cheap corrugated cardboard box beneath had a hole in it, I'd have probably tossed it into my bag and delivered it as usual. But the flimsy covering was torn and I could see inside the box. I gave it a wee shake and heard the clinking sound that transported me back to a time of playing marbles in the street. The exposed opening in the parcel needed only some modest poking and that, together with a little more determined shaking, persuaded the contents to tumble into my palm.

In my hand were half a dozen small, dull looking misshapen rocks, akin to chipped ice cubes that haven't come away properly from their frozen tray. They were hard, sharp and warm to the touch and, while I had no idea what they were, my sub conscious fleetingly poked the bizarre notion into my head that perhaps I was holding some sort of hidden treasure.

As much as I liked my job, the rounds could be mind-numbing and one found that a fantasy world could all too easily drift in to ease the boredom – and sometimes it stayed with you just a little bit longer than it should.

I caught myself whispering, "Argh, Jim lad" and picturing an open chest on a desert island, its contents overflowing and glinting in the bright sunshine. But the treasure I was holding bore no relation to this fictional plunder. Perhaps the fact that it neither glinted nor sparkled nudged my thoughts into a different direction and so, with the soles of Paul Simon's shoes pushing Long John Silver out of the equation, I turned to my phone and Googled the word *diamonds*.

Once I scrolled past the seemingly endless offers of white engagement rings (from £11,207) and 3+ carat Blue Nile loose stones (upwards of £62,215.20) I edited my search by adding the word *rough*.

Pay dirt.

Now you may think it slightly ironic that I neither know much, nor care a great deal about stamps, but I do know how to price the cost of a package. More specifically, I understand weights and I reckon each one of these rocks came in at around five or six grams. Nothing likely to prompt excitement at this stage, but after spending near to 5 minutes looking at various sites: how much do rough diamonds cost?; what is a carat?; who is bugs bunny? (it's not always easy to type when getting excited), I thought each one of the stones I'd been mindlessly turning over in my hand might be worth up to a few thousand pounds, i.e. worthy of some serious thinking.

Having said that, the more I read the clearer it became that calculating the value of rough diamonds, if indeed these were what they are, was actually about as clear as the opaque stones I was holding themselves.

What did suddenly become clear was that, to find out their true worth, I'd need to get them to an expert - and therein lay my first problem. The packet had already passed far too many hands and checks for it to be "lost in the post". The worst amateur Sherlock in the world would need less than 10 minutes to eliminate the impossible and be left pointing the figure very definitely at me. No, the second best option was the only one I could take so, popping the largest of the stones in my pocket, replacing the other five in the package and covering over the hole with a strip of special tape we use for items of correspondence received by the Royal Mail in damaged condition, I went out to do my round.

I'd decided to travel to Birmingham and find some dodgy looking back street jeweller to "claim" my prize, but I was on duty for the rest of the week, so planned to make the trip at the weekend.

The good news is that I didn't buy my train ticket in advance. The bad news was that it seems I wasn't far off the mark as to how long it might take to be tracked down by a part-time detective. And the way my conscious had started constantly pricking me, that shouldn't have come as a surprise.

The day after I'd popped the almost complete package through the appropriate letter box, I found myself glancing over my shoulder - for no apparent reason other than a slight prickly feeling on the back of my neck.

Twenty-four hours later I was no longer turning around, but kept sensing that one or two of the innocuous looking people now crossing my path had also done so earlier on my route.

By the third day I had begun to relax with such thoughts and senses all but disappeared, although that changed the moment I stepped foot into my fourth floor flat.

The main door to the building was off the latch, not that that was particularly unusual. Nor was the absence of light on the first floor landing: the kids from the apartment below invariably pinched the bulb within moments of a new one being screwed into place, so I barely gave its absence a second thought. However, finding my apartment door ajar and two guys sitting on the sofa in my living room was not a typical occurrence.

After a few feeble attempts to feign ignorance and some very clear signals that there were very few ways this situation might end well for me if I didn't come clean - I came clean, produced their missing diamond (at this moment I was as good as convinced that was what this was) and slumped down in the sofa they'd by now vacated to await my fate.

It is hard in these circumstances to put a particularly positive spin on things, but.....let's give it a go.

In short (and by that I mean missing out the bits where it was made plain to me how some of my bits might end up in various different places if I didn't cooperate) it seems they were having a problem and I could just be the solution they were looking for. Or, at the very least, part of it.

The package of rough diamonds (I was indeed learning as we went along) I had chanced upon was one of several consignments destined, ultimately, for somewhere in Belgium. Of late, apparently, too many of these shipments had been intercepted. Not, they didn't hesitate to make clear, in the ridiculously clumsy and amateurish way that I had brought myself to their attention, but by the authorities who seemed to be getting better and better at their task. This, I was told, was the reason they were in the business of exploring alternatives.

I, perhaps unwisely, ventured that using substandard materials and trusting your cargo to the rigours (and trustworthiness!) of the postal service didn't seem one worth taking further.

The larger of my two visitors – and with both men weighing in at something over 18 stone, the distinction was somewhat redundant – told me they'd already come to that conclusion. It had been worth a go, he said: a shot in the dark. No idea was too stupid to discount without first exploring. "We reasoned the more stupid it seemed to us, the more stupid it might seem to the authorities: and they were unlikely to concentrate resources on ideas that were deemed too stupid."

Apparently, the *pop it in the post* method had actually worked the previous two occasions they had tried it, but it was their own authorities who'd decided it was all too much like a *cross your fingers and hope* option than a sustainable strategy.

Something else was needed. Someone else was needed. Someone who they had over a barrel and at their mercy was needed.

Bugger.

I say, bugger, but let's be fair. Things really haven't gone too badly since that cosy chat on my sofa. My newfound role turned out to be not too dissimilar to the one I'd been long pounding out, although it had been embellished slightly: I was still the Postman, but now I was also in packaging.

My task, on paper, was straight forward. Collect consignments of illegal diamonds being smuggled into the Republic of Ireland and smuggle them into England. Of course, taking this simple sentence off the paper and putting it into some kind of practice had its challenges – although I seemed to hurdle them fairly easily and at a far greater pace than many (including myself) might have imagined.

First of all, we needed to find a way to avoid the checks that the authorities occasionally carried out on direct trips between Eire and mainland UK. These often had a somewhat random feel to them. One never sensed there was a particular item on their wanted list and by not aiming for any one or two things with any real focus, they were invariably victims of their own lack of success; rarely uncovering anything untoward. But while adopting a scattergun approach to their customs work might often land in our favour, we couldn't really rely on it. There was always the risk of us coming unstuck as they stumbled across the very last thing they were looking for, and the very, very last thing we wanted them to find.

By contrast, no one in any of the six counties ever appeared to be the least bit interested in a humble mechanic travelling between two towns in the United Kingdom. And the crossings between Northern Ireland and the Republic were also invariably trouble free. Indeed, if driving from, say, Belfast to Galway via the N54, you'd do it by accident about half a dozen times without the police or, for that matter, you yourself realising it. The border controls such as they were – and there were precious few of those – were mainly on the lookout for whiskey and smokes. You might occasionally see a sniffer dog on the hunt for guns, but, since the Good Friday agreement, the necessity for such checks had greatly diminished, so were really very few and far between.

The most sensible travel arrangements therefore for our purposes would be to take a plane from England to County Antrim in Northern Ireland before then driving down to my ultimate destination in County Cork in the South. All we needed to find was some solid justifications for me to be making such trips – and on a regular basis.

The solution came about, slightly out of left field, with the purchase of three run down car repair shops.

I needed somewhere to be able to hide in plain sight, and I took the idea for my cover from my previous, previous occupation. No matter how well a vehicle is manufactured, it will, at some stage, need fixing, so a functioning garage in any community is rarely under suspicion. If we could set up the new arrangement as an English company with yours truly in charge, then me popping up at regular intervals, going back and forth across the Irish Sea, or up and down over the border as I kept tabs on our Irish investment was unlikely to set many tongues wagging.

THE HUNTRODDS COINCIDENCES

It sounded plausible, but would clearly require a fair bit of organising to pull things together. However, any thought I had that there'd be a relaxing lull in proceedings while the necessary arrangements to create this front were put into place, was seriously misplaced. Within a matter of weeks my new employers had acquired a dilapidated business in Maidenhead which would act as the Head Office. They'd also taken on a couple of loss making garages in Ireland: one in Ballycastle in Northern Ireland, the other, nearly 400 miles due south in a town called Baltimore, in the Republic. The former is a bleak coastal settlement that you really wouldn't go out of your way to visit unless you were en route to play golf at Portrush to its west, or perhaps on the return journey from the course to collect some of your balls that could easily have been blown the 17 miles east by the Atlantic gales.

By almost no contrast at all, Baltimore (pronounced balltimoree with a lilt, not bawltimor with a drawl) had even less going for it, other than the minimum interest it ever caused the local constabulary; its easy rowing distance proximity to several small nearby islands; and its craggy coastline of caves and inlets. All three attributes made it the perfect location for landing contraband gems and, in my new guise as Chief Mechanic for Sparkle Car Works Ltd, it was a place I began travelling to from Maidenhead, via Ballycastle regularly.

The first dozen or so trips went without a hitch.

We had a PO Box set up through which I'd receive details of my jobs. Obviously I needed to know not only when a consignment would be delivered but also from where I would make the collection. There had been as many pickup points in and around Baltimore as there had been actual collections, which I suppose kept everything and everyone as fresh and on their toes as possible.

The calculation of the arrival date was far from an exact science and often involved a great deal of heel kicking while waiting for a ship to come in and its Captain to deign it safe to offload his cargo. This enabled me to see much of the Republic's southerly most parish and meet one or two people outside the immediate confines of the diamond business. If you're someone who is not against smoking the odd bit of weed – and trust me, if you weren't so minded beforehand, a few mind numbing hours in places like Knockanmorough on Cape Clear Island, or an overnight stay in the Horseshoe B&B on Sherkin, will make you an instant convert – then making a few contacts with relevant contacts of their own in that market can only be a good thing.

Back to the job in hand. Once a pickup had to be made, the garage would sort out the necessary arrangements for me to travel to Ireland, leaving a paper trail justifying and therefore legitimising my reason for visiting our two outlets and being in the country.

Although my wheel in the cog was key, my actual role was pretty straightforward. So long as I could read the instructions properly and locate the park bench beneath which the parcel had been taped, or find the hiding place in the toilets of the designated bar or restaurant, or, let's be honest, even stumble across whatever other ingeniously chosen means for concealing the goods had been selected, my task was half done.

Once back in England, I just needed to make some sort of not dissimilar arrangement so that the next stage of delivery process could progress.

Things might have been made more challenging if we'd also had to manage the money side of the business, but that was never the case. I was paid through the garage for my legitimate mechanic "activities"; and direct into a French bank account under the guise of holiday rentals for my extra curricula tasks. What the person I handed the baton onto did with it, I neither knew, nor frankly, cared. He had always been at the end of the line whenever I had dialled whatever freshly supplied phone number I'd been given; and he'd always collected the goods by the time of my routine check the following day. Everything couldn't have been sweeter. But then Charlton Athletic lost in the League One playoff semi-final to Shrewsbury Town.

To be fair, putting the trauma and tribulation created on our business down solely to the South East London's side's lack of footballing skills that day is a tad unreasonable, some may even suggest completely unrelated. But the day Shrewsbury advanced to the Wembley final at the Addick's expense, was the same one that my *Mr Collector Guy* went AWOL.

A delivery was to be arranged during the week of the match. We'd lost the first leg of the doubleheader at home the week before and I remember traipsing back from that game depressed, but not so far down in the mire that I couldn't check the arrangements for my next drop off. The message I was given dictated collection had to take place in 72 hours - on the eve of the return fixture. Well, I thought, that puts paid to me attending the match. Trying to look on the bright side I decided that at least I wouldn't have to watch us being knocked out. Or so I assumed. The parameters I was given was "somewhere in Shropshire". Perhaps I could sort out this business and go to the game as well.

I searched online for accommodation in Shropshire, settled on *The Lambs Inn* in Edgmond, on the eastern side of the county, and booked a room for a couple of nights. I pulled into the pub's car park on the Friday afternoon and was pleased to spot the sign promising a selection of fine Cask Ales inside. As I checked in I could see that they were clearly going fast and loose with the definition of the word *selection*, as there was just the one beer engine standing at right angles to the bar. My heart sank a little further when I saw the solitary liquid that would be pulled up from the cellar below was Bass bitter. I hate Bass.

I went in search of a better class of beer and my quest was rewarded barely a few miles away down a couple of rarely used country lanes. As I drove along what appeared to be the solitary road in a small hamlet called Tibberton, and approached what looked suspiciously like it might be a pub, I spotted a large black notice board suggesting that *Kevin and Loraine were keen to welcome me to The Sutherland.* I pulled into the empty car park, fearing that Kevin and Loraine may have long since gone the way of many other landlords in such remote areas, but peering through the window saw – Loraine? – merrily straightening up the stools and tables. I could just make out the wording on the badge stuck on one of the beer pumps: *Pedigree.* I was in luck. If Budweiser is labelled the King of Beers, then that could only be because the modest central England brewery, Marston's, creators of Pedigree ale, with its palate of biscuit malt, spicy hops and light fruitiness, had so sanctioned it.

When Loraine (I was later to find out that it was indeed she) looked up from her domestic chores and saw me standing/drooling at the window, she tapped her wrist a couple of times and mouthed "five o'clock". I glanced at my watch and realised I had a little under an hour before opening, which, despite the lure of the ale, actually quite suited me.

I decided a quick on foot survey of the village would do me and it wasn't long before I found what I was looking for.

I'd tried to navigate a broadly circuitous route, which, as I could see from Google maps, looked doable: turn left out of the car park; right into Plantation Road; and right again into Back Lane. Carry on to the end and take another right and the Suthy would come back into view. It was soon clear that these were the major arteries of this village, but I found the wee vein I was seeking mid circuit. Hay Street had the look of a road long forgotten. The broken down remains of a ramshakled house, last occupied many many moons ago, was visible, but this aside, Hay Street's sole function seemed to be to stand in defiance of the local farmer as it did very little other than dissect a perfectly serviceable, large and fine stretch of his farmland in two. And I wouldn't have given this road to nowhere a second glance had it not been for a concrete barrel shaped object buried in the verge and all but completely obscured by cow parsley.

On closer inspection, I saw this municipal waste bin had seen better days. It looked like it was still used, although it was barely a third full and from the date of the discarded newspaper on top not actually emptied all that often. This would do me fine.

I completed my recce just as the clock metaphorically struck five, so I strode into the pub where I was indeed made extremely welcome by Loraine (sadly no Kevin) and settled in for the evening with several large and well-earned beers. The last piece of the jigsaw I needed to put into place was to relay the coordinates of the pickup to Collector Guy, but that would have to wait till the next day when could find somewhere in this county that had a mobile phone signal.

On the day of the match I drove west towards Shrewsbury, stopping in Hay Street to tape my parcel to the underside of the waste bin.

My plan for the rest of the day was to drive to the ground, watch the Mighty Charlton overturn the one goal deficit then, on the return journey, make a modest detour via Tibberton for a routine check that the package had been removed from its hiding place, before continuing on my way to the M54 and returning home in triumphant.

By the time the match had finished and I'd parked up in a quiet spot along Hay Street, I was, as the Americans would say: nought for 2.

For the second time in a handful of days, I'd seen my team go down 1 – 0 to these Salopian rivals. Getting out of the ground was no problem as the home fans were celebrating wildly on the pitch and had no intention of leaving anytime soon, so within barely 5 minutes of the referee blowing the final whistle, I was back on the B5062 heading east.

For five pm on a Sunday evening the roads were extraordinarily clear. Even now I can hardly remember seeing more than a couple of cars for the entire 15 mile journey to Tibberton. There were even two vehicles less than that in evidence as I pulled off the main thoroughfare (is a B road main?) and into leafy, deserted Hay Street. I was approaching things from the other end of the road than I had done previously and it took me a few moments before I spotted the grey stone bin with its coat of cow parsley. However, any concern I might have had for the state of the roadside flora was soon mown away when I fumbled around the base of the concrete structure and found the package that I'd secured there less than four hours ago was still in place.

I instinctively jolted up and looked around, but I doubt anyone other than me had passed this way over the past seven days – and I remained alone now. I hastily untaped the parcel, stuck it up my red Charlton Athletic Pringle sweater and jumped back into my car.

To begin with, I think I was just a little numb. Looking down, I should have been able to see my red and white CAFC belt, rather than what looked akin to a lumpy beer gut. I went over the details and instructions I'd passed on the day before: nothing untoward had been said, nor out of place had happened, so there was no reason I could conjure that meant the pickup shouldn't have been totally successful. And yet my protruding stomach was saying otherwise.

There were strict protocols to follow depending on the circumstance, and while several circumstances were possible, there was only one I was worried about: why hadn't The Collector collected?

The reason in the end was pretty straightforward and to cut a long story short, it was because he'd been "collected" himself – by the police! I suppose the more accurate term is "arrested", but, either way, the result was the same.

I never really got to the bottom of what had actually happened that weekend, but it was soon made clear enough that it would be better for me all round if I didn't dwell on it further – so I didn't. In any event, I had a new "partner" to break in: they had allotted me a Cadbury's Milk Tray man – and we had some work to do together.

Chapter 12

Two trains; Two houses; Two orphans

MAN

Sometimes you have to accept the truth and stop wasting time on the wrong people (Anonymous)

I don't recall the exact moment I dreamt up "the plan", but it can't have been kick-started too many days after she had answered the Person Friday advert. She'd put her head around my office door and asked if she was in the right place for the interview. She was sorry to disturb, but there was no one at the desk outside to ask.

My first thought was the same I always had when in the presence of someone so stunningly beautiful. The second thought was that if I hired this one, I'd have to make up something pretty convincing at home to deflect the inevitable suspicion. Maybe the reverse of Mr Kratz in the Killing of Sister George: instead of pretending that the minger in my office was a stunner, I could suggest it was the other way around.

Anyway, I told her that the reason for the advertisement and interview was because the previous person employed to sit at that desk had decided she no longer wanted to do that, so would she please come in and make herself comfortable.

The moment the rest of her body came into view as it followed her head through the doorway, my solitary thought was, *delightful*. Things might have progressed with a little more comfort had I not actually said that word out loud, but we somehow got past that.

I remember absolutely nothing about the interview other than me just repeating the *D* word on some sort of continuous loop – though definitely just in my head – apart from me finishing the meeting in the same way I'd started, saying, *delightful* (audibly) for a second time and then asking her when she could start.

As soon as she'd drifted out of the building, I drifted off to the beach combing, sea spraying, sand wrestling place I always seemed to end up in such circumstances, although this time the reverie didn't follow the usual pattern. She and I were both in the picture: her Halle Berry to my Daniel Craig, but in the background and cresting through the waves on a body board was my wife.

Now at this point I should be saying something about how much I love my other half, that she means everything to me and I wouldn't hurt her for the world, but there's a time and place I want to be with her, and this is neither one of those. To be honest, at that moment I suddenly realised that I didn't really love her, she doesn't mean a great deal to me anymore and if there was any way things could be manoeuvred so that I never had to spend another moment with her ever again then, well, perhaps *bring it on*.

I don't want to suggest this was some kind of epiphany but it was a bit of a Johnny Nash *I can see clearly now* moment: there had been a sufficiency of straws blowing my way over recent years and the one that had just arrived had more than dented Mr Camel's spinal chord.

Playing away in a marriage, as I had been doing for some time, should, at least, leave one with a sense of doing wrong. Yet here I was, coming to terms with the fact that not only didn't I feel guilt, I felt nothing other than the certainty that I really wasn't in a place that I wanted to be. We'd been mulling along for so long, I'm sure the residents of Tobermory would have welcomed us with open arms and given us the freedom of the town.

This clearly couldn't continue, especially now that I had this new found clarity (and a gorgeous Person Friday), but the issue was what to do about it.

A few random and diverse options wandered into my head, though most were immediately tossed aside. There was no question of doing anything physical or particularly untoward. Everything would be fine and amicable. We'd separate, divvy up the furniture, the cat and CDs, and my assistant and I would just quietly slip away.

Although, separation could easily become divorce - and that would have financial implications. Actually, thinking about it, *implications* is such an insufficient a word for what there would be. The house and business were in joint names (for tax reasons, apparently. Bloody accountants!). The two cars were about the only things that weren't, but they were both HP'd up to the hilt. I had access to the firm's working capital, but that's small beer: the real seven figure money was in the house and the business itself. And let's not gloss over the two old Victorian houses in South East London left to my dear wife by her father when he'd passed away.

Her parents had met in a south London pub sixty odd years ago. It was a Monday evening in July and their customary commuter trains; *hers,* the 17:32 from Charing Cross, *his,* the 17:40 from Cannon Street, had pulled into Blackheath station on time and, as usual, within minutes of each other. Both made to start their respective and walks home as they had each done over a thousand times before, totally oblivious and unaware of each other's existence. However, *Fate* had obviously got fed up with this and so decided to throw down the mother of all sudden and totally unpredicted downpours, forcing both of them – almost involuntarily, but certainly independently - to take refuge in a hostelry neither had ever frequented before, the adjacent *Railway Tavern.* My future mother-in-law was first to arrive and instinctively moved away from the hubbub near the door and towards what appeared a quieter area at the rear of the pub. My father-in-law to be ran in moments later, but went no further than the bar, plonking himself down on the nearest stool.

The tale as to how this gap was bridged that evening has been told, retold and embellished by the family many times over the years; so often, in fact that my head usually drops whenever I hear the opening salvos of the story being rendered. I have long since stopped rehearsing it – even quietly to myself. Suffice it to say, bridged, the gap certainly was and - assisted further along the way courtesy of Mrs Fate, a loving relationship grew.

One thing that helped fan those early flames was their realisation that night that they lived, (1) in the same road, and (2) in houses no more than seventy five yards apart. His parents had died in extraordinary circumstances two years earlier when an aga had exploded during a Celebrity Bake Off demonstration they'd attended in Marylebone. This left him, their only child, alone and without a cooker in number 23 Granville Place, a huge Victorian house on four levels. (The first time I relayed this tale I threw in that it had once been five floors - but that was another story).

By absolutely no contrast what so ever, she lost both her folks around the same time in a freak three legged roller skating accident when a wheel had got caught in a storm drain. The tragedy left her the sole occupant of number 4; a mirror of the building ten doors down and one across.

At this point in the family story the narrator of the day will usually pause to enable the narratee to absorb the bizarre and horrendous demise of both sets of parents. And any teller worth their salt will also nudge their audience towards the incredulity that, despite living more or less across the street from one another for almost twenty years, neither had ever so much as laid an eye on one another prior to that afternoon in *The Railway*.

But once these aspects have been absorbed and the tale resumed, it quickly wanders into a happier-ever-after mode as the listener learns that the couple were rarely to be found apart thereafter.

Both houses remained in their possession. Sometimes they'd sleep at twenty three, sometimes at number four, but it was always one or other; and always together.

Their daughter's arrival brought a bit of focus – they really didn't want either the constant upheaval of relocating a new born baby every few days; or the expense of buying two lots of toys, so they settled in one (his: it was nearer to the station) and rented out the other.

Her mother's death: the result of a one in a million accident in the Carr's cracker factory in Carlisle where she was conducting an audit, happened on the afternoon of her 17th birthday. Her father never got over the loss of his soul mate. He stopped turning up for work in the Group Department of the Sun Life Assurance Company of Canada and spent most of his days wandering aimlessly around Greenwich Park; and all of his evenings at *her* table in *The Railway*. Within nine months, the pain, anguish, heartache and alcohol had combined to terminal effect.

I had arrived on the scene shortly after her mother's passing, and while my wife to be was happy then to continue residing in number 23 Granville Place, the day she lost her father was the last night she again ever set foot in either property.

Renting them out was no trouble and the monthly income from a pair of such desirable properties certainly helped us in the early days of our marriage while we worked on developing my chocolate business.

The long term rentals over the years have remained nice little earners, but their estimated sale values (on which I have kept a constant eye), currently standing at £1.75 million each is always in the back of one's mind.

Returning to my current deliberations, there was no getting away from the fact that my financial position is short on cash/long on assets – so there was no chance of *sliding noiselessly out* of anything. More to the point, with all the money held in joint names and tied up in bricks, mortar and business I needed a *walking out* option with a twist. If I was to vanish to some far-flung place, without a trace (but perhaps a Friday) – and live in a style I would like to become accustomed - I would have to liquidate everything. Coming up with a ruse to get total control of the finances and slip away without hindrance would certainly require a bit of cunning.

An idea began to form in my mind. It was a longshot but if I could make it work it would hardly be a more perfect plan than if my wife's name really was Trace.

Chapter 13
Two pagers / One aroma

WIFIE

I should have known better with a boy like you (The Beatles)

Of course I should have seen it coming. No one should ever get to the stage after the event and realise that those fifteen pointers which looked innocuous on their own collectively added up to the bleeding obvious.

I can sort of excuse myself from not having picked up on the little things that had gradually stopped happening. I can't for example remember the last time he'd turned up with flowers for no reason; or noticed I'd had my hair done. Even his reaction to my appearance in a new Joseph Ribkoff top, asking if the kettle was on, didn't set any hares running.

But if I let these misdemeanours pass without actually realising they'd wandered anywhere near my nose, then surely I should have sniffed the odd felony when it presented itself? Instead, it was as if I simply failed to notice how he'd started to continuously talk down to me; or belittle me in front of our closest friends; or just not turn up to dinner dates we'd spoken about barely a few hours earlier.

In the end, the light bulb moment came not with something crude like a Monty Python fish slap with a two-foot trout, but rather more subtly in the form of an en suite bathroom.

I had always wanted one. I'd almost vetoed the purchase of our first home all those years ago on the basis that the master bedroom had no adjoining facilities. The loo in the council house I'd grown up in Tooting Bec, an area of southwest London, was in the back garden and the bath was beneath a formica'd worktop in the kitchen. The weekly bathe amongst the pots and pans and nightly gauntlet run over the cold cobble stones were rituals I always vowed I would make up for in spades the moment I moved into a dwelling of my own.

My dream, I'd pleaded at the time, was to be able to glide straight from bed to bidet with nothing in between. He argued that his dream was being able to carry out his ablutions with more than a centimetre of plasterboard between him and his divan.

In the end, I settled for a contract in the minor suits: a downstairs' loo and a bathroom a few strides along the landing.

And so it remained, through all the belittling and ignoring, the lack of flowers or compliments, until one evening after dinner he suddenly announced he wanted to build an extension onto the rear of the house.

It was about nine months ago and he'd just returned from yet another business trip to Belgium. I remember thinking that the increased frequency of these continental trips seemed to have coincided with the arrival of his new Girl Friday, sorry, PA, sorry, Secretary, though at the time I did little more than allow that thought to be popped into the misdemeanour box. He told me the chocolate people he was working with had a construction company in the UK that had hit a metaphorical brick wall. They'd put a good number of their eggs in a solitary local authority social housing companies' basket and this week, without warning, their building contract had been frozen. He said it had left them *zat in rivier met stront zonder peddel* (although my Dutch is not up to much; I got the drift) and, in short, we could get a great deal and I could get the en suite I had always wanted.

This new found desire to satisfy a dream I'd let go some time ago gave me a slightly warm feeling, but I was given little opportunity to build on that as he was off *unbuilding* our home. Thoughts of my ablutions were pushed to one side as he began talking of knocking through walls and fitting out dens and sticking in huge bay picture windows. I think there was even a bit of landscape gardening thrown in somewhere along the line, though I can't quite be sure about that. While all this did come from a tad out of the blue, as soon as he bought in to my suggestion of a glass ceilinged conservatory – enthusiastically I recall – I became as wrapped up in the idea as he was. We were making decisions together again, and it was my wishes, as well as his thoughts, that were being accommodated. It was like old times.

I slept well that night, more as a result of us having actually discussed something together than the thought of being able to see *Villeroy and Boch* printed on the porcelain, though that prospect did indeed warm the heart and the memories of a wee four-year-old girl from Tooting.

I remember this all being raised on a Monday, because the next day I was playing in the monthly Ladies stableford. I'd come back into the clubhouse to change (35 points – not bad) and found 5 missed calls from *"BAND"* on my mobile: (just after we were married I'd accidentally omitted the first three letters when I edited his details in my contacts and never bothered to change it). I was trying to recall the last time he'd phoned me once during the day, let alone five times on the trot and was about to press the *return call* button when he rung again.

He said he'd been on to the builder people and they'd come straight back with an outline plan and quote. Blimey, I thought.

They must have really been left in the lurch and keen to grab any business that was going. It was, he said, a great deal: mate's rates and, at under £100,000, virtually cost price. It should be three times that and would add tons to the value of the house. We'd fund it through the firm eventually, but for speed it was easier to pop it onto the mortgage then clear that with a Director's loan in the new financial year. The building society just needed us to sign a few papers, and we'd be good to go. We could look over the plans at the weekend and that if he could be in charge of the exterior, I could have carte blanche of furnishings.

Maybe I was being swept along in the moment and while, at that very moment, I had no inkling anything was amiss, three things were about to happen that would change all that.

The first blip on my radar screen pinged the following morning when his Secretary knocked on the front door. She said *He'd* asked her to drop off the papers from the Building Society and while that simple piece of dialogue should have been more than enough information for me to work out who the stunning creature standing on my welcome mat was, I was still left somewhat fazed. It wasn't so much that we'd never met before, nor that I wasn't expecting that gap in my mental contact list to be filled there and then, it was that she was just so gorgeous.

Now, ordinarily I wouldn't be thrown simply by the appearance of a beautiful person, however unexpected the circumstances, but on numerous occasions he'd described, indeed almost dismissed the new girl as, "*functional, certainly not decorative*". He had deliberately led me to believe she was much more in the mode of Mr Katz from an old film we'd seen the other night, rather than say, Halle Berry in, well, any old movie she'd ever made. His past form dictated there was really only one reason he would have done that. Of course, while all this evidence was barely circumstantial, it would be less than six hours later that something a little more concrete landed in my palm.

The second pointer wandered into my psyche shortly after lunch when he breezed through the door. That in itself was unusual; indeed, I couldn't even recall the last time he'd come home from work during the day. He said he had a meeting to go to later, and he'd spilt something on his suit so needed to change. In any event, he wanted to get the papers for the mortgage sorted out (had I signed them yet?) and thought he could kill two birds, so to speak.

As it happened, I hadn't put pen to the papers because, I told him, I wasn't quite sure where to start. There seemed so many of them. He said it was much worse than it looked and I should just follow his lead. He then proceeded to flick through the pack, stopping each time he came to a little piece of yellow tape marking the place to scrawl the date and his signature, then sliding the bundle across to me to do likewise. Within 30 seconds he was tapping the documents into a neat and ordered pile and clicking shut the clasp on his briefcase. He emptied the contents of his suit jacket onto the table and took to the stairs, two at a time, up to the bedroom.

I didn't notice it at first, but as I pushed his pile of coins and car keys away from the edge of the table, I saw the dark grey plastic pager. Half a dozen hours ago I wouldn't have been able to distinguish a pager from a cheap Christmas cracker gift, but I'd seen the identical model to this one earlier that day. His secretary had been fiddling with it as I'd opened the door to her. She looked up and, I suppose, in response to my slightly quizzical look offered, "He's bought us the latest in pager technology and we're both still wrestling with it."

Picking up what I assumed was the male part to the female one I'd seen his secretary pop quickly into her handbag made me wonder why on earth a chocolate box seller and his minion would need the latest technology in anything.

The final thing to raise my suspicion level up to *there's-something-you-need-to-do-something-about* mode, hit me a few moments after he'd leapt down the stairs, this time three or four at once, scooping up the pile of stuff emptied from his pockets earlier and left, pulling the front door closed behind him. Perhaps it was the calm after the storm. Perhaps a strong breeze collected something that had been swirling around our porch. Perhaps I just realised that the scent I'd smelt over the past few months, with greater intensity and even greater frequency, had made an appearance earlier today. Well, one thing was now certain: I could sure as eggs put a face to that smell.

Chapter 14

Spike's box set and Sue's book club

WIFIE
I find television very educating. Every time somebody turns on the set, I go into the other room and read a book (Groucho Marx)

She wasn't the first of his secretaries that he'd experimented with. Come to that, she wasn't the first of other people's secretaries that he'd gotten close to, but somehow I sensed this one might be different. In the past I had just let things pass, but there comes a time............

The question was, what should I do about it? Actually, before tackling that, perhaps I should be clear about what I *wished* to do about it.

It took me all of 5 seconds to decide on the answer to Q2: take him to the cleaners and take him for everything he's got. I didn't just want to take his trousers down; I wanted to paint his arse red as well.

Formulating the response to Q1 took a little more time, though one thing was clear for sure – I'd need some hard evidence before I could even consider taking the lid off the tin of crimson emulsion.

There had been other women. Not lots, but certainly more than one. If pushed I could have brought each of them back to mind, although of the many things I was considering at that moment, spending time recalling his trysts and conquests was not something high up on the to do list. Not that any mental note I produced would have included the bimbos' pen picture, as I'd never actually met any of them. It was always, "Oh, I'm seeing Bill's old school friend, or Simon's new and progressive rabbi, or the trainee auditor" etc, etc. And while I knew it was going on, I was prepared to live with it. After all, I'd had my own few goes early in our marriage, so was on less than solid terrain to take either the moral high ground or offence. Not that it didn't irk me, of course it did, but never having seen any of the ephemeral loves of his lives somehow made it easier to brush it all under the carpet.

I think that's why, when I finally saw one of his conquests, it had such a shattering effect. Coming face to face with her as she as good as rubbed mine into the dirt, crystallised everything and I could see the neat little cocoon I'd packed myself inside for the ineffective wrapping it really was. It looked pathetic, as did I, and I was not going to let that continue. We were quits now. In fact, if I was suddenly being honest with myself here, we were *quits* a few goes ago. Giving me this Technicolor picture, however accidental, was one go too far. I was determined it would prove to be the start to the end.

Deciding on the core of my strategy was easy. There were a couple of ways he could be seriously hurt: Attack his reputation or separate him from his money. The former wouldn't work on two levels. His business relationships were well established and the way he talked about them, I suspect planting something untoward into the minds of his contacts might only make them love him more. Further to the point, even if I did ruin him, there would be no upside for me. Sure, I'd be able to wear a smug and satisfied grin for a while, but that don't buy many tins of baked beans at Waitrose. No, his Money, or rather our money and making it all my money, would be the key. What I didn't realise at the time was that both the metaphorical and physical piece of metal I needed to get me started was already waiting for me in my kitchen cupboard.

Despite us almost living on top of one another, Sue and I didn't actually meet until a plumbing calamity sort of threw us together. Gosh, was it really three years ago?

I remember getting ready to leave for my usual Tuesday afternoon duplicate bridge club meeting when the phone rang: it was my partner to tell me that there had been some sort of flood and the village hall was out of action until further notice. Much of our conversation centred on the pain and disruption to local life this would cause, though I sensed we were both secretly cursing our rotten luck. Having scored 76.4% the previous week we were due many plaudits from our fellow sharps and in a single gush, a burst water pipe had washed away our moment of glory.

Through the empathy and the ruing, our conversation turned to what we were going to do instead. South, (I enjoyed being in charge and scoring so invariably played North) mentioned his book club taking place later that day and said I should come along.

The fortnightly book club was just one of South's endless streams of activities to which he was constantly trying to entice me. He had a core list of mainly weekly events inked into his diary: Lunchtime pool in a local pub on Mondays; four weekly bridge sessions (Monday night and Tuesday day with me, Tuesday night and Thursday afternoon without); table tennis in the village hall on Wednesdays; Badminton Thursday mornings; and cards (anything but bridge) in his local later that evening. No regular entries were permitted on Fridays, which were kept free for the various non-weekly things he had to cram in. He went walking twice a month: one, on the first Friday to come along, was a "short" four or so mile amble open to anyone from the village who turned up.

The other, coming in at eight or ten miles, was slightly more serious and would normally involve catching a train to some distant starting point. I could never get on board with the idea of catching a train in order to go for a walk, but he appeared to enjoy it. In amongst that lot he'd fit in, and organise a monthly village bike ride – similar to the amble but on the third Friday and three or four times the length. There was also some sort of gardening club he dabbled his fingers in, though I never quite got to the bottom of that one. It seemed to involve going to different places – walking and cycling continued to feature - to look at plants and stuff. Not my cup of tea at all and, even though I believe they'd usually finish these horticultural dalliances with a few cups of China or India, he never managed to persuade me to join him.

Until then, he'd had a similar lack of success getting me involved in the 14 day book cycle. But my diary was looking very sad, like something that might inspire Procol Harum, and the thought of filling this unexpected gap by sitting around and playing Computer Bridge on my own seemed bleak. I knew I'd regret it the next day and spend the following thirteen working out how to get out of making a repeat appearance, but I said "Why not?" Hopefully that wouldn't sound too enthusiastic and might serve me well in the event that an exit strategy became necessary. Then I asked what book they were reviewing.

I must confess I was taken aback when he said, *Puckoon*, though perhaps slightly relieved that at least it wasn't *Adolf Hitler, my part in his downfall*. I simply said, "Balls". He replied, "Caw! I see you know it. Funnily enough, we're meeting just round the corner from you: I'll knock for you at three."

On the appointed hour I saw Nick pull his midlife crisis BMW convertible onto the drive, but he'd already put the roof's closing mechanism into action before I'd managed to pick up my tattered box set of Spike Milligan's greatest work and join him outside. He said we were going to Sue Morrison's house, so could he leave the car here? He was surprised when I told him I'd never heard of her. "Does she live near here?" I asked. By way of response he simply moved a few feet to his right and, on reaching the fence that boarded my front garden from next door, pointed at the houses that backed onto ours in the next street along.

"That's her." he said. I turned to look towards a house I must have glanced at a million times before but never actually seen. Standing at an upstairs window was (I don't wish to be unkind, particularly from fifty or sixty yards, but) an elderly lady who was either waving enthusiastically at us or cleaning an exceptionally stubborn mark on the glass.

My first thought was that this could make my exit strategy slightly difficult, though I needn't have worried: as things turned out, that was to be a path I wouldn't choose to take.

We were at her front door within moments and straight away guided into the room at the rear of her home. It seems we were the last to arrive and Sue (yes, I can't believe we've never crossed swords before either, how extraordinary) pointed us towards two empty chairs at the end of an oversized dining table. I barely had a chance to catch more than a glimpse of my house through the window as we took our seats (what on earth is that hanging out of the gutter?) before I was introduced to the other worms: a Mary, a Hannah and two Tracys, all clutching their Milligan box sets (maybe *Puckoon* was never sold without its three paperback mates?).

Of course the coincidence of our houses being so close together served as the ice breaking topic of conversation for the new girl, although once the questions started, Nick sort of took on responsibility for providing my answers. At first I felt slightly irked at being cut across in this way, but it did give me the opportunity to take in a longer gaze out of Sue's rear window.

119

Our two rear patios were separated by our abutting back gardens. Until relatively recently the physical demarcation had been marked with quite a high fence (ours) and a line of leylandii (Sue's), although they'd become diseased about a year ago and were uprooted. For our part, we'd decided the fence was more than sufficient: we joked that our Norwegian friend, Gunnar, a six foot eight (and a half) inch tall ex Grenadier Guard would have still needed a stepladder to see over it. In any event, our garden had a slight upward slope, front to back, which accentuated the privacy our wooden screen afforded us.

I was suddenly aware my card and now book partner had moved away from how he and I first met and onto the losing trick count we'd recently adopted to impressive effect at the bridge club. Sue, realising that Nick had lost his audience, called the meeting to order and started quoting dialogue from the novel on the table before us.

While most of the modest plot lines from a book I'd not flicked through for over twenty years had long since escaped me, I was able to chip in occasionally as a familiar phrase or two cropped up. However, there are only so many times one can say, "Balls" or "Caw" without feeling little more than a tolerated by-reader, so I mainly sat listening to the others. I was on more solid ground when the talk turned to the underlying message of the book and the oft time comical situation along the Northern Ireland border with its Republican neighbour that Milligan was clearly poking fun at. I'd worked in Belfast in the 1970s, lodging in nearby Bangor. My guest house was in Queen's Parade overlooking the harbour (beautiful), but less than a hundred yards from the Marks & Spencer store bombed by the IRA a few months after my contract had ended (not quite so picturesque). My first hand insight served me well for this round table purpose and, fairly soon, I was feeling like one of the girls (+ Nick).

I must say I was actually enjoying it all. This was a very different level of intellectual engagement than I was used to on a Tuesday afternoon (or most other afternoons come to that). It wasn't like we were solving world peace or the Middle East crisis (although those two might be one and the same thing) but it involved personal opinions and articulating them in a way that made sense, or at the very least, didn't make me sound stupid.

We'd segued onto the Good Friday Agreement, but before I had managed to wax lyrical on what I consider being Mo Mowlam's pivotal role in bringing the whole thing together, Tracy (number 2) had hopped onto Tony Blair, skipped on 5 years and jumped into a diatribe on weapons of mass destruction. Sensing the mood had changed, Sue - I found myself really warming towards this woman of perception - suggested we leave things there and think about the topic for the group's next session.

Nick started patting the outside of his ever present jacket and jerking his head around. This was a familiar routine: he'd lost his wallet. When I say wallet, that was certainly the core item he was searching for, though it was the contents he was really after. Sure enough, there it was on the floor beneath his chair: a blackened and worn leather fold over wallet, wrapped around what were at least fifty scrappy and torn fragments of paper. The whole wodge must have come in at three inches thick and was something more akin to a 1980s Filofax than a simple container for money and plastic. Reunited with his filing cabinet, he tugged at one of the particularly well folded pieces of A4 and spread out it before me, revealing a list of titles beneath an underlined heading that read *Book club*.

Top of the list was *The Handmaid's Tale* (January). I'd read this when it was first published and was rather waiting for the sequel. This was followed by *Wolf Hall* (February). Ditto. When was *Bring Up the Bodies* due out in paperback? Next came *Dracula* (March), *The Tale of Two Cities* (April) and *Lolita* (May). I felt glad I'd missed the spring meetings.

Then there was June's selection that we'd just completed. I recall thinking *Puckoon* really was out of left field but, unlike the company it was keeping from earlier in the year, at least it wasn't a book that made you rush to your Leonard Cohen collection for cheering up.

The next on the list sounded mysterious and exciting. It was a new one on me, though if I'd have had even the remotest of ideas that *The Jewel of Seven Stars* had been penned by the same author who wrote *Dracula*, I'm not sure I would have darkened the group's door ever again. But at the time, I was ignorant of *The Jewel's* provenance; I just knew it would please Nick to have introduced another woman to the fold and, in any event, I quite liked the (majority) female company – so I committed to giving the club at least one more go.

To be honest though, that commitment was tested to the limit when I sat down to wrestle with the Stoker tome we'd been directed towards. From memory I gave it a quick going over, attempted a few cerebral points at the July meeting, then, once home, did little more than toss it onto the bookshelf while flicking through the other novels lying there to seek out the subject of our August task: the battered copy of my favourite novel in the world, *Pride and Prejudice*. I could never understand Tom Hanks failing to get to grips with it in the film, *You've Got Mail*. In my book, that would have been grounds enough for Meg Ryan to at least hesitate before ending up in his arms. I'd really enjoy immersing myself in it again and, based on the discussions of my first two meetings, found myself thinking of how everyone might approach getting under its dust cover.

Mary would do what she usually did: analyse the humour and show how the latest comedian to join the *Mock the Week* panel had simply lifted his (it was always the guys she had it in for) material from it. She would also refer to every character in the book, be it male, female or animal, in her broadest of Midlands accents, as, *me ducks*. I had no real idea as to what Hannah might come up with, though even if she did say anything extraordinary, I'd probably miss it. If I had a single hour left to live, I'd choose to spend it in Hannah's company because she could make sixty minutes seem like an eternity. What she'd do with P&P in that time, I'd be afraid to even think about. Tracy (1) would relate the book in question with other works by the same author – so we were actually in for her comments on any number of different books, rather than just the one we'd all read. Tracy (2) would identify the Marxist threat that the writer was really trying to signal. Talking of signals, Nick had already made it clear he was in the Hanks' camp, so we could expect very little beyond him simply belittling everything.

I wasn't quite sure what Sue would make of it all. I just remember metaphorically crossing my fingers and really hoped, almost prayed that she'd love the story at least half as much as I did. As it turned out, she liked it twice as much as that, and from there we became close friends.

Of course, being back yard neighbours as we titled ourselves, helped forge the friendship. Living so close to each other deleted any chance of making a flimsy excuse not to be able to pop round for coffee, or nip down to the shops (or the wine bar!) together, not that either of us seemed at all interested in finding such an excuse. On top of the book club, our caffeine fuelled mornings became regular (her place on Tuesdays, mine on Thursdays), joint shopping trips not unusual and early evening preprandials not infrequent.

There are few people whom I really love, and still fewer I feel really close to. Sue was one of those people so a month ago, when she suddenly rushed off to Spain to help look after her grandchild, I just felt vacant and lost.

I remember her turning up distraught on my doorstep the morning she'd received the news that her daughter-in-law had suffered a dreadful accident and would be in hospital for the foreseeable future. Her son was beside himself, and Sue decided her place was beside him. Someone had to help out with her granddaughter, Josie. She told me she was trying to organise a flight out that very day and asked, almost pleaded for me to look after the house for her while she was away. She'd have no time to clear out the fridge, cancel the papers etc etc. "It would be such a load off my mind while I try to focus on just getting out to them."

Despite standing in my open doorway and begrudging her going, even before she'd made a move to go, of course I agreed instantly and shooed her away. I told her she could leave all the domestic matters in my hands and reassured her that the key I'd long since swapped with her for one to my front door was hanging safely on a hook in my kitchen. "Now go" I said, "and ring me when you can to let me know how things are panning out."

That must have been on a Wednesday, because I remember it being a day before it was her turn to fire up the percolator. About 10:30 the next morning I trudged the few hundred steps it took me to reach her house, though this time instead of ringing the bell I simply let myself in.

Of course I'd been inside a thousand times before, but never on my own and never with nothing but such silence and my own thoughts. I decided to start off with a full recce of the place to check if there was anything obvious that needed some attention. I'd wandered upstairs into Sue's bedroom where everything looked in order. I started staring absentmindedly out of the window where I'd first seen her "waving", looking out across our respective lawns. Had I not been so immersed, I might have seen the face of the woman my husband had just shepherded out of the back door. I could see his car on the driveway but by the time I'd turned towards it all I could glimpse were its rear lights as it drove away without revealing any further clues as to the passenger's identity.

124

It was that thought that returned to mind as I mulled over what to do about his goings on. I wandered into the kitchen and opened the cabinet door where I kept the candles and other house essentials. On the shelf, between the AAA batteries and the clay pot full of thumb tacks was Sue's front door key, attached to a fob in the shape of a cartoon cat. As I turned it over in my hand, I realised I knew the perfect spot from where I could keep an eye on him. And her. And get whatever evidence was needed to take the adulterous bastard to the cleaners.

Chapter 15
Magpies always come in pairs

MAN

What we anticipate seldom occurs. What we least expect generally happens (Benjamin Disraeli)

Despite my bravado with Vlad and the fact that I was striding away from the restaurant with as much of an air of confidence as I could gather, I was depressingly aware that I'd learned hardly anything that might offer a clue about where I should be actually going or, for that matter, what on earth was going on.

As I made my way onto Whitby Bridge, I was distracted by a familiar black and white bird attending to some road kill. I greeted him in the accepted manner taught to me by my mother, 'Morning, Mr Magpie' and, as if she were standing my side issuing instructions, I scanned the skies for his partner. No Mrs Magpie. How sad. They would rarely travel or hunt alone unless something untoward, usually involving an urban fox, had happened. One for sorrow, two for.......

"That doesn't bring me joy, only sorrow. Go. And wait. You know where."

The Magpie café! I'd forgotten it was the diner picked by the Accountant as the *payment venue* on my first job. I say, forgotten:

it was more the sort of thing one just sub-consciously selects not to remember, because there's never going to be a reason you have to. Or at least, almost never!

Funnily enough, it would have been my preferred choice for lunch today. I'd visited it a few times now, and the fish was always moist and the batter ever crisp: I'm sure Seckie had only plumped for Hadleys because of its proximity to the meeting.

Still, while at least I now knew where I was supposed to be heading, that piece of knowledge was hardly being crowded out of my memory banks by other known facts: I had no idea where my car was; not an inkling where the diamonds might be; what could possibly have happened to the drugs; why the Accountant had blown me off and sent me scuttling across town; nor for the life of me where Vlad fitted into all this.

In short, I didn't really have a clue what on earth was going on. However, as I cleared the bridge and turned right at the corner into St Ann's Staith, I knew I needed to increase my pace and work up an appetite. I had a feeling I was about to order my second haddock of the day.

Chapter 16

A big yellow taxi nearly took this girl away

ACCOUNTANT

Of course the hunt is only as interesting as the prey is clever (MD Elster)

I froze solid, my soles welded to the sidewalk, as I watched the all too familiar shape of the staggery drunken man, or Dean to me and his friends, begin swerving his way over the bridge. He had all but drawn level with my contact, although they both remained across the road from each other. I know he said he would be in Whitby too, but I certainly hadn't expected him to pop up out of nowhere quite like this.

I suppose I had been concentrating on these two with such intensity that I'd absentmindedly wandered off the pavement and was almost run over. A flash of lemon, a loud blast on a taxi's horn, a screech of brakes and some – I will admit, well merited – verbal abuse, proved sufficient warning, and I managed to avoid any coming together. What is it about me and big yellow taxis? This was the second time in recent memory that I was nearly ferried to my Maker by one. At least this one didn't have an "Oh so hilarious" novelty horn. Nevertheless, I'm certainly going off Joni Mitchell.

I could see clearly into the cab, but other than spotting the chap in the back now lying prone on the floor, no other harm seemed to have been done.

As my near death experience drove off, I regained some composure just in time to catch both my men of interest complete the river crossing simultaneously. I breathed a sigh of relief as Dean turned left and my man veered right.

My close cab collision prompted me to refocus. Questions of what on earth my partner was doing here and how did he come to stumble, almost literally, onto the tail I was following had to be left for a calmer moment. I needed to carry on, assume nothing had gone horribly wrong and concentrate on the reason for my own presence: was my quarry kosher, where were the diamonds and what lead he would give me on the drugs.

Him turning right off the bridge was a good sign. There were few reasons anyone who had just eaten a plate of fish and chips (my £20 had bought me some detailed intel) would have chosen this course. The road does little more than circle back on itself so unless he'd decided to pop into the array of amusement arcades towards the top of the hill, or Whitby's RNLI Museum, I was more than confident he was aiming for my café.

As things now stood, my diminutive partner had become surplus to requirements, although it needed another £20 note to convince him to bugger off. I could handle things from here. I was now as sure as I could be that this was the right guy and I didn't have any shenanigans to deal with outside of the core brief of finding out why he wasn't handing over the money for the stones.

Of course, I'd thrown this cunning plan together somewhat on the hoof. It has been a few weeks since I had been in this windblown neck of the woods, so I wasn't even sure if *The Magpie* would be open. As I walked up the hill I was relieved to see the Quayside restaurant was doing a fair trade. Competition here is strong and you could be pretty confident that if one establishment has its lights on, the next one a few houses up will have also flicked their electricity switch. Now all I had to do was hope they had a spare table for two.

As I progressed into Pier Road, the distinctive black and white building overlooking the harbour of *The Magpie* café came into view and I breathed another sigh of relief. The stoop leading up to the entrance was clear. This was one popular venue and in the tourist season people would often be found standing outside in line, waiting for a table. Demand generally diminishes the more distant summer becomes, but it can still be strong, so you need to be lucky – and it seems I was. The weather had clearly had a detrimental effect on takings today: at last a reason to be thankful for these woods being windblown.

I hadn't actually seen him go in, but was as sure as I could be that he had, so delayed my entry to give him a chance to sit down and stew for a few moments. I tugged my collar up a tad more against the elements, continued on towards the museum and pulled out my phone to fill a bit of time. My default check is the BBC website, but I bypassed that: a text from Dean had just arrived saying, "Didn't mean to shock you. All's well. Carry on". Cue relief sigh number three.

Back to business, I crossed the road to be river side and lent up against the iron railings that followed the line of the Esk out to sea. Looking back, the street was empty. There was no traffic (the road works seem to have cut off this wee section of the town - RNLI's takings will also be hit) and no shitty coat wearers dashing along the pavements. Even the seagulls had decided to steer clear.

I strolled back to the café and up the stone steps. The door is flanked by two huge bay windows and, although he had his back to me, I could see the man I was looking for sat at the table on the right.

The restaurant's layout is mostly open plan: not 100% ideal for a cosy tête-à-tête, but the seating in the bays is sufficiently distanced from the others to enable at least some form of private exchange to take place. He'd chosen as well as he could, and I told him as much as I slipped into the chair next to him. Actually, that was about all I had the chance to say before the door opened, allowing not only the sounds of the town to make their way across the mat, but also Dean.

Chapter 17

Accountants and Goffers: hiding in the Bushes, with another Loraine

POSTMAN

> Coming together is a beginning, staying together is progress, and working together is success (Henry Ford)

It had been over 24 hours since I'd put my unsteady runner onto the case, but he hadn't deigned, as yet, to provide me with an update on his progress. I really can't understand why removing your Clark Kent style glasses and staring so intently at a telephone doesn't force it to ring instantly. Given the effort I was putting in, you'd have thought that at the very least I would have been rewarded with the handset melting into a pile of plastic goo. But I suppose I shouldn't have been that surprised. To be fair, he generally comes up trumps for me, but it's just so hard to make yourself believe that everything's going to be alright in the end when his methods and general demeanour fill you with nothing other than impending doom. And it's not as if he hasn't always been like that.

Our first ever meeting had been in *The Bushes*: a proper Irish pub, set in the middle of the Square overlooking the harbour. I'd given most of the other hostelries in the town a chance to earn my custom but, as fine as they were, they fitted more like OJ's glove than Cinderella's slipper. Now, whenever I needed to pass the time waiting for shipments, this was where I felt most comfortable gravitating towards and where I became a bit of a regular.

It only took a few weeks before I was on first-name terms with the ever present barmaid, Loraine. She was as welcoming and jolly as the landlady in the *Sutherland Arms* had been, and the coincidence of sharing the moniker with a fellowess beer pourer meant I was unlikely to ever forget it. And it was barely another day or two before I no longer had to submit a formal request for a glass of *Smithwick's*, my Irish red ale of choice. Our relationship had developed such that she would be halfway through pulling my first pint before I'd reached the bar and have my refill ready almost before I'd realised myself I was in need of one.

It took a tad longer to get to know the locals by name. This was the sort of pub where everyone was pleasant enough, but bought their own drinks. There were never any rounds purchased, even by groups of guys – and it was mostly guys in Bushes – who had come in together. But over time I picked most of them off, albeit in dribs and drabs. A friendly nod or wink as you entered the bar towards a man you'd been stood next to a day or so before breaks the ice. Soon you overhear someone mention his name, which you repeat casually later that evening. Somehow you slip your name into the ether and from there on in the winking and nodding is replaced with more personable greetings.

One by one my mental list of regulars' names grew and while most would never go beyond the casual acknowledgement stage, I developed a much stronger relationship with Martin, Dean and Aisling.

THE HUNTRODDS COINCIDENCES

I became first name friends with Martin a month or two before hurdling the nodding phase with Dean. Had the encounters been simultaneous – or perhaps the other way around – I might have found it hard to get beyond Rat Pack references. Our conversations never wandered much into personal stuff: the Gents in *The Bushes* (there has to be a joke in there somewhere), was the only place our paths or sprays ever crossed.

While it is fair to say that personal material among the pub's patrons was rarely traded, as the newest comer to the pub I felt I should, if not provide my entire life story, at least explain my presence in these here parts.

Martin and I seemed to find ourselves standing next to each other at the bar more often than not and, now I think back, he was the more inquisitive out of the two of us: where was I staying; how long was I here for; if I was not sipping four pints of *Smithwicks*, how was I passing the rest of my time here. General sorts of gen.

I don't recall the question of recreational drug use cropping up much before he'd digested a reasonable outline of his new found drinking partner. I do, however, recall the night it did raise its head and within an hour I had purchased a *wee bag-'o-weed* as Niall Robertson, an old Scottish Smoke Bud of mine from the Orkneys used to call it. Later that evening, strolling home along the harbour and toking on my newfound friend removed the last semblance of the almost negligible hesitation I'd had about resuming a relationship with the plant I'd left behind long ago. My thoughts were as light as the breeze off the sea and while I certainly wouldn't let it overtake my life – if there's one thing I can do well, it's control my emotions and what I do – I was sure the occasional smoke or two would be the perfect distraction to break the monotony of the waiting game I often had to play in Baltimore.

I didn't spend every evening in *The Bushes*, nor did I see Martin every time I was there, but when our paths did coincide, the beer flowed, the conversation was varied and if the odd dime bag was passed my way, all well and good.

One night, towards the end of an unusual dalliance into an evening's fifth pint of ale, I asked how he had come to be the local purveyor of grass. He looked slightly quizzical at first, but seemed to shrug off any thought of stopping this line of enquiry in its tracks. Before continuing though, he steered us in the direction of a quiet corner table and lowered his usual high singsong tone a notch or two. He explained that the weed was but a small side line he was permitted to follow by his suppliers. It provided his beer money, which was fine, but the real cash came from the business this was on the side of, which was harder and far more serious stuff: Crack Cocaine. Why, he wanted to know. Did I want some?

I was slightly taken aback. I liked to keep a clear(ish) head: two glasses of best was usually my limit. Five pints and a puff of wacky backy and I was like Baloo the Bear: gone man, gone. Mixing that in with Coke or Snow or whatever you called it was not something I was remotely interested in exploring.

He was nodding along with what I was saying and, despite clearly being a few drinks ahead of me, suddenly looked particularly focussed and said, "Good. I like that. We might just be able to do some business together".

And that was how it all started. It turned out that his set up was something almost identical to mine. For my car mechanic, swap to his potato merchant. For garages in Ballycastle and Cork, read farms in nearby Munster and Donegal on the border. We were the same guys, doing the same things in similar businesses, and it looked like I was about to start paying a little closer attention to his.

I was Martinless the first time Dean and I elevated our relationship to speaking actual words. I'd just come into the pub and spotted, couldn't fail to miss really, his enormous frame sat on his usual bar-side seat ordering a drink. I often felt self-conscious about my shock of red hair – *Duracell* was the nickname of choice for many of my school friends, though my piercing green eyes prompted some of the slightly crueller and less subtle among them to opt for something far more direct, like *Spooky Freak Boy*. What I would have paid to have been next to this guy in the playground where he would surely have absorbed the unwanted attention I was getting. My uncle Norman, an avid fan of all things horses, would have described him as a magnificent beast, before gauging his height, in hands, to within the width of a horseshoe. My equine mathematical skills were several furlongs shorts of his, but I would have felt on solid ground to have ventured Dean was one, if not two hands over six feet – and almost the same across the shoulders. His hair was as rich a copper hew as mine, and if that wasn't enough to help pick him out from a crowd, he always seemed to have a silly little emerald hat perched perilously on his locks: it looked as small and out of place on his head as he did whenever he was stood alongside more regularly sized mortals. Our paths had crossed so rarely that we had barely reached the nodding stage, but on this occasion I caught Loraine mentioning his name as he exchanged a five Euro note for a pint of what apparently was called a Blacksmith. I asked her what on earth was in that but Dean replied for her, "Guinness," (obviously I thought – he'll put me down as totally stupid), "and Smithwicks." (which, I judged, was slightly less obvious so stopped beating myself up over not being able to win at the guess the provincial drink game). Anyway, our conversation drifted on from there.

He'd seen me on and off at the bar and asked what my story was. At least, I think that was what he asked. The accent of those who live in the south of the island is far less harsh than that of their northern brethren, but it still requires a degree of concentration so as not to lose anything in the translation. Added to that, this clearly wasn't the first pint of Blacksmith he'd purchased today, and the alcohol was beginning to challenge his articulation skills. In short I really was a long way off 100 per cent sure of the exact line of questioning he was pursuing. Taking a punt, I more or less rehearsed the lines I'd previously given to Martin and just hoped my side of the discussion was relating, even in some small way, to the conversation he thought he was having with me.

As it turned out, it seems my skills did include the ability to interpret *slury-lilt* and our relationship grew from there. His father had always wanted him to be a mechanic, and he appeared particularly interested in my work, both here and in England. He'd done a fair bit of travelling, certainly to Limerick and Galway and once as far as Dublin (well, at least to the outskirts thereof), but the concept of crossing the water to go further afield seemed quite beyond him. He'd arrived in town a short time ago and, from what I could make out, he was only stopping here because he had run out of land on which to aimlessly wander.

One other thing that was clearly somewhat out of his grasp was money. He always had enough to buy his own strange hop and malt concoction – just as well as, after all, this was *The Bushes* – but whenever talk wandered beyond the mundane, his story invariably veered towards tough luck and hard times. Houses? I rent somewhere cheap when I can. I can't afford to buy. Restaurants? Not at those prices. Beans on toast often does me. Transport? You can't get better value than the Marylebone Coach. He must have caught my vacant expression because, without me even asking, he explained it was some weird Tom Waits' term for walking referenced in one of his songs. He thought he'd heard it on a CD he had once borrowed from a friend.

He didn't come across as particularly unhappy discussing his financial situation – it was a topic that had cropped up between us far more than once. But the fact that there really wasn't all that much substance to discuss certainly hadn't held him back from bemoaning his luck. It soon became clear that while some might curtail this conversation by leaning back on their stool and saying, "I may be poor, but I'm happy as I am.", Dean was not one of those.

"Well, you're never going to make any cash by staying around these parts." I told him. "Have you really never travelled more than a couple of hundred miles from this tip of the island? If you truly want to fatten your purse, you'll just have to do *something* different."

Until then, I hadn't been talking with anything specific in mind. Despite his general state, which, to be fair was rarely totally pissed, (although to be equally just, seldom dipped below quite tipsy), I had warmed to the man. As such, I was constantly on my guard not to offend him by letting him see how pathetic I thought he really was.

When he asked me, therefore, what I might suggest, I was somewhat at a loss. What on earth could I recommend to a failed mechanic of many unfixed abodes?

I didn't know it at the time, but I would eventually provide him with an answer to that question as a result of something that cropped up a couple of months later over a pint I was sharing with a third new friend, Aisling.

The sharing pint thing was a bit of a private joke developed on the back of our first meeting. I was getting ready to leave the garage not long after lunch one wet Tuesday afternoon when I received some disappointing news. The latest delivery I was due to meet had suddenly been put on hold: the knock on effect of some interest expressed by a few overly exuberant coastguards in Libya a couple of days ago.

I picked up my coat and was mulling over what I was going to do with this unplanned gift of time. It was far too early to pop into the pub – never before six o'clock was my usual mantra, but the mother of all downpours put paid to any immediate thought of venturing out, so I remained holed up at the garage. The flash of rain was intense but, as is often the case in this part of the country, short-lived, so resigned to an afternoon of bingeing American sitcoms on Netflix, I took advantage of the lull in the weather and set out for my digs.

I had barely reached the Square as the slightly annoying drizzle that had been lightly dampening my ginger hair abated, but only to allow the deluge to return. With *The Almighty* having just turned the taps on full blast and my lodgings still a couple of hundred yards away, my judgement that I was but a few steps from the welcome mat of *The Bushes* made my next decision easy.

As I pushed the pub's door open, it was clear that the weather had dissuaded many others from venturing out. Indeed, if you discounted the bar maid my appearance did no more than double the number of people in the bar.

As I crossed the floor shaking the worst of the rain from my coat, Loraine was apologising for the fact that the *Smithwicks* had just run out. Worse still, she couldn't get into the cellar to put a new barrel on for a good half hour because the Governor was down there in the middle of a stock check.

This afternoon was going from bad to worse.

I was just coming to the conclusion that nothing could happen that would improve the situation when my solitary fellow punter chipped in and said, "If you can find a straw you'd be welcome to share my Guinness."

Now, any sort of contact between strangers in this particular bar was rare; indeed some would view such an unprompted advance with great caution, so these words caught me somewhat off guard.

I was nudged further out of kilter with the sudden realisation that the person I'd mentally classified as my solitary *fellow* punter was not a fellow at all. In my defence, clients of the female persuasion were as rare as casual conversation in *The Bushes*.

Here was a bright, blonde, blue eye belle, looking in my direction, wiping her hands with a towel and apologising for dripping all over the floor. She was clearly in a bit of a sorry state having been caught out in the rain and so, when she implored me to be her knight in shining armour and rescue her from her own thoughts on such a dank and dismal day – how could I refuse.

While that meeting was to herald the end of my six o'clock mantra – at least on Tuesdays (and so it would transpire, Thursdays), it also proved to be the beginning of quite a beautiful relationship: though not in that way. In such games I was more of a Friend of Dorothy, not that she gave me any reason to think she might be at all interested in playing anything with me. She just seemed happy to welcome a friendly face and have someone to chat with on a miserable weekday afternoon.

The damsel I had saved was called Aisling O'Toole. With a name like that it came as no surprise to hear she was originally from Ireland. I was, however, slightly taken aback (though on reflection I'm not completely sure why) when she said she was involved in finance, employed by a firm with offices in England and Northern Ireland and working on something to do with negating the UK VAT liabilities of her clients. She'd been trying to develop a money saving scheme on the back of the liberal tax haven regulations in Shannon, a town a few counties away on the east coast. So far she'd had very little success. She was now in Baltimore, following up on a rumour that a similar but more ambitious set up was being considered by the authorities in nearby Killarney.

There was also something about investing in a business exporting four leaf clovers to America, but this had, ironically I thought, been hit by a series of misfortunes that had stopped the idea in its tracks.

She laughed that, given her diminutive stature (uncle Norm would have had a stab at her being at least a hand under the average five foot two for a woman) her bosses always joked that she could bring any deal in under the radar. Alas, she explained, irrespective of her vertically challenged powers, it seemed things were so bogged down she was doing little else other than bouncing between her Head Office in Yorkshire, their hub in Belfast and a couple of nights (Tuesdays and Thursdays) in Baltimore. And there was no end in sight for this triangular tripping until her (taller) Powers that Be got their game in gear and directed otherwise.

Until that moment I had lost track that, in the absence of a straw the last forty-five minutes had been a dry old do, but then Loraine appeared by my side placing a fresh pint of ale on a new and unsoiled beer mat in front of me. Had she not done that, had she simply called me up to the bar with a cry that the *Smithwicks* was back on, I might have just taken it to another table, nodding farewell politely to Aisling, but leaving the two of us to go our separate ways. But I was really enjoying her company. I even found the way she spoke, with an odd sounding Yorkshire accent Dick Van Dyke would have been proud of, kind of cute. Equally endearing was her habit of always placing the emphasis on the final syllable of any three syllable word. I appreciate many people might find hearing Russell Crowe's famous line in Gladiator pronounced, my name is maxiMUS deciMUS meriDius, commanDER of the armies of the north, as irritating as coming across Chandler Bing asking, for what was probably the millionth time, "...could I *be* any more annoying....?". I, on the other hand, found it no less than charming. And so charmed was I that, throughout that evening, I remained at her table, in a seat I have returned to virtually every Tuesday (and Thursday) since.

Over the weeks, our conversations were varied. Sometimes mundane: the overhead camshaft on her car hire had stopped doing what it should (I knew what that was – she didn't). Sometimes political: How can American Senate Committees just block judicial nominees put forward by the President? (More her territory than mine). Sometimes niche: the correct title of Steve Harley and Cockney Rebel's hit single is not, Come up and see me, make me smile, but Make me smile (Come up and see me). Sometimes, even interesting: the sun is about 20 galactic years old, which is the number of times it has orbited the centre of the Milky Way. OK, let's leave interesting to one side for the moment but one thing's for sure, we never touched on anything personal.

Well, perhaps once.

I'd just returned from my near miss in Tibberton and the loss of my partner. His replacement had been sorted out and I must have had that well and truly on my mind because I told Aisling I had a slight *business difficulty*. I said it looked like I was about to start working closely on what I described as some very sensitive stuff, with a guy I knew absolutely nothing about. If it turned out that he was dodgy in any way, I could end up in big trouble but, the deal was being arranged in such a way that made it almost impossible for me to make the sorts of checks on him I wanted to do.

It was time to get a refill, just for me – this was *The Bushes* after all – and in any event, Aisling was still nursing her Guinness. On my return to the table, the conversation remained focussed on my little problem. So far, I'd kept away from any specifics - I'm not sure when the time actually becomes right to disclose to a relative stranger that you are a diamond smuggler – but something I said must have struck a chord because she suggested maybe this was her chance to return a favour and come to *my* rescue as my princess in shining armour. She said that if anyone could carry out due diligence on a businessman in the UK, she was my woman. She was back and forth to the mainland, as she called it, all the time and, given the glacial pace her current project was preceding, *all the time* was something she had plenty of.

143

I didn't jump in and accept her offer straight away: instead I shut down the conversation and manoeuvred the chat towards cats. She'd once gone on for what seemed like hours about her own moggy (called Sid, apparently) and I felt that would be an easy topic to slide into.

But after mulling things over for a few days, all I could see were up sides. At the moment, the only thing I knew about the replacement *compadre in crime* being foisted on me was, well.....nothing actually. Any intel Aisling sourced would, at worst, give me more than I had at present. And with luck, any financial dirt she found would almost inevitably lead towards a clearer picture of the new mystery man – and give me a better feel of whether I needed to keep just a casual eye on him or create an additional point of vision in the back of my head.

And so began the second chapter of our relationship.

She had returned to her usual seat in the pub the Tuesday after giving her the brief, armed with a sheath of papers. Once she'd finished providing her general overview of this confectionary salesman, I probably knew more about him than his Secretary did – and she was sleeping with him! This gossipy info was all well and good but I needed to concentrate on the meat of what Aisling had put together so returned to my digs to finish reading. I wanted to make absolutely sure she'd done a good job. I needn't have worried. As I turned over the last page of her report I knew I could have taken on his wife in a competition of Mr & Mrs - and won. I pretty much knew everything I needed to about this man, including that there did not appear to be anything "dodgy" to learn.

He was successful in business and from everything she saw – and Aisling insisted she'd seen everything – he was not only above board he was hovering six foot above it. He had a niche little business, a well-established connection of sellers and buyers, and he filed both VAT and income tax returns months before their deadlines. He was a tad creative with his overheads – she joked that that unless he was doing something ridiculous like travelling first class on Eurostar everywhere he went he was over egging the cost of his expenses – but, if anything, that gave me a modicum of comfort: at least she'd found *something*. Mother Teresa was not the ideal candidate for this line of work.

Aisling's commentary on Confectionary Man was just the gen I needed to feel at peace about the new arrangements I would be working under – and perhaps that laid a solid platform for us because within a few months it was clear as day that he and I were a perfect team. There had been a couple of hiccoughs, but they were, shall we say, administrative errors rather than personnel issues and things I think we could have lived with.

Alas, *they* didn't agree.

To be honest, I was extremely wary when the proposal, or more accurately *instruction*, came along. Why on earth did I need some sort of managing coordinator overseeing my actions? I well remember the apprehension I'd felt the last time a new body had been foisted upon me, and this addition seemed far from necessary. This time, however, I had someone on hand who could placate my fears. Within ten days, Aisling was reporting back, placating away and giving me absolutely everything I could possibly want to know about Confectionary Man's secretary. There were even a few things I would have been afraid to ask about, such as some questionable commentary to do with her *flexibility*.

It was good to have satisfied myself that the new post would be filled by a person I would be happy to work with, albeit one chosen by the new boy. That point seemed pretty clear to everyone because, when I made the case to add in a body of my own choosing, no one argued.

That Thursday, I told Aisling everything that was going on with my ever growing rough diamond exploits and how I needed someone I could trust to handle the money side of things. She didn't seem at all fazed at what I'd outlined. Indeed she appeared more than happy at the prospect of filling her dreary downtime days in Baltimore with some excitement that it took no more than a few moments for her to agree to be my new link in our rejigged chain. And so began the third chapter in my relationship with this lovely Yorkshire lass. My Accountant had been picked. Others could do their own checks on her if they wished.

When our conversation turned to practical matters, she asked whether I had anyone outside of the bracelet I went to if ever something "delicate" needed handling. I didn't, but that was some tasty food for thought. Having such a character I could call, who could, perhaps, also be my eyes and ears should I require such independent organs, might not be such a bad idea.

It was less than 24 hours later that I found Dean, almost sliding off his stool. It took me far less time to convinced him his fortunes could, at the drop of his hat and a ferry trip across to the mainland, change very much for the better.

Chapter 18

A young addict dies when budgets are tight

DEAN MARTIN

The number one rule of fishing is be quiet. Don't scare the fish
(Carole Radziwil)

At first, when I was given the opportunity to investigate the death of
a young boy in Cork, I just thought it was my chance to get back out
into proper policing.

I'd been placed on traffic duty, as they call it, following
accusations my team was behind the fitting up of a minor player
in the Dublin heroin business. It was total nonsense, of course: the
toe rag was bang to rights on a charge of supplying and his fate
was sealed. Given where he was heading, even if he'd been stood on
Mayfair, he would not have been permitted to pass GO. The sign
writer had all but started work etching his name on one of the cell
doors in the capital's dank Victorian fortress that would be his home
for a good double figure stretch. The case was so open and shut
that I gave it no thought beyond anticipating the several large pints
of *Blacksmith* I'd be downing on the evening the inevitable guilty
verdict came in.

I'm guessing he didn't grasp the hopelessness of his situation until somewhat later but, around the time the jury was being sworn in, I got the sense that something in his demeanour had changed. His, "bring it on coppers" cocky attitude had suddenly vanished and was replaced with a resolve that he wasn't going anywhere – and certainly not Portlaoise – without trying any and everything he could think of: and he certainly wasn't going to let logic or truth get in his way. Alas for me, and some of my team, his most bizarre thought was also to be his most convincing. His tale was that the real villains of this piece were the Garda's Drugs Unit, or, more specifically, me and a couple of my lieutenants. He said that we'd been overseeing the narcotic activities in the capital – and filling our boots with as many bungs as our hearts desired – for years. He looked all doleful as he tried to persuade anyone who would listen that he was "just another innocent bystander being framed by the Guards".

Of course his story didn't wash which, given the risks he, as a good-looking man, would face when using the *off suite* facilities to the cell the judge could mandate he reside in for the next 17 years, is rather ironic because, I'm thinking, nor would he – at least not on a regular basis.

But so ridiculous was his claim; so full of holes was his suggestion; so totally implausible was his accusation, that people thought gosh, that's so bonkers there must be a ring of truth about it!

The top brass knew it was all rubbish, but the press decided this was a tale worth getting its tabloid teeth into. Being true to their code, they didn't let the facts get in the way of a good story, and despite the Force's best efforts, we just couldn't shift it off the front pages.

Soon the whiff of something dodgy was clinging to my plain clothes and my superiors took what they felt was their only option: rip my mufti off my back and swap them for my old uniform. While "things died down", I was to be bonded to a desk: reduced to organising paperwork and counting and tagging the very bags of illicit substances I had hitherto been taking directly off the streets these past three years.

I spent every waking hour at that desk ruing my lot and wondering when on earth the powers that be would decide sufficient dust had blown over that they could risk letting me out of the closet and back into the real world. The answer came twenty six months, one week and seven hours after taking up these *administrative duties*: the day a 16 year old lad overdosed on cocaine.

To begin with, such travesties are fortunately rare but, such a dramatic rarity usually translates into seismic news. The Chief not only had to act but also be seen to be acting. Of course, that's quite easily said and, had the Department of Justice and Equality in St Stephen's Green not been forced to slash the force's budget in half following the recent banking crisis, it would also have probably been quite easily done.

However, the cuts had been made and, when the majority of your costs are in personnel, that's where the majority of the savings will be identified.

In short, the country's Drug and Organised Crime Bureau had taken a far less pleasant hit than the daily doses enjoyed by so many of their clients. And the day Michael Cornacchia's mother discovered her son's body in his bedroom on Cork's Southside, the Head of the DOCB found he didn't have a single plain clothes Inspector to call on.

So I was put back into my civilian suit and onto the case.

The tests confirmed he'd overdosed on a synthetic drug called U-47700. This substance had already been implicated in dozens of deaths, including that of the singer, Prince, who died after taking a cocktail of drugs the year before.

It seemed pretty likely to me that the poor boy had taken the hit in the belief it was cocaine. There was unlikely to be little more to it than that, and therefore, this was where my investigation would no doubt end and my journey back behind the counter would begin. Or so I assumed.

As sad as this whole tragic narcotics related death story was, the thing that grabbed the headlines was not the victim, but the substance. Michael's was the first known fatality from U-47700, or *pink heroin*, in Ireland. If the austerity measures hadn't also resulted in a considerable reduction in the number of telephones in the station, I think the Justice Minister would have rung mine off its cradle. As it turned out, it was the Bureau's Deputy Commissioner who took the call, although it was the Commissioner herself who I accompanied to Steward's Lodge for a briefing with the Taoiseach.

Now drugs are a comparatively minor issue in the Republic. I'm not saying we are problem free: far from it. We have our fair share of smack heads dotted around the 32 counties, but, as a proportion of our population, nowhere near as many as most other countries – and our Prime Minister wanted to keep it that way.

His orders were simple. I was to head up a team to discover how these hard drugs were getting onto our shores and who the bad guys were.

On the face of it, this seemed quite an obvious brief. Let's be honest, investigating what has happened and trying to find out who has done whatever it is you want to find out about, is hardly a ground-breaking approach to detective work. But there was to be a modest wrinkle. We would be doing it undercover. Deep undercover.

This was all unfamiliar territory for us. We certainly had no idea the extent of the gang's network. Come to that, we didn't even know if there was an actual gang, but we began working on the premise that we were dealing with some form of organised group anyway. One serious concern was not knowing if they had managed to infiltrate the police, judiciary, or indeed the government. This meant we didn't really know who could and couldn't be trusted and so it was decided my team needed to be smart, small and select.

I leave to one side that it must be quite rare for just two people to be referred to as *a team*, but I suppose at least the Commissioner had the courtesy of including the word small in our description.

My partner was drafted in on secondment from the UK's drug squad in the West Yorkshire police force, so was a very fresh face. And with me having been hands off anything other than a stapler for so long, none of the current pushers or dealers would have any idea the two new people on their block were undercover cops.

Not that this seemed to help us all that much in the beginning.

Despite starting with the obvious places and snouts in Dublin, it was ages before we made any genuine progress.

But after months and months of grafting, we had a breakthrough. A hitherto small-time pimp, well known to the authorities, not only for his work in the capital's bordellos but as one who also did a little bit of dealing on the side, seemed to have shot up several levels – and onto our radar. The nickel and dime bags of blow he'd long been hawking to the girls in the back streets of Monto had recently given way to more serious material and to swankier people in swankier parts of the city.

The more we found out about him, the more we were sure he'd gotten, or fallen, in with some dangerous individuals and that he could be the key who would lead us to centre of the operation we'd been charged with locating. So we started surveillance. Serious surveillance. Or at least, as serious as two undercover operatives can manage between them.

The suggestion that his base might be in Limerick happened early on. There seemed no real rhyme or reason he might have chosen that part of the country but, as senior officer and man most wanting to succeed and take all the glory, I put myself on that case. I left my partner trawling areas of Dublin's Quays and Liberties in the south inner city and boarded a train out of the capital. I was optimistic, but also a realist. If this didn't work out, there would always be another track to follow. Failure at this stage wouldn't necessarily leave a nasty taste in the mouth. Little did I know then that, first off, that wasn't true and second, the taste would be smoky bacon.

The initial trip west was a dead end, and I did little apart from stroll the length of O'Connell Street bouncing between Bobby Byrne's in the south and *The Locke Bar* at its northern tip. My second sojourn proved to be just as big a waste of time as the first, although I was at least beginning to find my way around town a bit better and had managed to sneak out the quieter coffee shops that charged less than €8 for a latte.

I returned to Dublin and was badgering a well-known grass for grass related information. As I handed over €12.30 for two cardboard cups of tea that had not been brewed in a previously warmed pot, nor presented with a cosy, I was genuinely looking forward to any form of info that would keep me as far away from Munster as possible. The assured cast iron lead I winkled out of *Grassman* was that my quarry was doing business in the dark nooks of Jerry Flannery's pub in Upper Denmark Street. Neither the bar nor the address was familiar to me, so I asked him where the hell that was. I suppose it really shouldn't have come as any surprise when he said, "Limerick".

I had not been to that part of the city, but after putting out a few gentle enquiries I soon learnt it had a reputation that proceeded itself. If there had been any dirty dealings going on, nobody would have been the least bit surprised. It wasn't much, but, in the absence of any other lead it was just enough of a carrot to haul my arse back there for the third time.

For three days and nights I was holed up in a box room on the fifth floor of a town house across the road from Jerry's. If the intelligence was right, I needed to remain in situ and out of sight. I'd been promised a fully functioning kitchen to help ease the pain of such incarceration – which indeed there was; and a varied and well-stocked fridge – which indeed there wasn't. Over the course of 72 hours I ate BBQ beans on toast, Brazilian BBQ pot noodles on toast and BBQ hotdogs on toast. Had more than one of the toaster's elements been working, I might have ventured a change in the diet with a go at toast on toast.

By the time the fourth day had wandered its way into my cocooned homage to the American diner, I decided this had been just another not particularly wild goose chase and the moment to accept that staying here would not lead me towards the gateway to Ireland's illicit drug distribution centre was nigh.

Feeling thoroughly fed up, and extremely underfed, I attempted some sub conscious aversion tactics and Googled *Nigella*, hoping for a sexy-looking Chinese concoction. The search results looked amazing. So good, in fact, that I barely glanced at Ms Lawson's pouting features, skipping instead directly to her recipe. My stomach immediately took over and, convincing my subconscious that I really no longer had any cover to blow, I ventured outside to the corner Spar for the necessary ingredients. I must confess that I felt locating Lychee in this neck of town might be a tough ask, but I thought, in for a penny, and so ask I did.

I wasn't totally surprised when the green-haired girl behind the till said, "...it might be next to the bacon, on the shelf with the other cheeses..." but it did give me a modest feeling of despair for my fellow man. I was shaken from this slight depression by my phone. It was my partner, insisting there was, at last, some super news to tell me.

Now I'm not saying, as I stepped out of the store and onto the pavement, that I greeted this revelation with total scepticism, but, at that moment I felt slightly more optimistic about green-haired girl appearing at the shop door waving a jar full of sweet white scented fruit.

But it was apparently me of little faith.

I sat down on a nearby bench, untroubled by any green follicled lady and, with no more than modest expectation that our investigation might have in any way progressed, said, "Arabella Ogden hyphen Tewksbury. What an absolute delight".

Picking, or rather being allocated a partner can be an arduous task. You want someone with experience who knows what they're doing. You want someone whose personality doesn't clash with yours. If they are to be your subordinate, you want someone who will follow your instructions – willingly, but you also want someone who has some initiative. I spoke about this in depth with the Deputy Commissioner, just before he made it plain that actually what I should want is the someone I was going to be given. And that turned out to be Detective Sergeant Arabella Ogden hyphen Tewksbury.

To be fair, she was many, if not all of the things on my hoped for list. She was also as class an act as her name suggested. And what a name. If Charles Dickens, Robert Browning and Thomas Hardy had been ordered by Queen Victoria to dream up the most quintessential English moniker imaginable, I doubt any of them would have landed all that far away from Arabella Ogden hyphen Tewksbury.

My softish Irish brogue seemed to lend itself perfectly to twirling my tongue around every syllable, especially if I also articulated her punctuation, which, slightly to her annoyance, I found it difficult not to do. Actually, despite her name, she was a working class act: father a nurse, mother a bus driver, and she'd followed her two brothers into the force. When it came to the time to specialise, A O hyphen T chose not to follow her siblings into the Firearms branch (I suppose having three Ogden hyphen Tewksburys in the same department would have made the morning roll call take too long) opting instead for the Drugs Squad. She'd taken to being among the low life better than most, which, fair play to her, is a tough environment to live with day and night. During the first four years in the department she'd developed a reputation for getting results undercover: earning the trust of those she courted and the plaudits of those who paid her wages. A year later she was promoted to Detective Sergeant based in some place in Yorkshire I can't pronounce. Eighteen months after that, she found herself on special assignment in Ireland, to the Garda Siochána – which was something she couldn't pronounce. So, at least we were equal.

She started giving me a breakdown of what had been happening at her end while, she said, adopting a pathetic imitation of my accent, I'd been sitting around on my Irish arse for four days. (I let that pass – it was a fair cop).

The Limerick thing, she'd discovered, was some sort of code word, not a place. She'd explain when we met but, it seems while we had been generating solid intel to follow, we'd just not been using it to navigate in the right direction. I say *we*, but of course it was only *me* that had been hunting this particular goose in this particular part of the country. Arabella O-T had been looking for a different bird altogether – and, it seems, with some success. His name was Martin something or other and he seemed pretty well established and comfortable in a tiny village in western Cork called Baltimore, a few hours' drive south from yours truly. She was sure he is the guy we've been searching for: one of the main suppliers helping to transport and filter the hard drug lines into the heart of the country.

There once was a copper in Limerick. Who kept coming back to the thick of it. It took him three goes, but in the end it just shows: something else'll turn up – if you're sick of it.

AOT had booked me into The Stone House; a quiet B&B in one of the village's many small side streets. I checked in, climbed the stairs to my allocated room and pushed open the door with my holdall. She was sitting, waiting, on the end of the bed but, ignoring any pleasantries, dived straight in and began bringing me up to speed. We'd decided it would be best to do that here, away from public gaze, at least until we had the chance to put together some sort of strategy.

It looked to her like the nooks and crannies around this sleepy little town's coast were central to how the goods were getting into the country. The problem we were facing was that history was not on our side. There is a reason in the 1600s this was a major pirate base. At the time it was thought that not only the justices, including the vice admiral of Munster, were involved in skulduggery but all the women of Baltimore were reputed to be either wives or mistresses of buccaneers.

If you'd have asked Long John Silver, Black Beard or, come to that, Captain Jack Sparrow, to design a haven into which they could ply their trade, then a shape akin to that of the Baltimore coastline is almost certainly what they'd have come up with.

Arabella's nooks and crannies were many in number: far too many for one person to even consider monitoring; which is why she hadn't even begun to try. And it was futile to think the effective doubling of resources my arrival had brought would enable us to make any more headroom. We probably needed a five hundred fold increase in boots on the ground for that to happen. But, until we pulled together some credible evidence that would convince our superiors of the merits such a dramatic and costly exercise might bring, our success lay in keeping tabs on Mister Mystery Martin and hoping we could get him to lead us to the big fry.

From the very beginning of this operation our luck had been like the old Dublin trams: all bad and bundled together in threes. There were the three wasted nights we had spent following three different guys along the banks of the Liffey before finding out they were organising a treasure hunt based on bridges in the Capital. This was not long followed by the embarrassment of having to explain to the manager of a Supremes' tribute act why we thought Florence Ballard, Mary Wilson and Diana Ross look alikes might be part of a wider drugs network we'd been tracking. My fruitless prial of Limerick experiences was only the most recent example of our troubles.

But while trams and trollies and buses the world over may continue to appear in triplicate, in Baltimore our fortunes suddenly changed.

Our early leads had all come from information gathered in drinking establishments. Perhaps, we mused, he felt safe in such public situations where a quiet corner for a quiet word could always be found. Perhaps a place where being seen talking to a stranger was more common than not, making contacts with his buyers and, hopefully, his sellers easier. Perhaps he just liked a drink. Whatever the reason, our best chance for establishing a strong covert contact was to find the right place, Martin's place, and blending in. With luck this could all be done before he'd spotted us. We'd then just hope we could move things on from there.

Of course, time was marching on. We'd had precious little positive notes to report back and with just the two of us verses the fifteen plus hostelries in the village, the maths was against us making an early landing on whichever drinking hole Martin had made his regular stop. We thought we'd start by spreading ourselves as wide as we could and selected two very different places to check out.

Option one was *Rolf's Country House and Restaurant*. If Martin wanted something quiet and five star, Rolf's was in a tranquil spot off the beaten track and a quality establishment. Arabella Ogden hyphen Tewksbury would blend right in.

Good luck number one came with our other choice; *The Bushes*. We went for this given its very central location, and, in case Martin was a man's man, wanting a proper pub, with proper beer. Peering in through the window, I spotted a stool at the end of the bar that looked as good as any to claim as my own

I'd been popping in early doors and plonking myself on said stool for three or four days the first time I saw Martin. The picture we had was recent and his features unmistakable. He greeted the barmaid by name and I stored Loraine into my memory bank.

We didn't speak, I'm not even sure we bothered to nod. He took his *Guinness* to a table and pulled out a paper, paying as much attention to the few other punters around him as he had with me.

Of course, had he been more engaging, I would have been ready. Rule one in undercover cop school is: make your part/live your part. There was nothing I could do about my size other than play to it, so my base coat was that of a big lumbering Irish ox. I wondered whether donning a dopey green hat and keeping it permanently balanced on my frizzy red locks pushed things over the top, but AOT, possibly with a half hidden smirk, had convinced me to go with it. We also felt it could help if I played at being a little vulnerable. Someone who is needy. Down, though not quite out, tends, at least in the first instance, to prompt a sympathetic ear. Throw in alongside that a tendency to have a drink or two too many and people might feel they can take advantage of you. Either way, I didn't mind how, just so long as I was taken.

For the next few nights I could be spotted, half slumped on my stool at the bar, doing my best to display the appearance of a man who'd had several more beers than I'd actually been nursing. Whether Martin spotted me was not particularly clear. He certainly didn't give any indication that he had and indeed, we continued sipping our pints some distance apart. He would often just sit quietly reading his paper, though he had begun spending more and more time in close company with a red-haired/green eyed guy who seemed to come into the pub as often I did.

Although I spent much of my time trying to think of ways to make at least some form of contact with Martin, the last thing I wanted to do was make the initial move. I didn't want to give him even the faintest of ideas that I might actively want to speak with him. However, as wise a strategy as that sounded, it wasn't helping me make any progress and I was beginning to wonder how on earth I was going to resolve my problem. The solution appeared at my side one evening when I heard a chap ask the barmaid what a pint of *Blacksmith* was.

Welcome to piece of good luck number two.

Glancing over my shoulder, I saw the enquiry was coming from the slightly spooky looking bloke who'd been spending so much recent time with Martin. Apart from his shocking follicles and stand out pupils, he had the letters PAT tattooed on three of the knuckles on his left hand. I chuckled to myself as I wondered if he was a postman.

It hadn't been difficult to get Loraine to verify that a bit of recreational grass dealing had been going on between these two guys for some time: she didn't mind as long as they bought their drinks and did nothing stupidly blatant that might make her open her blind eye. And nor did I mind. This might just be the opportunity I needed. If Spooky Mail Carrier had got in close enough with Martin to start buying some weed, then maybe other relationships had also been forged. I know there's a possibility that the enemy of my enemy could become my friend, I just had to hope the same might work for the friend of my enemy.

Laying the base was fairly straightforward. Pat seemed to accept without question the sort of down and out and slightly hopeless persona I gave him, and it was a tale I found just as easy to emboss with each new session we shared. Within no time I think I'd convinced him that I was nothing short of being just a pretty useless guy who had no money, no prospects and not really anywhere specific to go.

I was cautious about gilding the pathetic lily I had planted, but just as keen to get as close to him as I could in order to get equally adjacent to his friend. So when he started talking about me having to look at ways I might fatten my purse, I took a chance and asked him if he had anything in mind. Almost immediately I wondered if I'd pushed too far as he ignored my question and moved the conversation away from the subject.

The more I thought about things, the more I became convinced that this imitation mailman was our best bet for getting to Martin and his suppliers. To be fair, of course, he was actually the *only* doorway we had, but either way, I couldn't afford to mess things up. For the moment, at least, I'd taken things as far as I could and in order to keep said things moving we needed to come up with a means of generating piece of luck number three.

That was when we decided it was the time to introduce Arabella Ogden hyphen Tewksbury into the picture.

Chapter 19
My first yellow taxi

AISLING

> I've always wanted to play a spy, because it is the ultimate acting exercise.
> You are never what you seem (Benedict Cumberbatch)

Looking back, it seems obvious. But at the time – not so much.

Dean had got about as far as he felt he could go with his new postman buddy, so we felt it was probably the right moment to bring me into play. We'd put the finishing touches onto my prepared back-story and were beginning to focus on how to actually integrate me into the equation when the question of my name came up.

"What should we go for?" he asked. "It certainly can't be Duchess of the Manor, Lady Arabella Ogden hyphen Tewksbury! Leave aside that this part of Ireland is about as provincial as it gets, we don't want to fall at the first hurdle by drawing any unnecessary attention to you. Putting you in the mix with three names and a fancy punctuation mark would be just about the easiest thing we could do to make you stick out like a quartet of sore thumbs."

I briefly wondered whether the likes of Marion Morrison, Maurice Micklewhite, or Harry Webb had offered up any argument when the similar proposal had been put to them. I guess it made sense that if we were moving away from something quintessentially English, we may just as well adopt an obvious Celtic alternative. And, we reasoned, while a hoity toity Anglo Saxon label might prompt some awkward questions, a blatantly Gaelic title was unlikely to raise as much as an eyebrow.

We approached the task scientifically. I'd seen an Irish comedian, Aisling Bea, on the comedy circuit and thought her first name as green as I was likely to get. On Googling her I discovered her proper name is Aisling Cliodhnadh O'Sullivan, but we agreed that might be going a little too far. Instead, Dean said his father had always loved Peter O'Toole – and if we used that, I could end up with the same initials as my own. We weren't immediately sure if that was going to be any help, but it is not unusual for many an undercover villain in an Agatha Christie book to have been found out with the wrong monogram on his, or her handkerchief, so reasoned it couldn't do any harm.

"Welcome to Baltimore, Aisling O'Toole", Dean announced with a wave of his arm as if inviting me into a grand ballroom. I quite liked the sound of it (and was particularly relieved that he hadn't articulated the apostrophe into my new moniker).

We could now move onto the actual business at hand: how were we going to feed me into the story without raising suspicions. An exciting new level to be moving onto, though not always as easy as it sounds to pull off.

Throughout my time as a police officer, I'd been on stake outs, search outs and inside outs. Occasionally they'd turn up trumps. But for every time you picked up a flush or, let's dream big, three tens, there would be two hundred times you'd be dealt little more than a three of diamonds, a four of spades and a seven of, well, it really didn't matter what suit it was; it would still make a bum hand. But, even by the law of averages, a prial has to turn up once in a blue moon

THE HUNTRODDS COINCIDENCES

or, as it so happened, on a dank and dirty rainy lunchtime on the Irish coast.

We'd already decided I couldn't just wander into *The Bushes* one evening, snuggle up to the Postman and trust to luck we might sail on successfully from there. Even a blind rat with a cold would see straight through such a pathetic story and just as speedily sniff me out as a relative.

Unfortunately, the only other plans we could conjure up had two key things going against them: they were pretty lame and hardly any less likely to avoid producing the whiff of rodent.

When I say *plans*, it was basically two variants of the same idea. In scenario one, I would hang around in the shadows by the village square waiting for Postie to make an appearance, before running into him, metaphorically, under the guise of a lost tourist. The second option also started out with me hanging around in the shadows by the village square waiting for Postie to make an appearance, but had the subtle difference of me tripping up on a cobblestone and running into him, physically.

We didn't think either approach had much of an edge over the other, by which I mean both had the same likelihood of failing, but they were the only ways we could think of prompting my introduction.

It was day one of operation *skulk in the bushes and spring out without trying to scare the bejeezus out of your quarry*. I was concentrating on identifying my skulking place of choice, dressed casually in line with the weather forecast for the day: fresh but balmy. It was around one o'clock I that discovered Ireland had their own version of Michael Fish beavering away in their Met Office. To be fair to Mr O'Fish, it wasn't exactly frogs and petulance I was being subjected to, but well, let's just say that with stair rods pinging down on one's head, I felt he was playing pretty fast and loose with the definitions of both balmy and fresh.

The sky had turned a shade of Guinness all punters crave but few landlords outside this island can achieve. At that moment the only thing I wanted was to get under cover and, with my hands and tourist map completely failing in their attempt to protect my head from the elements, I made a dash across the square. From nowhere the amplified sound of the opening bars of La Marseillaise pierced my ears and I looked up just in time to see a New York style cab swerving to avoid knocking me over. While successful on that front, the driver was not skilful enough to miss the pool of rainwater at my feet: Suddenly I was being systematically drenched from both ends. The odd Irish/French/American amalgam of yellow taxi disappeared around the corner and, with no further vehicles to block my path, I made it onto the pavement and dived into the doorway of the nearest building.

These last few moments had happened at pace and in a bit of a blur, and it took a couple of shakes of the head to dislodge the rain that had blurred my vision and clouded my brain. Within moments, however I could see from the name on the welcome mat on which I was dripping that this random place the Gods had chosen for my sanctuary was *The Bushes*.

I instinctively turned to leave. We'd been working on ways to subtly segue me into the equation: bursting through the front door unannounced felt some distance away from that. Yet, here I now was, and in fully justifiable circumstances. If anything, it might seem odd just hightailing it back outside into the Celtic monsoon without so much as a *by your leave*. Perhaps I should give this serendipity an opportunity to unfold and see where it takes us.

The place was deserted apart from the barmaid who beckoned me in. With no other customers on whom to focus, I received a little more of her attention than I might otherwise have done. We shared a tale or two about the weather in these parts before she presented me with a towel and a freshly pulled pint of Guinness. Now this wouldn't have been my tipple of choice but hey, I was undercover so why shouldn't the persona we'd invented consume pints of stout?

I picked out a table where I could begin to dab myself dry and looked around. I'd only seen the inside of this pub from the outside, through the large window pane facing the square. Once Dean had started taking up residence, it seemed to make sense for me to stay away. It struck me as being large, dark, brown and, not wishing to be rude but, shabby: typical of bars the world over. What is it about some landlords: Don't they realise there's a market for having their place looking, at least *a little* clean and bright? It is legal to serve alcohol without sawdust and spit being present. If only more would make their establishments somewhere people might also want to drink, say wine or a cocktail they might just double their potential audience.

I moved on from my wee internal rant and was trying to work out which stool Dean had laid claimed to when the door flew open. A fellow drowned rat had rushed in, presumably in search of cover and, judging by the puddle forming at his feet, a place where he could dry out his mop of copper coloured hair.

While the colour of his hair wasn't anywhere near enough for a solid ID, the piercing green eyes beneath the wet thatch that was dripping onto his tattooed knuckles was good enough circumstantial evidence for me. It was Postman Pat.

My first thought, having stumbled across him in this way was what a waste of time it had been working on the cunning "*entrap your quarry in the Square*" rouses. But at least I was prepared, ready to dive in and engage in conversation with him: this was, after all, the whole point of the aforementioned plans.

There seemed some problem with the barmaid serving his drink, so I decided on an opening gambit of asking if he fancied sharing mine.

He looked slightly suspicious but I did my best to appear lost and forlorn, which seemed to do the trick as he made to move towards me. Then, in what I later reflected on as quite a nice, if not ingenious, touch I apologised for the dank state of my matted hair and told him I'd got caught outside in the mother of all downpours so had shot in here for cover.

He sat down, eyeing the clump of towel by my side, smiled and sympathised. It seems Michael Fish had caught him out too. He was quite happy to talk and not particularly keen to leave. Not that I was getting any sort of sexual vibe from him. There was no dabbling of a toe into a moderately riské innuendo, or an accidental brush of his hand against mine. It was just a comfortable and relaxed chat between two wet strangers in an empty pub.

I must say that much of his conversation bordered on the somewhat inane, although I am a bit of a 70s music fan and was interested to learn the proper title to the iconic Cockney Rebel song. But, banality apart, I was certainly not going to have any better opportunity to gently roll out my prepared spiel without him feeling it had been rammed down his throat. So, doing my best to keep hold of the embellished Yorkshire accent I had decided to go with (against Dean's recommendation) and trusting to Rule number Two in the Undercover Handbook, I deposited my background story, harsh vowels and funny pronunciation on the table. They'd be fine there: available for him to pick up at his leisure.

Back at the Guest House, Dean and I worked out a bar schedule for the two of us. I couldn't be in there *every* Tuesday and Thursday afternoon – he and I certainly didn't want to be there at the same time – but we had to keep our man hot and interested.

We decided I should give Pat gentle notices of when I was and wasn't likely to be at *our* table. "I need to be in London for a few days, so I won't be able to share a drink with you again until next Tuesday." That sort of thing, just so he was aware I hadn't forsaken him. As it happened, my first real break came about on the back of one such bulletin.

He was speaking about needing to check out a new business partner, but really didn't know how to go about it. I said I knew the very person to help him out: me! Perhaps he'd been fishing and was hoping I would volunteer my services but, who cares: it seems at last, I was finally getting somewhere.

I obviously did a decent job (which wasn't a total surprise given I'd handed over the task to a CID colleague in Yorkshire – these fraud guys are excellent!) because my services were in demand a second time when, some weeks later he needed someone else examined.

I was certainly edging closer to him and told Dean I didn't think it would be long before I started making genuine progress. He mumbled, slightly ungraciously I felt, that it was about time we had some actual news on that front. To be fair, it had so far been a bit of a slog. One always expects to be in for a huge and dreary haul on these sorts of cases, though not that that ever tends to ease the pain very much. However, on the Tuesday following his mealy mouthed commentary on the situation, good news appeared.

Pat had been sharing more and more information about his various *business activities* and I'm sure he will have been aware how dodgy it all might be sounding to me. Perhaps he'd been testing me out: would the thought of being involved in dubious dealings send me running, or draw me closer to him.

Well, if I had been on trial it seems that the jury had chosen that afternoon to come in smiling and with 24 sets of *thumbs up* pointing in my direction.

He hadn't even taken a sip of his beer when he sat down and just started talking about his smuggling operation and how he needed some help. I can only assume that the background checks I'd done, and the way I had approached them, had finally tipped the balance and lulled Pat into the false sense of security I was hoping he would stray.

Was I in, he asked. You try stopping me, I thought.

I must say, however, that, as quickly as it arrived, my euphoria was slightly tempered when I focussed on the commodities being smuggled: diamonds! Add to that the fact that the intended destination was in mainland Europe, and suddenly we seemed quite some distance away from our quest of finding the source of the heroin being distributed on the streets of Dublin.

Pat was still talking but I concentrating more on trying to make sense of where black market gems fitted in to all this and if they had any chance of getting Dean and I any closer to Martin's drugs. I could only hope that going along with this diamond game would, at best, lead us, and at worst, enable us to stumble across what we were really after.

Once I had a handle on my new role, which seemed to include me including spending a bit more time in places like Whitby than I might have hoped for, I decided to chance my arm and see if I could somehow get Dean involved. I asked Pat if he had any "personal" hired help, or confidant he turned to for some mindless duties: an extra pair of eyes and ears, perhaps? I tried to be subtle in suggesting that to have someone on hand you could trust, or at least paid him enough to earn their trust, could make a great deal of sense, especially given the business he was dabbling in. He said he hadn't but, keeping Rule number Two in mind, I left the thought hanging with him.

Less than 24 hours later, Dean came back to the Stone House from his evening session in *The Bushes* to announce that, as of this moment, we were now *both* on the Postman's payroll.

At last, the game really was afoot.

Chapter 20

The Rookie and crate of salmon

DEAN MARTIN
> Success is the ability to go from one failure to another
> with no less enthusiasm (Winston Churchill – *again*)

Well, didn't I just come up smelling of shamrocks. Not!

As I made to leave Hadley's fish restaurant, I caught a glimpse of Arabella, sorry, Aisling, looking my way from the other side of the street. I feigned tripping up on the pavement, trying to let my collar slip just enough so she could spot me. As I turned to follow in the wake of my target who was now striding out over Whitney Bridge, one question flashed through my mind. How on earth did my once enormous and intricate operation become barely more than some pathetic and tacky surveillance job on the east coast of England?

It had been six months since Arabella, sorry, Aisling, had got the two of us in nice and tight with the Postman, and during that time I'd been reduced to little more than a goffer. To be honest, it was pretty much my fault. I'd decided to allocate myself what I considered to be the sexiest of tasks: getting in close to the sources of the supplies of both the crack and the stones. Surely this would be where the action was? As it happens, it's not until you're at the beck and call of a smuggler that you experience, first hand, what a mundane role it can be. Driving here. Waiting around there. Never meeting anyone face to face. Driving back to the place whence you first came, and then waiting for the moment when you can do it all over again.

Meanwhile, Aisling had become an integral part of the smugglers' dirty diamond deed department and was now the key link between the Postman and his deliverer. She was also amassing stacks of evidence about said dirty deeds that were making her the toast of the Belgium Federale Politie in whatever the Walloon equivalent of a bier Keller is.

But as delighted as the Antwerp fraud squad was with her efforts (and the fact that they were being given a rock solid [pun, ha bloody ha] case all tied up with a neat Irish bow, why wouldn't they be?), it wasn't getting us any closer to the origins of the narcotics.

And the longer this state went on, the more concerned I became that this would not end well for yours truly. What if, while I was faffing around in Postie's wake, someone else, who possibly didn't even realise there was anything untoward happening, appeared out of nowhere and tripped over the Dealers' supply route into the country? My paranoia then really took over. I could see these unknown personnel begin to crack the (my!) case wide open, take all the plaudits and leave my boss mouthing the inevitable question: "so what has Dean been doing all this time - perhaps he'd be better off back behind his desk?"

As the Chinese might very nearly have said, *beware of what you don't quite wish for*, because, needless to say, that is sort of what happened.

I was on my way back from running an errand for his nibs in Tuam when I heard the news. Unlike the Saw Doctors, and irrespective of how marvellous the stone walls looked or green grass smelt, I'd preferred to have been in my room at The Stone House. At least there I could have hurled a glass against the wall in frustration rather than having to be satisfied with screaming at the top of my lungs as I continued the drive along the N17.

This unwanted intel actually came via two calls, from two separate sources, and within a space of two minutes of each other. First up was a very panicky Postman Pat who took no time or breath to run me through the extraordinary scenes in Baltimore. It sounded as though the Country's entire police force had descended on the town and were all camped in the Sherkin Island Ferry car park. When he did pause to inhale, he must have taken the opportunity to flick through his copy of The Penguin Books of Idioms, because he felt people breathing down his neck, hard on his heels, looking over his shoulder and lurking in the shadows. The up side was at least he didn't seem to think that the paranoids were after him. Not that that stopped him repeating the same eight words on a continuous loop, "What on earth am I going to do!?"

I'd pretty much got the whole drift by the time I was able to slide a word in. I couldn't stop myself mentally flicking through my own stack of hackneyed phrases and asking if he had reason to believe that someone was actually about to feel his collar. "Not really." He said. "I've been meticulous about covering my tracks and keeping people off the scent."

In an effort to get him to throw the damn book out the window, I waded in with a dramatic suggestion. "If you genuinely have been operating so far under the radar, why don't you just......pack up your troubles in that funny tartan bag of yours and simply....smile while casually walking out of town?"

This, it seems, is exactly what his self-preservation instincts were telling him to do. However, the avaricious side of his brain was busy reminding him that two of the things he'd have to pack into his plaid bag were €1,000,000 worth of pink heroin and €250,000 of uncut diamonds he had taken delivery of earlier in the week. "This was to be the big one." he shouted. (I really couldn't believe he'd wandered into 1920s gangster movie dialogue, but I suppose it was clear what he meant).

The success of our recent missions had given both the drugs and diamond guys the confidence to up the ante several mega levels. Unfortunately for *us*, he said – suddenly it seemed as if I was being lassoed into the mix – it would appear that Sod, Finagale, Melody and Murphy had been out on a bender together last weekend and decided that the very moment both the narcotic and gem parties should do the upping would coincide with the instant every police officer on the Island was being instructed to congregate outside *The Bushes*.

Yes, he agreed, *we* – it would seem besides the lassoing, my wrists were being tied and hooked on to whatever you call the funny little nob on the front of a saddle – should leave of town, but we had to take the stuff with us. He'd been in the final throws of finalising the details for this *special posting* and if we were smart, he said, we could still fence the merchandise. He could then pick up the money – I spotted my sudden absence from the equation – and get out and away Scott free.

He hung up with an instruction that I should flee (overly dramatic) to England, board a ferry, go to my digs and wait for his call.

Barely had I heard the magnified sound of his line going dead echo through the car's speakers than my phone rang again. Flicking the voice control button on the steering wheel enabled the dulcet tones of the Police Commissioner to float around the car.

She could barely conceal or contain her excitement as she proceeded to sing me the *Ballad of Baltimore* from her side of the fence. Apparently an ordinary police officer – actually, not even an ordinary anything: a Reserve Gardai, from Cork - was in Baltimore looking for a case of fresh Atlantic salmon for a party he was throwing for his father's 60th birthday. To cut a long fishy story short, he goes down to the dock, finds a boat that's unloading its cargo, does a good deal with one of the ship's hands (who throws in some shrimp for good measure) and drives home happy as a clam at high tide. However, his joy is halted as soon as he hoiks the crate into his garage, prises open the lid and finds it full to the Sally Gunnels of 20 kilo bags of chalky white powder, pink heroin, beneath a thin layer of ice. It would be fair to say he had anticipated something somewhat healthier, and a slightly deeper shade of red.

The ruse the Chinese drug barons had been using to sneak their unwanted goods into the country alongside legitimate fish exports had been thwarted. The fact that they would simply move on and find other legitimate exports to conceal their wares around – and other countries into which said wares could be slipped - mattered not to the Commissioner or the Irish Prime Minister. As long as it wasn't on her emerald and pleasant land.

And just when I thought nothing could make me feel any worse, she tells me (and Dean, she said, you'll laugh at this) "he had only signed up for the voluntary work with the police because his wife thought he might look good in a uniform!"

It was as much as I could do to manage a high pitched, "ha".

She obviously failed to register the dismay in my voice because she continued, "and if you think *that's* funny, wait till you hear that he'd only been out of training for six days when he had stumbled across his unexpected catch!"

The despair I felt in that moment would only be compounded a week later when PC Brilliant was photographed, stood rigid, flanked by the Bureau's Commissioner and the Taoiseach, in my rightful place, on the lawns of Steward's Lodge.

Having concluded her tale of *Reserve Police Constable Marvell's Coup* and detailed how the raid on the rogue ships in Baltimore dock had ensured they wouldn't be returning anytime soon, I sensed she was about to grope for some conciliatory words to soothe what she no doubt (and correctly) imagined would be my bruised ego. In fear that she might also be leading up to ordering me back towards the rear side of my old desk, I cut in before she had the chance. "I'm guessing you'll want me to wrap things up neatly at this end and bring the Postman in for questioning? He's sorting out the logistics of his final deal as we speak, and I (and Ms Ogden Tewksbury, I mumbled) are in touching distance of his collar."

I hoped I wouldn't have to mention that, in addition to the quarry, I'd also be bringing back around a million Euros' worth of heroin. I wanted to keep that back as a nice little surprise and, just in case I needed one, a bargaining chip.

She mulled it over for a few seconds then, without troubling to ask any specifics about the quantity involved, told me to go ahead, but report back by the end of the week.

As I reached the far side the Whitby Bridge, I saw my prey turn right. He could only be heading for *The Magpie*, couldn't he? Aisling must have somehow arranged to meet him there: maybe to double check he was who he was purporting to be.

I decided to veer the other way and hole up in the doorway of a local bank, just to confirm my guess was correct. Sure enough, Aisling was not far behind me and soon I watched her turn toward the café. Leaving a suitable gap, I followed in her wake.

The plan, such as it was, was perhaps not the most sophisticated ever concocted, but it was the best we could come up at the time: scare him – no, petrify him – into giving us Postman Pat on a plate.

THE HUNTRODDS COINCIDENCES

As I approached the café's steps, I looked through the front bay window. She had found him and was sitting down by his side. I decided two against one could only improve our chances of success: perhaps we could slip, albeit totally unrehearsed, into a bad cop/bad cop scenario. Anyway, confident in the moment that AOT would soon get over the shock of me turning up unannounced, I bounced up *The Magpie*'s stoop and through the door. I walked over to them, pulled up a seat from an adjoining table and, ignoring my partner's slightly surprised and quizzical look, turned to the man sat opposite her. He was wearing an even more stunned expression. As I lowered myself into the chair I said, "Hi. This is Aisling and I'm Dean, but you can call us Your Worst Nightmare".

Chapter 21
The Agent in the High Street

MAN

I'm the Vice-President of panic,
and the President is missing (Paige Lewis)

I watched the two, now no longer, undercover detectives leave the restaurant. I suppose the good news was that while barely half an hour ago I didn't have the faintest idea of what on earth was going on, at least I'd reached a place where I was totally up to speed. Not that this new found intelligence was providing any degree of comfort.

I knew the drugs thing was a big mistake. I know: let's welcome here on stage for your delectation and delight, *Mr Eyes Suddenly Wide Open to the Bleeding Obvious.*

There was no messing about by either of them, although I was soon aware that their focus seemed 99% on the narcotics and fractionally less than bugger all on the diamonds.

They already knew I didn't have the stones, and when they discovered I was just as devoid of the heroin, they started babbling to each other as if I wasn't there. They wandered around several potential scenarios: who did/didn't have the drugs; or the gems, or the gems AND the drugs.....before seeming to decide any further guess work was fruitless. If I was telling the truth and holding nothing back (and I think they'd long realised I'd been scared so far out of my wits that I already had to make a trip to the dry cleaners) then they needed to concentrate on the Postman. They seemed equally convinced that the goods weren't still *in his mailbag*, so to speak and he was therefore likely to be panicking just as much as me. I doubted that, but chose not to contradict.

Whatever the score, the two plods seemed sure Pat would be the one making the next move - and that it would be in my general direction. Dean wrote down his mobile number, Aisling's mobile number, his land line, her land line, his email address, ditto hers and, for good measure, he gave me a pager code and dog whistle. Well, perhaps just the pager code. It was stressed that there could be no understandable, acceptable, or for that matter, unfathomable or unacceptable reason why I would not be able to reach either of them the second I'd had any contact, whatsoever, from him. "Do that;" said Dean, "ensure we catch him bang to rights, with the drugs in his hands, and we'll put in enough friendly words for you with the Powers That Be that you might even get off with a suspended sentence." I will say that I have heard slightly more convincing lines from a chap I once saw in the piazza in Covent Garden shuffling three well cornered cards on an upturned cardboard box. But at least he had three cards. I seemed to be holding three less than that at the moment, so really, I had little option but to go along with what they were saying.

In an effort to curry favour I asked them what they wanted to know about the diamond business. Actually, on my first go I must have whispered something that even the dog whistle wouldn't have picked up. When they realised what I was saying they began to toy with me a little – not too much but enough to reinforce the need to visit *Sketchleys*. It seemed slightly odd but they didn't appear to have the slightest interest in that side of things. Or at least not as far as I was concerned. They already had sufficient evidence for the continental cops to make their move on the jewellers with whom the stones were ending their journey. Ordinarily they'd also want to wrap in those involved on the transportation side, but they had bigger fish to fry than even the chef in *The Magpie* had ever seen. So, if I, this pathetically poor excuse for a DHL driver, could help them catch the guy holding a serious quantity of Class A narcotics, then my status would suddenly be elevated from persona very non grata to their bestest mate. Some form of immunity for such whistle blowing activity could easily be put on the table and possibly even take me out of the conviction equation. As a parting shot, they left me a snapshot of the Postman. While this was the first time I'd laid eyes on him I felt this was unlikely to be of much help past at least knowing in advance what the chap who would tear me limb from limb once he'd found out I had turned Queen's evidence looked like.

We'd been approached four times by the waitress keen to take our orders but had successfully waved her away each time craving "...just a few more minutes...". As the only one now left at the table I felt the least I should do, on this her fifth passing, was ask for a coffee. If nothing else it would allow me to mull all this over and delay the moment I'd have to leave the sanctuary of the restaurant and return to the real world of cops, robbers and red-haired, green eyed, black-ink tattooed Irishmen.

On the face of it, I appeared to have very few options. Complying with the terms and requirements Mulder and Scully had given me seemed a sensible one to stick with. However, having some form of back-up plan able to be triggered into action after (or, the thought flashed into my mind, before) I'd handed them the Colourful Celt, might not be a bad idea.

The coffee arrived. I avoided having to add to the lunch I'd eaten on the other side of the estuary by turning away from the server and putting in a call to Jonny at *Go Travel*. He'd been my go to travel man – I'm sure he never got tired of hearing that joke – in days gone by when I used to book exotic family holidays. He was on what the Directors of *Go Travel* actually called the *Exotic Desk*, though I mustn't take the mickey out of that. I suppose it was meant to be a title easily remembered and, as it had attracted me back on a number of occasions, it seems to have achieved its aim. You would go to Jonny if what you wanted was quirky; or imaginative; or stylish. He would also be your first call if any element of confidentiality was required. The surprise trip for the wife, for example (unlikely), or the Secretary (now you're talking): that type of thing.

He also had an extra sense that enabled him to bring clarity to the trip you kind of had a vague idea in your mind about but really couldn't make it much less foggy than that. He once told me he knew Margaret Thatcher well; she and Dennis had booked many a Hoseasons boat trip through him. "Not tremendously exotic," he confided, "but a little sexier than the occasional Butlin's holiday they used to take in Bognor until they realised how close that was to Broadstairs and Ted Heath! In fact," he said, "it was me who'd put her onto the Francis of Assisi's lines about *where there is despair, may we bring hope* that she used before entering Number 10 following her election victory in 1979. At the time," he continued, "I had the text of that prayer hung on my wall in the office. It was perhaps slightly over offering and a tad irreverent using a saint's appeal to God to help promote a Cox & Kings luxury package to Mauritius, but it seemed to work - and she seemed to like it."

The voice on the other end of the phone promised Jonny was just finishing off with another customer and I fleetingly wondered if it was Tony or even Boris: either of their extended families would bring in a fair commission. He was true to the receptionist's words and in no time I had him trying to peer through the fog of random ideas and fixed requirements I was putting into his mortar for pestling.

I'd given him as much as I could think of on the hoof: Remote. Confidential. Away from it all. Very confidential. Not easily traced. Secret. Oh, and did I mention, this should be kept confidential?

I think he got the drift and promised to get back to me soon, "Without error or doubt" he said.

He had brought me faith, but I needed to keep on top of things so cut him off and pressed the speed dial number for Seckie.

As soon as she answered, she jumped straight in and started providing a progress report on my car. Actually, I think she was anticipating a rant from me and wanted to get in first to say there was, in fact, no progress – it was still AWOL.

This certainly didn't in any way ease or advance my situation, but the spectres of Dempsey and Makepeace were still looming large in my head, muscling out any other thoughts struggling to slip into prominence. I gave her as coherent a run-through of the dog's dinner of my day as I could muster, leaving to the end the cherry on the pedigree chum of the undercover cops and their instructions. I told her that finding a way out of this was far from assured, and our only chance rested on us being able to address, stamp and deliver the Postman into the hands of John Steed and Emma Peel: though how we do that, I had no idea.

Not surprisingly, she seemed to be having a little difficulty digesting all of that, so I took the opportunity to continue talking, throwing in my half-baked plan of organising some form of exit strategy.

As it turned out, it was me that was thrown by her response. "Yes, though perhaps it's our disappearance act we should be focussing on." She said. "We can't just leave all this to chance and the promises of the detectives who've been chasing this case for so long."

It was her use of the word *our* that had caught me off guard. Of course I'd assured her numerous times that we were a team and promised on at least as many occasions that once we'd amassed a sufficiently large egg, we would flee the nest together. But that was when I was dreaming about us wandering off into the sunset: when everything was going so fine and dandy. As it was, things had now moved closer towards dreadful and dull. I had not pressed the self-preservation button – or more accurately, Jonny's phone number at *Go Travel* – a few moments ago with the motivation to grab anything other than a one-way ticket – anywhere - for one.

I'm not sure exactly how long it took me to reply, so I could only hope that if she had picked up even the most modest of hesitations she would put it down to no more than the rather unnerving situation.

Just in case there were cracks that needed papering over, I attempted a reassuring approach, saying she should get onto that for us straight away. "Conjure up a few ideas we can leap on together at a moment's notice – and perhaps bear in mind we could need to jump before, as opposed to after, we try to deliver on my promise to the Dynamic Duo."

I pondered for a moment, wondering what she might come up with and how it would compare to Jonny's offering: not that it would make any difference. I was clear in that split second that I had no intention of either joining her trip or factoring her in on mine, but I had to keep her very much onside - and not only until all this was behind us. Money was going to become even more key and so the minor matters of liquidating the company's assets and selling the three properties from underneath the nose of my wife needed to be kept on top of. I'd had Seckie working on both tasks the day she had left the house with my briefcase stuffed of papers adorned with my wife's signatures.

The early feelers she had put out resulted in a sweet little bidding war for my business between *Hotel Chocolat* and *Thorntons* that I very much liked the taste of; and *Alaine de Payne and Co* had produced a number of interested buyers for our family des res and her two old London abodes within 72 hours of receiving the instructions.

Since then, all sales had been progressing so well that just two days ago I'd been quietly optimistic, nay loudly confident that serious amounts of cash were barely moments away from joining the proceeds of the – hitherto – successful black market exploits being fed into my Swiss bank account.

It was time to move on, so I brought the conversation to a close. "Let me know if you hear so much as a whisper about the stolen car, or the stolen stolen gems, or the drugs. And we need to manufacture a way to get the Postman into the path of the Batman and Robin. Can you think of a ruse to contact him? Perhaps you could convince him to deliver himself."

Chapter 22

Titan on line meets Agent in the High Street

SECKIE

I can see clearly now the rain is gone (Jonny Nash)

The phone went dead. Batman and Robin? Blimey, those two cops eally had got to him, though as I paused to think about things, maybe that was a reasonable condition for him to be in. It wasn't taking an extraordinary stretch of imagination to picture the mocked caped crusaders breaking through a foggy London scene and running in my direction like an episode from Only Fools and Horses.

I needed a moment to think about exactly what I should do now. It felt that mixing stuff up a little might be the way to go: at least for starters, but first things first. I flipped open my laptop and began downloading a *Titan* travel brochure for later viewing over a cup of tea (or something stronger).

Next I thought if the time really had come to pick up my very real cat, Sid, and hurl him into a metaphorical flight of Red Sheffields, then I needed to make three calls.

First off, I punched a familiar number into my phone. The Postman answered almost before I'd pressed the final digit on my device.

I told him the police had just been in touch and had found the car somewhere down in Kent near where he'd left it. It didn't seem as if it had suffered damage of any kind, nor been involved in anything untoward (as far as they knew!), so if someone wanted to come down to the pound to pick it up – they could.

He asked the obvious question, but I told him the sergeant had said the golf bag was still in the boot. It certainly didn't sound as if the Force's finest had carried out a great deal of investigation much beyond taking the silly looking kangaroo head cover off the three wood. I said they'd already emailed me the notice letter authorising collection so there wasn't any more palaver to go through apart from actually getting to the recovery operator pound. "I should have it back by sometime tomorrow. What do you want me to do about the goods?"

He said he wanted to check everything out personally. His first thought was to sort out the car's collection himself, though he moved away from that idea once I'd reminded him in whose custody the vehicle was at the moment. He agreed that he probably didn't want to risk getting into a similar state. His second suggestion was that I do the pickup and drive to some remote spot where we'd meet. I vetoed on safety grounds. Mine. Instead, we settled on somewhere I convinced him would be neutral territory. "I have the keys to a friend's house who's out of the country." I said. "It's in a quiet residential street, near to a graveyard where the neighbours – on both sides of the cemetery wall - mind their own business. I'm expected to turn up now and again while keeping an eye on the place, so my pulling onto her drive in an unusual car won't look - unusual. Nor will having a friend with me."

I got him to write down *Third, Secret* and *Venues*, which would take him straight to the house. The line went quiet. I presumed he was testing out the geocode. It turns out I was right because a few moments later he said the app had whisked him off to Elkhorn Nebraska and to get my game in gear. "Didn't I realise how serious this whole situation was becoming?" he yelled. I checked the code and said I certainly did realise the critical status of our plight and suggested he should heed his own advice and be a little more careful. "Try making sure your sausage figures added an *S* on the end of the third word and you'll find you'll be in both the right country and at the correct address for our meeting."

After another brief pause, I heard a sort of wimpish "OK. That seems to work now. See you tomorrow at three".

My next call was back to my wobbling jelly of a boss. I told him that no sooner had I put down the phone on him just now than the Kent police rang. I repeated my fictional story about the car and the golf clubs, the time both they and the Postman would be at his house – and to make sure he was there too.

"My house!?" he spat out. "What on earth are you doing pointing him that close to me?"

I told him I'd said it was a friend's house. "He has no idea it's really yours."

In the end, I think I managed to placate him by saying it made total sense to have this meeting on our turf and on our terms. Not that those words of attempted comfort in any way stopped him spending the next 10 minutes hurling numerous questions at me about how I'd let all this happen. I spent a similar amount of time trying to drag him away from the various deaths by a thousand cuts he was envisioning an unholy alliance of the Belgium Police and Chinese Triad members inflicting on him.

Eventually he begrudgingly seemed to accept it as "...a better outcome than was looking likely earlier on today...." and said he'd get to the house early tomorrow, around twoish, just to steady himself.

"At least," I told him, "you can get straight on to Cagney and Lacey and give them the bone they'd asked for. Such speed of action can only hold you in good stead." As I let that thought sink in, I wondered if that theory would also hold good for me.

I rang off and was about to make the third call when my phone started vibrating. I didn't recognise the incoming number but answered it anyway.

It was some chap named Harley from a firm called Go Travel. I'd sort of guessed the line of business they were in before he told me. I hesitated for a second while wondering if his surname was Davidson and was about to deal with him in the same way I usually handled all SPAM calls when I heard him say, *Titan* in a tone slightly more proud than I might have gone for. He proceeded to inform me, in significantly greater detail than I needed (or wanted), that Go Travel is the recognised agent for *Titan* in the area and that my earlier on-line request for a brochure had been forwarded to him. "I wouldn't ordinarily bother you direct" he continued, "but my boss, Jonny had received a similar enquiry for the same address as I'd filled in on the contact page. He just wanted me to double check: was this in fact a booking for a single traveller, as he'd been given over the phone a few hours ago, or a two people booking as per my Googled request?"

I can't immediately recall whether or not I actually resolved his issue before pressing the red circle with a white receiver on the face of my phone. Not that it really mattered; an answer either way wasn't going to result in a booking. Not now that I'd discovered I was being sold well and truly down the river. I sat back in my chair, closed my eyes and let the steam finish coming out of my ears before returning to the task at hand and completing my third call. The number I was about to ring was the same one I'd been preparing to dial when Motor Bike Guy had called. The substance of the call I was about to have, however, following my conversation with the efficient Harley from Go Travel, would take a very different course. Mr Davison's enquiry had prompted me to decide on an issue I'd been wrestling with for some time: it was to be Plan B.

As soon as the boss's wife answered the phone I said, "It's now or never." and things went on from there.

Chapter 23
My third secret venue

POSTMAN

If you give more than is expected,
you might just get more than you deserve (Chris Brady)

At first I thought it slightly ironic that *Third, Secret* and *Venues* should be the very phrase to direct me to the third of the secret venues I had travelled to this week. At least it would be easy to remember. Unfortunately, what was also fairly simple to recall was that I'd chosen this, of all deliveries, to go *all in*, when even the likes of Victoria Coren Mitchell, Rusty Ryan and Henry Gondorff might have picked caution over impatience.

In my defence, the police raid in Baltimore had sort of forced me into action. With what seemed like the entire Irish Garda and the best part of Interpol's forces within touching distance of my collar, it clearly wasn't the most ideal of times to have a million Euros of drugs, let alone a quarter of a million Euros in illicit uncut diamonds lying around in plain sight.

I did think, momentarily, about just skipping town and leaving it all behind, but that didn't really seem a likely option. True, I would have been safe, alive and not incarcerated, but I would also have been considerably poorer. In any event, surely every interested party on either side of the law would be after my tail. No, even before I spoke with Dean, I guess, in my heart of hearts, I already knew I wouldn't be vacating my lodgings empty-handed. With that decision made, the only genuine issue was dealing with the quantities involved.

To date, the gems I had been passing on were in very manageable lots; the bags were not much bigger than a packet of sugar. Ditto the drugs. After all, I'd only really managed to lure the Chocolate guy and his secretary into the narcotics world with talk of it all being small beer; a nice little earner with no actual risk. I remember telling his secretary that what we'd be doing was nickel and dime stuff, "...too minor league for the authorities to worry about". Now here I was dramatically upping the ante by the odd eight million five and ten cent pieces; and from a few bags of Tate and Lyle to a dirty great big coal sack.

I decided in the end on a plan that, while some considerable way short of cunning, was still one I'm sure Baldrick would have been proud of. "Cross your fingers, say nothing and see what happens".

When they eventually retrieve the car and - assuming the police have indeed become none the wiser and left everything exactly where I'd put it only a few days ago - got around to looking in the boot, they'd find just what they were expecting: some rough diamonds stuffed in the bottom of a golf bag and packets of pink heroin in the well where the spare tyre normally rested. The fact that it would be instantly apparent that the volumes they were staring at were some twenty times what they had been used to handling would not matter. Not to me, anyway. They'd have to do what I was doing: get on with it and sort it out.

Of course the money would be key: even with my Irish base having been compromised, there were diamond bosses and drug barons expecting their cash. Provided the two deliveries were carried out *as per usual*, all would be fine and dandy. The payments would be made in the well-practiced ways through the well-organised channels. But without the goods, nothing particularly usual was going to happen anywhere.

I've no idea what journey the car went on after I'd driven it to the agreed drop off point and left the booty, so to speak, in the boot. That would be the subject of a conversation to be had at some future date. Providing everything was found exactly where and as I'd left things, then the topic could be raised at leisure, perhaps over a brandy after the celebratory meal we'd all no doubt have.

However, if the cupboard was bare, the discussion would need to happen a great deal sooner than that – probably sometime close to three pm tomorrow afternoon.

Chapter 24
Why was his caravan there today?

MAN

    I always feel like somebody's watching me (Michael Jackson)

As the minicab pulled up outside my house, it was a relief to finally see my car in its rightful place on my drive. I hauled myself out of the taxi, waited until she'd driven off, checked my watch and scanned the street. It was just after two and not a soul was in sight. As I approached the front door I spun around quickly as if I was in the middle of a game of frozen statues trying to catch them out. Nothing. I thought, gosh, they're good.

    I had called the Krankies the second Seckie had rung off. I gave them my address – with a bit of luck the sale might have progressed far enough for me not to worry too much about that having been brought into the equation – and the timings for the meeting. I didn't disbelieve for a moment that they'd not come good on their simple promise of, "We'll be there". Whatever happened, they weren't going to let this chance pass them by.

    I then tried some rather pathetic negotiations in a desperate attempt to enhance my equally pathetic position. My plea was simple: surely delivering the Postie sooner rather than later must be worth some extra points and consideration? I received little back other than the reminder that my current state of liberty was significantly greater than I had any right to expect: "Just get on with it, allow us to make the arrest and then we'll talk about what happens next".

To be honest, as I stood on the welcome mat outside my humble abode, I fully expected to be able to see - at least some semblance of - the intrepid undercover team right now. But as I looked out across the grassy area in the middle of our crescent, I couldn't for the life of me spot the cover I assumed they were already under. There are several trees in a sort of horseshoe design around the edge of the pavement standing guard to protect the ring of houses that faced them. But these are too thin and bare to aide even the most slender of hiders: and certainly not a six foot six plus square of a man with a silly green pork-pie hat and his blonde haired midget, Annie Oakley sidekick.

The only real modicum of shelter was my Niggly Neighbour's mini white caravan parked up on the other side of the road. It was unusual seeing it there. I remember the day he'd bought it home from the garage it took him over three hours to negotiate the sharp turn off the road and get it onto his land. I'd gone out to offer a cup of tea. "I thought you might need a break" I said, not able to suppress a snigger. He said his new purchase may be small, but its turning circle is the opposite of tight. "It'll be seven blue moons before I try parking the damn thing here again!" Well, I can only assume we've had six since then because, there it was – back outside his garage.

Actually, I didn't give a monkey's where he stuck it, as long as he didn't chew up the grass verges in the process. Anyway, the sloping drive on which it now stood enabled me to see straight through underneath it: wherever they were camping out, it wasn't there.

I'd run out of options and had started scanning the rooftops when I saw my living room curtains twitch. I hadn't even considered they might be holed up inside. Very clever, these spooks. Where better to catch their prey (about which I suppose I had a passing interest) and protect any harm from happening to me (which role I felt should immediately be railroaded way beyond *passing interest* and become *Consideration Numero Uno*). I suddenly felt calmer than I had been for the past 72 hours and quite reassured by their presence. As I entered the house, I thought the least I could do was make them a cup of tea while we hung around for events to unfold. And maybe I could check things out in the car boot while waiting for the kettle to boil.

Chapter 25

What can you see out of a friend's bedroom window

WIFIE

> In life, the only thing that you can expect,
> is the unexpected (Joan Rivers)

The morning alarm introduced Radio Four's piercing pips into my slumber. It was 7am. My first thoughts, even before the sixth beep had sounded, were about what needed to be done by the time he was due home at 2:00 this afternoon. His secretary had returned to Sue's house last night, so I knew she'd be ready and able to have the car on our drive by noon. It had been tucked up nice, neat and out of sight in my friend's garage for the previous three nights, but today it had to be here and visible well ahead of his arrival.

As I looked out of my bedroom window, across the lawn and towards Sue's house, I began thinking back on how I had arrived at this point in my marriage.

I think the crunch point was the occasion I snatched that glimpse of him *And One Other* in my house the day I was over at Sue's. She had just left for Spain and I was checking all was well and aimlessly peering out of her bedroom window. Although I hadn't actually laid my eyes on the prize, so to speak, I was still pretty sure who *AOO* was. Even so, it took around a fortnight camping out every day in that upstairs room before I caught sight of them returning and could make the positive identification: him with his furtive glances up and down the street as he stepped out of the car – our car; and the hussy who some time ago had dropped off bank papers for me to sign, getting out of the passenger seat. She was carrying what looked like an overnight bag but, I was guessing, it could probably be relabelled an hour and a half holdall.

As things turned out, an eighty-seven minute sack would have covered the deed. He'd had the unwitting decency to close our bedroom curtains, but that's about as much kudos as I was prepared to give him.

He had left early the following morning for a meeting with a buyer from Fortnum's so I knew when I called the office he wouldn't be there. When she answered the phone I simply asked if she had lost an earring, ".....either on that occasion you dropped off those banking papers, or perhaps (I paused for dramatic effect) sometime yesterday?"

I put down the receiver before she'd had a chance to reply. I thought it might take her a few hours to concoct some form of response she could bear to give me face to face: as it transpired, barely 45 minutes had passed before the front doorbell rang.

I'm not totally sure what I'd expected her to say. Mea culpa was a phrase Jake Thackray had a knack for squeezing into his songs, but he was from Yorkshire so often had something to apologise for. No, the tale she started to replay wandered in from so far out of left field it would have surprised both Babe Ruth and Mickey Mantle.

To be fair, she came straight out of the blocks, holding her hands up to having an affair with him. But I didn't have a chance to smell, let alone relish this act of contrition before she'd moved onto the account of the two Belgium twin sisters he'd been working, mainly in shifts, sometimes individually, for the last three months. She was livid and said how dreadful she felt, not only for her but, placing her hand sympathetically on my shoulder, for me as well.

I couldn't help thinking this hadn't made me feel quite as placated as she was probably going for, but she was in full flow so certainly didn't notice my lack of gratitude.

She called him a cheating, conniving so-and-so (I felt she deserved some credit for avoiding the obvious alliteration, so allowed her to continue) and said she'd been mulling over what *we* might do about it all. I let the "we" pass for the moment, not least because I was fascinated with what on earth was going to come next. "It came to me," she said, "that day I drove back to the office with the documents you'd just signed."

I'm guessing at this stage I wasn't wearing the expression of someone who was sharing her line of thinking or giving the impression that I was even coming up hard on the rails, because she added, "The *joint* papers." emphasising the middle word. "He wanted you to sign over your rights to the business, the house you are standing in – and let's not forget your parents' houses in London - so he could sell them from under your nose, pocket the cash and run off into the sunset." I think we both knew she'd deliberately omitted the phrase "together with me" at the end of that sentence, but again, I let that pass. "Of course," she carried on, "while the documents did indeed enable him to do that to you, they also give you the power to do something not dissimilar to him."

This lull in her lecture gave me the chance to catch up. I was now not only well and truly on the same page as her, but three chapters ahead, so the pause wasn't necessary.

All our married life, our money, assets, everything had been held and run jointly. Blimey, we'd actually put both of our names down on the adoption papers for a cat. That's how it was in the beginning when all was fresh and lovely; and was how it had remained even though things had since become stale and ragged. Sure, he managed our finances on a day-to-day basis, but that was for no other reason than he was better at that sort of thing than me. It was just one of the many tasks of everyday chores that we divvied up between us when we started living together. I was cleaning and decorating; he was shopping, ironing and finance. Each job was carried out individually, but they were all for the benefit of us both.

This act of treachery pierced straight through my purse. In that instant, any doubts I may have been harbouring about whether it really was all over between us simply vanished. Any thoughts of perhaps patching things up, gone. And filling these voids was nothing more than the idea of hitting him where it hurt, in his Ted Baker wallet. The fact that this was nothing more than exactly what he was in the middle of trying to do to me just made it feel all the sweeter. The thing now was to move the objective along the bus and into some kind of action.

At this moment, his secretary seemed to pick up on these unspoken words and started putting forward variations on the joint financial arrangement that, until recently, I'd been in. At first I wasn't completely sure where she was heading, but it soon became pretty Tom Cruise *crystal clear* that her plan boiled down to a simple table turn. Instead of him leaving me high and dry by selling and running off with the proceeds of my properties in London, the house we lived in here and the business – I did it to him!

"The two of us are in this situation because of him." She said. "You have the power to pool all your hitherto joint goods into one neat stack. I have the pieces of paper that will enable you to do that. Separately we're like a couple of card sharps who are both holding a couple of aces. As things stand we cancel each other out, but together our hand would beat all comers. I'm happy to slip you my pair, just so long as you agree to let me have half of your pile. United, we can empty the tatty designer billfold of his. What do you say?"

THE HUNTRODDS COINCIDENCES

At first I didn't say very much. Up until now, my anger, annoyance and resentment had been split 50:50 between the two of them. The thought of accepting a spray from the *Prada Candy Eau de Parfum* bottle I was being offered by one half of the perpetrators of my misery was leaving more of a nasty smell than I suspect Meryl Streep ever aimed for. But what could I do?

I needed the documents she held to legitimise my claim and allow me to start playing the game; she needed my signature to release the funds and enable the fruit machine to pay out. Together we could have three sevens. Separately the best we could hope for was a couple of cherries.

"What do you have in mind?" I replied.

That was when I learned it wasn't just the brace of Belgium belles filling his time away from me: he'd also been carrying on elsewhere, but with much more serious and lucrative extra-curriculum activities.

She outlined how the entire process worked; how she'd met some postman or other in Antwerp, and how they'd been smuggling drugs and diamonds across various boarders.

Blimey.

Saving the best for last, she spoke about how we might concoct some sort of plan. The idea was to bring the Powers That Be into play in such a way that my husband would be held fully responsible, while we walked away, suitably enriched and free both from him and any repercussions. The problem was working out just how to achieve this.

Following the formation of this unholy alliance - and in an effort to bring this cunning plan to some form of fruition - we took the opportunity, whenever he was elsewhere, to meet or speak. The ideas we kicked around usually started out sounding pretty good, but almost always ended with at least one of us being arrested. And not once did we concoct a scenario where either of us came away with any money. Over the next few months our conversations remained broadly circuitous, right up, in fact, to her phone call about a week ago.

She said she'd just had a call from her postman chappy who was frantically babbling about the world having gone mad in Ireland. He'd told her the police were everywhere, and he had to get out. He said this was going to be his last delivery; and it was going to be a doozie! No Tanner and Farthing stuff: this would be, well and truly, the Lord Mayor's show to end all Lord Mayor shows. Then he told her he'd be transporting so much more gear than usual that opting for something like behind the cycle sheds, or in a yellow roadside grit bin for the drop wasn't going to work this time. "Perhaps going for a van or SUV might be better." he said.

I told her I didn't see where all this was going or how it was really offering us anything different to the various scenarios we'd been circling all this time, and to so little avail.

Her level of excitement had gone up a notch. "Look." She said. "It sounds like he's about to deliver every last grain of heroin, every last piece of rough diamond, in fact every last egg that he currently owns into our hands. This is his final hurrah and our one remaining chance to get things sorted." she said. "Think. How can we make this work to our advantage? Come on. No idea's too stupid."

We wandered around familiar territory, rehearsing plans long since abandoned. This was mainly because they *were* all too stupid. Very few of them ended with the desired effect of us girls successfully wandering off into the sunset. Those that did all had the downside of us being attacked by a mad and unforgiving mailman, inflicting injuries sufficient to ensure we'd never be able to wander anywhere, ever again.

Almost in desperation, I said "Well, if no idea's too stupid then, why don't we just nick the stuff ourselves?"

I didn't sense my idea had been grasped with any degree of either enthusiasm or, for that matter, understanding, so I tried to elaborate.

"You just need to set things up exactly as you have done on every previous occasion, but this time, with a wrinkle. Play this well and you'll be able to sit back, looking all coy and innocent."

Unfortunately, at that moment, the only vibes I got from her were ones of immodest guilt; and there was still no indication she had begun following my line of thought.

"Look." I said. "The Postman will be in touch with you shortly to sort out details of his drop. Tell him you've gone with his idea of the SUV and give him the usual sort of remote location he'll be comfortable collecting it from. By contrast, the address you suggest he drives it to for the drop off should be some place fairly public; where leaving a parked car raises not even the slightest of eyebrows.

Not for the first time did I then voice how ridiculously convoluted these processes appeared; only to be greeted with the usual response, "I agree, but that's the way it is and it's what we have got to work within. Anyway", she asked, "what's your wrinkle?"

I said, "Once you have everything confirmed with Postie, get onto my husband. Give him the Irish mayhem story and say that the Postman is spooked and has decided to liquidate all of his stocks of drugs and gems in one go and that the amounts of gear involved this time will be big. Explain therefore that the sort of vehicle we need is a large, but try as you might you've run round everywhere but can't find anything suitable. Tell my conniving little runt of a spouse that the only option you can think of at such short notice is to use his beloved BMW X7. He'll balk at that, so you'll need to convince him to go along with it. Perhaps tell him that you will be the one to drive it to the pickup point and that it will be back on his drive, the following morning, full of the gear, ready for him to make contact with the Accountant, as usual."

"I still don't quite see the wrinkle." She said.

I said it was sort of simple. "When we pick up the car, we don't drive it here to my house, where you've told my husband to expect it to be parked. Instead, we let him wake up and find it's not outside, where it should be on the drive. We then just sit back and let him put the felines amongst our feathered chums."

"The Postman will think he's just made a bog standard delivery. He'll no doubt wait, somewhere in the shadows until he sees the vehicle and his goods collected, or in this case, driven away, as per usual. To where, he neither knows nor cares. The fact that he could be being double crossed shouldn't even cross his mind. Nothing untoward has ever happened before and this will all look like business as usual. As far as he is concerned, his part of the process will have been completed. Successfully."

"Indeed, do this right and he won't think anything out of the ordinary will have happened until he finds out the following morning that the car has gone AWOL. That should be about a minute after my husband finally accepts that the vacant space on his driveway he'll have been staring at for ages, is not, in fact, going to be covered with his precious motor. By then, it will have been many hours since I'll have hidden the car someplace secure – I have the keys to a friend's house whose garage we could use to help us make it *vanish*. So long as Pat thinks the SUV was stolen from where he parked it, and you can convince your boss you have no idea why it isn't sitting outside of his house, they will both start panicking. It will be different types of panic, about their own respective side of things, but no matter. Our scene will have been set. Then, in a couple of days, when the moment is right, you arrange for both guys to meet us here, under the pretext of being reunited with the reappearing BMW. Once we have everyone and all incriminating evidence together in the same place, the Girls and Boys in Blue can come in to tidy it all up."

On this point I thought that my friendly Bobby on the beat would be able to assist. He always seems happy to hear anything I have to tell him, though I've often wondered if that's only because he just hasn't had the heart to tell me to get lost. Well, popping this little delicacy onto his plate will not only serve our purposes, it will also reward that compassion. Mental note: sort that out later.

Now I'm not saying that this was the most cast-iron of plans to go with, but it was as best as either of us could come up with. At the very least, it seemed to enable us to get everything pointing in the general direction we wanted things to be heading.

And so it had played out.

She'd taken the oversized SUV and parked it as planned at *wiped.brief.often* and crouched down barely 20 yards away at *open.focal.simple.* It was a well-concealed spot at this little used end of a golf club's car park, in a clutch of unkempt forest sandwiched between the 8th green and the grounds of the Steward's grace and favour cottage. She watched the Postman walk down the club's private road, carrying a hold all in one hand and golf bag over his shoulder. We both later agreed that this was quite a nice touch. He fumbled underneath the rear wheel arch for the keys she'd left resting on the tyre as arranged, pulled open the huge hatchback door and swung the clubs inside.

He removed the carpet revealing the space that, until a few hours earlier, had been filled by the spare Dunlop and carefully emptied the contents of his hand luggage into the recess. He replaced the mat and hurled the empty bag into the woods, falling short of my new found partner in crime's hiding place but still close enough to cause her to duck. By the time she looked up he was already in the driving seat and moments later the car's taillights were all she could see as he made his way back to the main road.

It took him about to half an hour from the moment she'd text me the letters POB to arrive at *third.secret.venues* (I was watching nearby at *forgot.laptop.snack*), but he wasted no time in jumping out of the car and looking around. I saw him casually move towards the rear of the vehicle where he bent down, apparently having dropped something. Within moments, he was back on his feet and striding down the road out of sight.

I waited a good twenty minutes before breaking cover and moving toward the rear of the car. I carried out my own play of bending down in search of something dropped. Coming up with the keys from their brief place of rest, I nipped into the driving seat and opened the glove compartment. There, appropriately enough lay a pair of driving gloves, made of the softest leather and costing as much as any item of clothing Victoria Beckham has even worn. Actually, the retail value was meaningless as they had been thrown in as a free gift from the BMW dealer. Of course it could be that the gloves cost £75,000, and the car was the gratis element. Either way, I'd made sure the size we picked was too small for *his* hands and took to wearing them whenever I was behind the wheel. Once I had pressed shut the dainty poppers etched with the German manufacturer's initials, I slipped the car into *drive* and zoomed off, passing at speed the spot between two parked Brake Brothers vans where the watching Postman stood.

Once on the road I flipped the speed dial button on the steering wheel and, when prompted, articulated, "Phone Shagger" as clearly as I could. His secretary answered my call almost immediately, leaving me no proper opportunity to savour the jokey handle I'd given her earlier that day on the vehicle's phone system. I told her I'd collected the car as planned and she should meet me at Sue's. "Google maps is saying I should be there in about three and three-quarter hours – don't be late!"

Three hours and 47 minutes later (a tractor had slowed things up a bit on the A5) I pulled onto my absent friend's driveway. Seckie had been waiting in her orange Ford Focus and although she'd started opening her door the moment she saw my beast turn into the road, I had the BMW safely tucked up and out of sight in the garage before she'd made it up to the house. I'd already pressed the fob button to close the electronically operated door, and she had to duck to avoid decapitation in order to follow me in. I pushed the button under the dashboard to release the hatch back which smoothly opened upwards causing her to sway for a second time to escape injury.

After such a long drive I was absolutely bursting for the loo and as I dived through the side door leading directly into the house and the nearby downstairs facilities I shouted over my shoulder, "Maybe you should just check the contents of the boot."

I was barely mid flow when she called out, "The rough diamonds are all neatly stashed in a golf bag. I've sorted through them: there must be a quarter of a million pounds' worth".

She yelled again, "And if you think that's a result, the heroin must be worth four or five times that! But it's in loose blocks wrapped in cellophane and sitting in the tyre well, so we'll need a case of some sort."

While I was keen to see what £1,000,000 of Class A looked like, I decided to delay that treat and went in search of a suitable receptacle. I found a tatty old green tartan suitcase under a dressing table in one of the spare bedrooms. Well, I thought, if Sue didn't need it for her Spanish trip then it was probably surplus to requirements and she hopefully wouldn't miss it.

I don't know why, perhaps all the subterfuge was getting to me, but I suddenly felt the urge to don some form of disguise. Nothing leapt out from a quick rifle through the wardrobes, although I did stumble across her vicuna cashmere serape. I had loved it from afar every time I'd seen her wear it. The subtle yet beautiful impala design wandering through the gentlest of weaves made me emerald with envy. However, the moment a Google search revealed Begg & Co retailing equivalent wraps from just under £3,000 was the same instant I decided I could never even hint at wanting to borrow it. Of course, she's currently in Spain and it is so hot there. And I'm sure I read somewhere that cashmere needed to be aired regularly. Anyway, it may not have been quite the *Spies R Us* product I was aiming for, but it would be as good a substitute as David Fairclough ever was for Liverpool.

I took the case downstairs into the garage and glanced over my partner's shoulder. I said, "You sort out transferring the drugs from the boot into bag – I'll get us something to drink."

I nipped into the kitchen and popped the kettle on. She called that we perhaps needed something slightly stronger than tea, so I detoured into the living room. I found an unopened container of limoncello and a half empty bottle of Bombay Sapphire on the floor next to the sideboard and, selecting the latter hunted out a couple of glasses. By the time I'd found where Sue kept the cut glass, ice and slim line tonic, Seckie had appeared at the doorway, suitcase in hand.

She hauled it up onto the sofa and slid open the zip. It was full of what looked like cling film wrapped bricks. "How do you know this stuff is all genuine?" I asked. "For all I know, we might have just cornered the market in yuckie brown sand."

She said this wasn't really the aspect of the business she was involved in. This, she told me in the tone of an aging school mam, was part of my husband's role in proceedings. She thought for a moment then continued, "He always said that the guys – and they were all guys – either side of our involvement in this enterprise did the real checking. If something like sand or mud did suddenly appear where it shouldn't, they would know exactly where the substitution had occurred. And I think he sort of relied on that. Anyway," she said, continuing in the guise of Miss Jean Brody, "what choice do we have? You're not able to verify it, are you?"

She was right, of course, but I still resented the snotty attitude. I responded with my own (somewhat pathetic) "Of course not" and attempted to hide my annoyance behind the Edinburgh crystal as I drained the last drop of Mother's ruin. I gave an involuntary shiver and said, "Just close up the case and get it back in the BMW."

I passed her the keys to the car and Sue's house. "Get home and get some rest." I said. "As soon as your boss wakes up in the morning and discovers his car is not where you told him it would be, he'll be straight on the phone to you. We'll then just need to sit it out, wait until everyone stops running around and choose the right time to start pulling all of our strings and bring everyone together." Nodding towards the fob in her hand I said, "Then you can come back here and collect the car."

With the softest of wraps draped over my shoulders, I left her to close up and began walking the few hundred yards around the corner to my house. I was barely half way down the street when I was overtaken by a blur of orange; an arm protruding from the driver's window and waving farewell.

As I reached the end of the road I realised everything was all but in place and there really was no going back now, even if I'd wanted to.

She phoned me two days later and, even though the only words blurted down the hand set were, "It's now, or never." I knew who it was; and what it must mean.

Of course, that didn't stop me from replying, "My love won't wait.", but that was only because it was but a knee-jerk reaction. During the absence of any reply I calculated that Elvis would probably have been dead over twenty years before she was born so forgave her for not continuing the lyric. I suggested she tell me more, though stopped short of introducing Olivia Newton John into the mix.

In short, it was all set for tomorrow at three. She'd stay overnight at Sue's and drive the car round here in the morning. My husband would arrive around two and the Postman an hour later. I just needed to make sure the police were on hand.

I watched her steer the BMW onto the drive about mid-day as planned, meeting her at the door as she tugged the case inside. I took the keys off her, pushed the auto locking button on the fob, and followed her along the hall. As she took up her position in the kitchen, I placed the keys next to my husband's passport on the sideboard beneath the Samsung Frame TV we'd recently had hung on the wall. I pulled open the curtains and secured them into place behind the vintage shabby chic tie backs we had picked up in an antique market just outside L'ille sur la Sourge in Provence: at a distant time when our marriage was at its peak. I settled down to peering out of the bay window towards the houses opposite, waiting for his minicab to pull up.

Not long later I watched him get out of the taxi and stride up the drive, quickly, purposefully. He looked round a few times as if to check whether he was alone and then, with a swift turn of his key, was inside.

I came away from the curtains and positioned myself on his recliner chair.

The hallway, as my mother-in-law would have described it, was lobbied off so I couldn't see him from where I sat. Of course, that meant he couldn't see me either; nor would he until he'd walked further along the hall. I'd remained silent and hoped, when he eventually caught sight of me, it might take him aback and knock him off guard. As it turned out, this is exactly, and most beautifully, what happened.

I listened as he took off his coat, slung it over the bannister at the foot of the stairs and made towards the kitchen. He stopped abruptly at the open living room door.

"What on earth are you doing in my chair?" he asked.

He'd always been the one to sit in this seat, although I do remember once coming into the room and finding him plonked in *my* usual chair, positioned on the other side of the room with its back to the window. At the time, I'd asked him what was up to. He half smiled, as if he'd amused himself – something he often did – and said, "Nothing, really" and just crossed the floor and returned to his regular place. I'd often thought how strange that was. Not strange with a capital S, but odd nonetheless.

Anyway, the fact I was sitting where I was appeared to throw him. "I've come to talk about the house." I told him. He looked vacant. "Our house" I said. "This house" I clarified, with a stabbing motion of my index finger towards the floor. "What are you planning to do with it?" He still seemed to be at a loss.

When I threw in that, while he was bringing me up to speed on *nous Maison*, he could also outline his plans for the proceeds from my parents' two properties and the business sale, he turned white.

"Cheating on me with other women was bad enough. That you were so rubbish at your attempted covert affairs made those little tawdry escapades laughable and almost bearable. But wandering into grubby territory and plotting to steal every penny we own puts you so far over the line you couldn't see it even with a telescope to your eye. Carrying on with your secretary in our house is one thing, but scheming to leave me out on the street as new owners moved into it and you sail off into the sunset is something very different. So," I said, motioning over my shoulder towards the kitchen, "*we've* decided to turn the tables."

At this point, and on cue, his secretary entered the room, wheeling the tartan suitcase behind her. If he was thrown before, he looked totally bewildered now. The sudden piercing ring of the doorbell at that moment didn't particularly ease his condition, but once we'd got him down off the ceiling, I suggested he better answer that. "It is, after all, your house". (If only for the present, I thought to myself).

Chapter 26
Two tartan bags

POSTMAN
The person who can smile when things go wrong
has thought of someone else they can blame it on (Robert Bloch)

It was nearly 3:00pm. I had been hovering around the end of the road for about 20 minutes, but hadn't seen so much as a soul. Given I was standing next to a cemetery, I found that somewhat reassuring, though not anywhere near as comforting as the sight of the enormous beast of a BMW I'd deposited the diamonds and drugs in three days ago sitting on the drive. I wandered towards it but stopped as I heard a car turn into the street and park up a few doors down. That the driver stayed in her seat made me wary at first, but then I noticed the local taxi company plate screwed to the grill on the front

Other than the sound marking UBER girl's arrival, it was spookily quiet and not only because of the close proximity of the graveyard: there really was no sign of anybody else. With as much nonchalance as I could muster, I tried the latch on the hatchback and attempted a similar level of lack of surprise when I found it unlocked. I peeped in and saw the golf clubs. The kangaroo head cover I'd used for the three wood was lying to one side, separated from its club, but other than that everything seemed to be as I'd left it. A quick fumble in the bag's front pocket told me the diamonds were still in situ. But even a more in depth search under the carpet revealed nothing other than that the spare tyre had been put back in its place.

I wobbled a bit and for no apparent reason looked over my shoulder. I may have left Baltimore behind but, given that heroin with a street value into seven figures had gone missing, the likelihood of repercussions following me here was still pretty high.

I clicked the boot shut, walked up to the door, put my left hand into my coat pocket and my other up towards the bell. At the same time as I stabbed the button with my right index figure, I hooked its counterpart on the other hand around the trigger of my Walther PPK 84mm, 564 gram double action pistol.

Different people like different movies. Some are fans of rom coms; some love everything Quentin Tarantino has done; some drool over the brilliance of the Coen brothers; and some consider *LA Confidential* to be the finest film ever made. There are even some, God forgive them, who rate Dracula pictures above all others. Me, I've always devoured and fawned over anything James Bond, so it was only natural that his gun of choice should be my first pick as well. Of course it having a delivery like a brick through a plate-glass window simply confirmed the suitability of my selection.

Through the funny little frosted bees on the front door's glass panels I saw a figure approach. I recognised him as the Chocolate Dealer I'd had Aisling check out at the beginning of this entire process.

Of course he didn't know me from Adam so, when he opened the door, I decided to help him out with four little words. "Hi. I'm the Postman."

He went an even whiter shade of pale than I'm guessing either Procol or Harum had ever bargained for. When I nodded down towards the bulge in my breast pocket and made plain the firearm was really not the sort of special package he'd want to take delivery of, his last few drops of colour vanished.

When a man just stares at you with somewhat vacant eyes and an open mouth for three or four seconds, that period can seem like a lifetime. I needed to get off the street; he needed to get a jolt. One swift twitch of my left hand did the job. He now saw the full outline of the trusty Walther in my jacket and that it was now pointing somewhere around his midriff. He started walking backwards and, reminiscent of Carter from Downton Abbey, announced, "We're in the living room."

I followed him in and found two women waiting to greet us. One, dressed in some weird outsized African scarf, was a total stranger: I'd have to come back to where she fitted into all this. The other was more familiar, and I instantly recalled the time we first met in a bar in Antwerp. It was there, over a couple of pints of Guinness, that we more or less laid the foundations that have led to us being in this room today.

I seemed to be centre stage, so took advantage. "Two things" I said, nodding in the direction of Impala Lady. "Who's this and what on earth is that doing here?" I'd directed everyone's attention to the large green tartan suitcase standing alone in the middle of the room. It was identical to the bag I'd left in my hotel room only a few hours ago and, while I knew it couldn't be mine, I still had to resist a natural reflex of stooping down to pick it up.

Pashmina girl answered. With a slight jerk of her head towards the frozen gawping man next to me, she said she was his wife, and that this was her house. "As for that", motioning in the direction of the Scottish bag we'd all seem to have encircled like four teenage girls at a disco, "that was exactly the same question we asked my husband when he arrived here about half an hour ago."

Frozen gawping guy had added ashen to the list of possible adjectives that could be pinned on him.

She looked to me and continued her story, "We watched him pull up and park his car on the drive as if it was the most natural thing in the world to do with a vehicle that everyone has been searching for over the last few days. He hauled that case out of the boot and wheeled it into the house with the air of someone returning from a week in the Highlands. My husband is many things: a cheat and a bastard are just two of them. But there's one thing he's not, and that's a good liar. He started saying he'd separated the heroin from the diamonds so that the three of us could run off somewhere together with the lion's share of the illicit cargo, leaving the gems behind in the car for you to be caught with, red-handed. There are a couple of Irish cops outside watching everything and waiting to move in. I've no doubt the bit about me and her," - did I imagine she spat out the word as she referred to the secretary? - "running off into the sunset with him became part of his story for the first time about 20 minutes ago. It was plain on his face when he got here that he hadn't expected to see either of us. I'm guessing he only popped in to pick up his passport," she nodded to the small burgundy booklet on the sideboard next to some keys, "and I'd put money on it that the taxi driver who pulled up outside just before you arrived has my spineless husband's name on her booking sheet - and that she is only expecting to be carrying one passenger, not three. Before you showed up, I thought there were only two people in this room who he was trying to do over. I think you've just increased that number by fifty per cent."

I looked at frozen, gawping, ashen, wide-eyed guy. He seemed to be coming out of his induced coma and, in what I guessed was a voice a few semitones above his normal pitch, suddenly added *Incredulous Man* to his increasing list of monikers.

"This is totally monstrous." He turned and sort of screeched in my direction. "I have no idea what on earth this barking woman is talking about. I've been running around the country like a blue arsed fly trying to sort out what happened to your delivery. I haven't seen my car for over two days and I certainly didn't drive it here: I came here by mini cab. I thought this meeting was all about getting to the bottom of all this nonsense, only to find this pair here spinning some bizarre tale that makes absolutely no sense. And what in heaven's name is this?" He moved across to the suitcase and started kicking it with his foot. "This isn't mine," he said "I've never seen it before in my life."

At this point his secretary chipped in for the first time since I'd arrived. "Well, if you've never seen it before, and your car is outside, how did they both get here? The cab that pulled up empty a few moments ago is the only one we've seen in the street all day."

Turning to me she proceeded to say that after she had spoken with me about the police vehicle pound in Kent, she'd done the same with her boss who told her he would sort out the pickup himself and deliver the car – and its contents – here in time for the meeting. Turning back to him she said, "Barely half an hour ago we watched from the upstairs bedroom as you parked the BMW on the drive. We saw you haul this tasteless piece of luggage out of the boot and into the house. By the time we'd come down it was sat here in the middle of the room; and your keys and passport had appeared over there on the sideboard."

At this point his semitones got higher, and the incredulity had segued into a rant. I had begun to have enough of all this palaver. Pulling Walther out of my pocket and jerking it in the general direction of the bag, I simply said to him, "Open it."

He was clearly shaken and seemed to have lost the ability to make zips work. He was almost babbling now about having no idea how this Scottish valise had made its way into his home, nor what secrets it contained. That mystery was soon revealed as he regained control of his digits and pulled back the metal slider. Four or five of the heroin cuboids I'd carefully wrapped and taken to the golf course barely three days ago fell out onto the floor.

He jumped back as if the bricks he saw were actually red hot and let out an involuntary yelp. His wife leapt towards him and started pounding his back and shrieking. "What are you doing with this sort of stuff and why have you brought it into our house? You're going to get us all killed. What were you thinking of?" She pushed away from him, ran to the window and buried her head in the curtains.

By now I really had had enough of all this. I told her to shut up, get away from the window, sit down and let me think. I motioned to her with a flick of my wrist and was then distracted by a huge blast and shattering of glass as the television on the wall exploded. I stared at the hole in the plaster where moments before the TV had been, but then noticed both women were concentrating on events a few feet below that. I looked down to see the man slumped over the case, his shirt completely covered in blood. The ranting had stopped but his frozen, open-mouthed, ashen and wide-eyed state had remained and for that instant, the three of us left standing in the room did little more than copy his every non-move.

I looked down. I'm guessing that, were this a spaghetti western, *A Fistful of Lasagne*, or whatever, The Man With No Name would be seen staring at a smoking gun and smelling whiffs of cordite. For my part there was the feint smell of some chemical or other that I couldn't quite place, and perhaps a wisp of mist from the tip of the pistol, though I might have just been imagining that. Removing the clip from the gun's handle showed one of the 380 ACP cartridges I'd loaded this morning was missing. I was staring at the two component parts of my pistol when the second explosion and smashing of glass to have filled the air within as many minutes happened. I watched as shards of frosted bees slide past the open living room door, closely followed by three or four characters in dark clothing all yelling at everyone to, "Get down! Get down!"

THE HUNTRODDS COINCIDENCES

In what seemed like slow motion, I looked down to the vacant stare of my erstwhile partner, then across to the shrieking women. Like a pair of synchronised swimmers in perfect unison, both had bowed their heads and covered them with their hands. I dipped my own head to look at my own upturned hands, each one cradling a separate piece of James Bond armoury. Together, they formed the finest handgun in the world. Apart, they were slightly less than useless. I looked back up and in what may have appeared to someone in the audience as a beautifully choreographed movement that any swimmer, synchronised or otherwise, would have been proud, I raised my arms out by my sides, let my knees bend to the floor, and did just exactly what the men and women in dark blue police uniforms were shouting.

Chapter 27

Lucky that caravan's here

PC42

I thought it was ridiculous to have two undercover policemen driving around in a striped tomato (Paul Michael Glaser)

The sign we'd been waiting for was given at 15:22 precisely. The second she appeared at the widow and flicked the curtains we knew the moment had arrived when we could catch everyone involved, not so much red handed as covered in henna from head to toe. This had been some time coming, but I was pretty sure it would prove to have been worth the wait.

I must confess that a month ago, when I was first called down by the duty sergeant to "deal with some batty woman", that this might be nothing more than the latest in a series of wind-ups we'd been playing on each other for the past few weeks. It had started quite harmlessly: He'd forgotten to record some overtime I had put in for, and I had tried to get him back by removing the tubes of ink from every one of the biros on the custody desk. He sort of returned the favour by buying a huge round of drinks for the entire station on my credit card. I felt he took undue umbrage when I said I'd found that a tad petty. He replied. "I'll show you petty." and placed an ad in the local paper advertising my car for sale. This toing and froing had carried on from there. My most recent retaliation; ordering 200 house bricks to be delivered and left on his drive, had been prodding at my conscience as being possibly one step too far so, I was already on the lookout for some form of reprisal when his call came through.

As I ushered the senior citizen into the interview room, I wondered whether I'd misjudged the situation. Here was a calm, obviously educated lady who perhaps genuinely just needed some help from the police. Such thoughts were swiftly banished, however, because no sooner had she sat down than her demeanour changed and what one could only describe as a rant began.

"My street is quiet and respectable, and this sort of thing really shouldn't be tolerated." She'd started quite gently, but soon got into her stride and, just as quickly, picked up the pace. "Instead of handing out parking tickets for leaving one's vehicle on a double yellow line when one is only popping into Waitrose for a moment on a Friday and I can never find a space in the car park for love nor money, the police should be getting to the bottom of this, stamping it out, nipping it in the bud and coming down hard on the person responsible and I want to know what you are going to do about it!"

It took 15 minutes before I had the faintest idea what *it* was.

While we are trained to stay professional at all times, I must confess that my heart sank just a little when I worked out she had been prattling on about a Peeping Tom. She explained, in slightly more detail than strictly necessary for my purposes, that there had been a significant amount of curtain flapping and even binocular glinting coming from a near neighbour's house than is proper, usual, or, for that matter, acceptable in her part of town.

She eased off a bit as we approached the final furlong of her tale, "Now I've not seen the lady who I think owns the house for ages - she may well have gone abroad - but I keep seeing someone peering out of her bedroom window. Lord knows what they're looking at, but they've been doing whatever it is for considerably longer than seems normal."

I knew this could be serious but, we're a long way from Coventry and, with the greatest respect to the woman sitting opposite me, she weren't no Lady Godiva. While I remained less than convinced that this wasn't all being recorded for use at the station Christmas party, without concrete evidence to that effect, I had to play this by the book. I told her to let me have the address where this was all taking place and I would investigate.

More often than not, when a man or woman in blue knocks on a door and asks to come in, the person we've called on reacts with suspicion. I've always found that quite ironic, given that invariably the reason I'm on their doorstep is that it's me who is suspicious about something they might have done. But there was to be no such issue this time.

The woman who answered the door all but wept at the sight of my uniform and dragged me over the threshold without my size twelves so much as touching the floor. Barely had I given her a hint on the reason I was standing in the hallway when she folded her arms, gathered herself, took in a breath and began hurling a series of disjointed and seemingly random pieces of information at me. And once she'd started, she just went on again, on again, on again and on. Again.

Apparently, this wasn't actually her home, she was looking after it for a friend who'd gone to Spain. Her husband was carrying on with his secretary, which was why she was upstairs in the bedroom where you could see straight across into her house in the next street; they have been cavorting in her own bed, "MY OWN BED!" she shouted. There is an Irish Postman and Belgium Wonka Factory guy involved; but thank God I had turned up to help catch them banged to rights and get them thrown out of her boudoir.

To be honest, I had sort of switched off around about the time she'd mentioned Spain.

In my defence, we have these sorts of nonsense tales and accusations brought to us almost every day, and the tirade I'd just been subjected to was more than likely to be but another one of those. The story we hear is often completely without substance, having been prompted by the complainant watching too much of something like late night Danish telly alongside too many bottles of Macon. But there is a process to follow, so I did what I always do in such circumstances. I took out my notebook and began going through the motions of occasionally nodding while scribbling things down (I try to make sure I keep my own biro to hand, rather than having to rely on a police station pen). In an effort to at least give the impression I really am taking this all very seriously, I usually stop every now and then to throw in an, "and what happened then?"

One thing was certain; she certainly wasn't using three or four words when she could tell her story in a couple of thousand. Jake Thackray would have been proud of her.

We reached the stage where stabbing my eyes out with sugar tongs started feeling like an attractive option about ten minutes into this one-way dialogue. However, assessing we were already some distance past the point when many of my contemporaries would have long given in, I decided that now was an acceptable moment for me to call a halt in proceedings and start placating.

I told her I would do everything I could to investigate this further, but she had to understand that for now all we really had to go on was her word. (It felt prudent not to add: and your slightly irrational behaviour with a telescope in a neighbour's house). I continued by saying she must appreciate that my superiors will need proof that her husband is actually involved in any wrongdoing. "It's only once we have some hard evidence that we can delve into things more deeply. But," and I did my level best to say this with as great a degree of sincerity as I could muster, "with your help, we will, I have no doubt, be able to catch him doing whatever it is he's been doing - be that with or without any of his hired employees, or representatives of the postal service - red-handed."

I also told her she should let me know every time she heard something – no matter how insignificant it may seem – about anything, anything at all that she felt was suspicious. Do that, I said, and you can rest assured, I would take things from there.

Placing my card in her hand and bidding her farewell, I left the house fairly confident I'd done a reasonable job shutting down the prospect of having to embark on an unlikely and time-consuming line of enquiry into a wine fuelled Scandinavian fairy tale. With luck, I would never hear from this Scorned Lady ever again.

Of course, I was as wrong as Dick Rowe had been when he closed his office door, turned to his assistant and said, "I think that will be the last time we ever hear of those Beatle chappies."

The first email report from her crow's nest was waiting for me on my pc (it's a laptop actually, but I'm sure IT technicians the world over would forgive a humble policeman the little pun) before I'd even returned to the station. It spoke of Africa and two-seater planes; Greek peninsulas and sleepy customs officials; Irish coves and Belgium confectionary. None of which made any sense, and all of which led me down a fairly obvious path: straight to the delete button. The second and third messages (waste paper bins and Charlton Athletic, respectively) arrived before my morning refs the following day. Both followed their predecessor into the virtual bin.

Over the coming days her communications became less frequent and, thankfully, a little more focussed. I was, however, still far from certain that I had the faintest idea what, if anything, was actually going on. Perhaps I was reaping the benefits of the lack of interest I showed the day I'd first interviewed her. It was becoming plain that we were now a ways on from simple philandering, and while I could feel in my water that some form of movement of illicit substances might be taking place, there was nothing remotely coherent here prompting me to rush past the washrooms and upstairs into the Super's office.

It was three or four days, and five or six further emailed jigsaw pieces, before the mists began to clear. It seems that some sort of smuggling was in fact going on, though her information that the commodities involved were diamonds and drugs sat awkwardly with me. They both begin with the same letter, but other than that, these are not normal bed fellows.

I desperately wanted this case, if indeed that's what this was, to be heading somewhere. Sure, I'd have been happy if it was just a good piece of intel that resulted in getting a few pushers off the streets. But some kind of huge drug bust and gem smuggling exposé could prove to be my ticket into CID. This was the stuff of an aspiring detective's dreams; though wishing rarely makes anything so. From a policing point of view, it hadn't been hard keeping this potential "crime of the century" to myself. And, despite my optimism, I was still someway off believing I could ever convince anyone there was anything here that merited further investigation. I needed something solid I could take into the Boss's room that he'd be able to hang his helmet on.

A few weeks after I'd first visited paranoid peeping woman at her friend's house, she phoned me. It was the first time since we'd met that she had contacted me direct. Whether it was her animated voice, or my desperation for her to come up with something concrete for me to grab hold of, I don't know, but within minutes it felt like sometime soon I might be presenting my superiors with one of the world's most desirable hat stands.

It seemed as if delivery of a massive pile of rough diamonds and huge mounds of heroin was about to take place. Something weird, by which I mean I didn't really understand what, had happened in Ireland; and whatever it was had resulted in every hare in the Emerald Isle running in whatever direction came to them first. Details were sketchy, but she outlined them as best she could and promised to get back to me with answers to the myriad of questions I threw at her.

"In the meantime," I said, "I think it's time for me to call at your house and have a little word with your husband. Don't worry; I'll come up with an excuse totally innocuous and unrelated to all this." I told her that making such a surprise appearance often plays havoc with the perpetrator's mind: it makes them question things that aren't actually there to be questioned and can lead to them making silly mistakes. "Nothing lost if nothing comes of it," I tried to reassure her, "but it might just be worth a go."

I said I'd pop round in the morning, towards the end of my night shift, a little after six. "Probably best if you're not there; that'll give me a clear, undistracted run at him."

As things turned out, (I was waylaid sorting out a domestic issue three streets away involving two banjos and a rather stunned tortoise) I didn't get there until 6:15. He was alone when I called, and whether or not it was down to my unexpected visit, he certainly seemed rattled about something. He struck me at first as being very distant; continuously looking over my shoulder as if in search of someone, or something.

I thought it a good idea to use part of the story that had kick started this investigation as my excuse for bothering him. I mentioned we'd had a report of a Peeping Tom in one of the houses in the next street overlooking his rear garden and asked if he had seen anything?

I wasn't totally concentrating on his reply, although it did have something to do with jumping onto the top of his wardrobe and needing to borrow some binoculars. What is it in this family about that they have the need to magnify everything? Anyway, I left feeling that Mission: *set-a-few-hares-running* had been successfully carried out, though, even if I say so myself, I think going back and ringing his bell a second time under the pretext of leaving my contact details was particularly inspired. Even if it had no effect at all, I still enjoyed it.

I went off duty and heard nothing further until the next day when I was back behind my desk typing up my own overtime sheet. The phone rang: it was Mata Hari with some specifics of what was going down. (Her words, not mine). "If all goes to schedule," she said, "around three o'clock tomorrow afternoon, everyone and everything to do with this caper [had I wandered into 1930s Chicago?] will be here, in my house. You just need to be on hand, ready to do whatever you need to do to stop all this nonsense and let me get on with my life."

The surge of euphoria I felt at that moment was immense – and not just because a crime might be solved and serious drug and diamond smugglers may be put behind bars. No, let's be honest, there must be room for shallowness as well. I could suddenly see my name being etched on the CID personnel board; my uniform being moth balled; engineers installing the detachable blue flashing light and siren in my car; and, of course, the look of amazement on Custody Sergeant Prank's face.

However, I temporarily stopped my cup from running over as I pondered two issues that required some immediate attention: one, the thing I had been putting off since this whole escapade began namely getting authorisation to actually investigate this "crime"; and the other, a brand new spanner Mata had literally only just thrown into my works. It seems a couple of Irish coppers had visited her this morning and wanted to meet me.

First of all, I needed to get my Superintendent on side. I marched boldly into his inner sanctum and gave him prologue, chapter, sentence and verse of the covert investigation I'd been running for this past month. His initial reaction wasn't quite as positive as I had imagined. He did not jump out of his chair, dance around his office, kiss me on both cheeks, embrace me as a long lost son or thank me for the prospect of boosting his command's flagging conviction rates. No. Instead he seemed determined to dwell on the fact that he was only just hearing about all this at the 13th hour. His rebuke was delivered from a sedentary position.

But at least he didn't throw me out and, after much consideration and, as he mentioned many times, against his better judgement, he declared I could lead an undercover investigation into all this. As if realising I was about to launch into my own form of tribal celebratory dance around his office, he stressed that granting me this *Leader of the Pack* role was little to do with his confidence that I was the police officer most likely to bring everything to a successful conclusion. It was more due to the fact that a flu epidemic had laid low almost all the station's detectives. As if to ensure that absolutely no trace of wind should remain in my sail, he said, "It's not that you're any good; there just isn't enough time to get anyone else up to speed. You can have four constables to assist, but there would be no asking the duty sergeant for any overtime." I resisted mentioning what a total waste of time that would be anyway and departed his office thinking he might want to work on his confidence building skills a bit. That thought soon left me though: I had been given the gig. Hurdle number one - hurdled. Now, if only my other difficulty could be resolved as easily.

I rounded up my four secondees and together we drove down to Ms Hari's house. The initial plan was to see the lie of the land and consider what preparations were needed for my stakeout of the next day's meeting. However, before being able to make any progress on those fronts, I had to deal with the problem of what to do with the couple of undercover cops with the Irish Gardaí who had appeared on the scene.

Apparently these two had been pursuing this case for ages and intended to be in on the kill alongside me. And it soon became clear that the idea of them working alongside me was little more than a figment of my own imagination; they didn't think me or my team had any role to play in this at all!

Our get together outside my contact's house started fairly cordially, although the balance of our conversation soon became somewhat skewed. I think I said something like, "Hello, I'm PC 42. Nice to meet you". This piece of information doesn't normally attract a great deal of negative response, but half an hour later I was still listening to the reply.

Neither I, nor the diminutive azure eyed female standing in the shadow of her huge, green bonneted partner, spoke a word as he took me down the Liffey, along the Shannon, off to Antwerp and back over to the east Yorkshire coast, all by way of explanation as to how the two of them had ended up in this neck of the woods. Now, all this background information, establishing how he, us, they, in fact everyone involved in this caper had come to be here, was interesting and, indeed, may one day serve well as the basis of a story for an excellent book. At this precise moment, however, it was more gloss than substance. I told him I already had all the information I needed to do the job I was here to do: catch and arrest the people involved in smuggling drugs and diamonds into the country. Of course the second I got these words in edgeways was the exact point this Anglo-Irish Treaty I had been subtly trying to forge was derailed and the troubles really began. "That," he yelled, "is exactly what we are here to do. And no *Bobby-in-blue come lately* is going to take this collar away from us!"

A few more valiant attempts to resolve matters were made, but to no avail. At one stage, in desperation and an attempt to introduce some levity into the situation, I suggested we could just try to do everything my way as I was here first!

We were getting nowhere.

The saving grace that popped along to, well, save us, was the eventual realisation, all round, that if everyone just kept sticking their heals in, nothing would end up sorted. And so, in an effort to stop any further laps around the houses, both sides tentatively agreed to put *the Treaty* back on the table and to at least try to join forces. The niceties could be sorted out once we had the nasties in custody.

I think I managed to move things along with the suggestion we needed to sort out from where we might best manage our "joint" operation. There were two of them and five of us. Clearly we all needed somewhere to sit, wait, and monitor.

The street was shaped like an elongated letter U, with identical four up/four down homes around the outside and a grassy area with a few trees in the middle. Number 7 over the road seemed the property of choice with an ideal line of sight across the green to Lady Peeper's abode. I was just wondering where we might all secrete ourselves when a white caravan honed into view. It looked as if the driver was Seven's owner as he started reversing the vehicle onto its driveway. Twenty minutes - and an extraordinary amount of toing and froing – later, he was still trying to complete this task.

Although his constant manoeuvrings were quite annoying, they didn't deflect me from the thought that this could be exactly the sort of thing I was looking for as our observation post. It was in the perfect position to keep tabs on the meeting due to take place the following afternoon, or, at least it would be once he had stopped faffing around and got it parked.

Once he'd eventually come to rest, I wandered over with a view to try and secure the caravan's occupation rights. I tried to break the ice by asking if, after all this effort, he might like a cup of tea. While that didn't go down quite as well as I thought it might, I did manage to get him back on side with mention of his chance to assist the police in closing a case involving the house opposite.

Almost immediately, he agreed to help. This was clearly either a very public-spirited person, or a blighted neighbour who hated the people across the road and was happy to be involved in anything likely to result in their comeuppance. However, whatever his motivation, negotiations stalled the moment the emerald *titfer* wearer involved himself – and it was soon clear that a three-way wrangle was not going to get us anywhere.

In the end it was slightly ironic that I should lose the debate because of the strength of my force verses theirs; or rather our respective numbers. As ideal as the site on which the caravan now stood was for a lookout, its size was somewhat of a problem. I'm guessing it could best be described as whatever the Americans would call the direct opposite of a Winnebago. It was a Honda Jazz to a Humber Super Snipe; a Mini to a Cortina. I'd never heard of a *Go-Pod* before and, with its proud owner from No 7 standing before it, I wasn't going to say anything derogatory. However, it was perhaps the smallest of attachments one might ever consider bolting onto a tow bar and driving off with while still maintaining a straight face or a modicum of pride. There was barely room inside for Hat Guy and his mute chum; the five of us would have no chance. So, we left the Celtic couple to settle into their cubby hole while Mr and Mrs Seven showed me and my intrepid quartet upstairs to their front bedroom with its panoramic view.

The Hudson Plan, so named because they would be downstairs to our up, demanded we were all in our places by noon; well before the arrival of our key protagonists was expected. We'd wait, counting them all in and, with due deference to Brian Hanrahan, hopefully do likewise as we assisted them on their way out. The signal would be the appearance of the Mistress of the house at the window and a shake of her drapes.

That was yesterday. Now, here we all were in situ, pent up like coiled springs. I'd left Little and Large to play Carry On Camping, while me and my trusty quartet retired to our upstairs lookout position. Everyone was waiting, straining whatever sinews they had in concentration, staring across the road; impatient to be triggered into action by the sight of a warmly wrapped lady at the living room curtains.

I'd rung my woman the moment we were all settled. She'd arrived home the night before and had slept well. As we spoke, I watched her appear across the street at the upstairs bedroom window, cradling the phone in one hand and giving me a vague thumbs up with the other.

Around midday, we saw the huge BMW sweep onto the drive. As if by magic, the boot flew open, and the driver got out: it was the Chocolate Man's Secretary. She went round the back of the car, hauled out a large tartan case and dragged it into the house. I'd not seen her before but knew she must be the third person in *a crowded relationship*, as it had once been described to me - at length!

It wasn't long before a taxi pulled up and the two women were joined inside by the one character missing from their ménage. Barely 20 minutes later, the last guest on the invitation list; a tall, slim, red-haired man with tattoos on his hands, walked into the street, up the driveway opposite and, after raking around in the boot of the BMW and what looked like a bit of faffing about with his coat pockets, was let in through the front door.

As we sat there waiting for the signal, I fixated on our Irish brother and sister in arms, cooped up in the caravan below. I couldn't stop thinking that the second they saw the curtains twitch their positional advantage would give them such a head start on us they'd be across the road and into the house before we'd even made it out of our bedroom and onto the landing.

As I played out the scene and watched my chance of entry into the CID vanish before me, my eyes refocused and settled on two oak fence posts lying on the ground below caravan's door. It looked as if Mr & Mrs S had put them there for use as steps. Suddenly, I had an idea. I dashed downstairs, crept outside and, grateful for the lack of any gravel on the pathway, heaved one of the pillars upright and wedged it into place beneath the *Go-Pod's* door handle. I was just reinforcing my makeshift lock cum barricade with the second post when my four comrades in blue rushed out from their hide and onto the street. I followed instinctively, and looking up, spotted the lady of the house opposite moving away from the window.

Within seconds we had crossed the street and were just running through the front gate when we heard an explosion and crashing of glass coming from inside the property.

My two MPCs were in the lead, side by side, closely pursued by the brace of WPCs, with me bringing up the rear. The three of us in the rear hardly had to break step as our burly vanguards hurled themselves at the front door. The wooden frame splintered into a thousand toothpicks, and the glass panels shattered into as many pieces as we ran unchecked into the house. We'd made it along the hall in double quick time but were suddenly stopped in our tracks. My boys appeared rooted to the spot, unable to comprehend the scene before them: the blood-stained shirt of the man lying on his back in the middle of the room; a ginger Christ-like figure kneeling by his side; and two women cowering on their left. My girls suffered no such hesitation and, before their male colleagues managed to shake themselves out of their trance, had the auburn deity pinned up against the windowsill with his hands cuffed behind him.

I crossed the floor, went through the motions of checking the prone guy for a pulse, and was staggered to find one. I yelled at battering ram Number One to get an ambulance and for Number Two to sort out a Maria (either colour would do).

I looked to the lady of the house. She stood up and said, "The diamonds are in the golf bag in the car's boot;" and, nodding across the room, "the drugs are in the suitcase."

The sounds of sirens interrupted any further intelligence gathering and soon the paramedics were among us doing their best for the poor guy on the floor. Whether it was tending to his wounds or considering giving him his last rites, I couldn't be sure. But they lifted him onto a gurney and carried him out without a sheet over his face, so I'm guessing he had at least a few more moments available to think on what had gone on this afternoon.

The Maria (white, as it happens) had arrived hard on the heels of its sister emergency service and Handcuffed Man was duly frogmarched into it.

I looked across to the wife of the prone chap who had just been stretchered out and mouthed, thank you. Then I turned to the Secretary and, in a somewhat sterner tone, said, "I hope you going to come along quietly, young lady"

Chapter 28

The driving gloves were no coincidence

SECKIE
Sin will take you farther than you ever expected to go; and will cost
you more than you ever expected to pay (Kay Arthur)

Ten words that came out of nowhere: I hope you going to come
along quietly, young lady.

Where on earth was he suggesting we went? We'd just gift
wrapped, stamped and delivered a couple of serious smugglers into
his hands: I was actually waiting for him and his chums to leave
so that me and my partner in solving crime could do some proper
celebrating and gloating.

I looked across to the woman I was in this with together. The
bewilderment on my face was met with a smirk on hers, suggesting
things weren't panning out quite as I had expected.

For sure, I'd been riding a canny, some might say dangerous race
with feet in a couple of different stables, but it seemed worth the risk.
Certainly, early on in this escapade, when *he* and I were so far out in
front, galloping freely, it was inconceivable that the two of us would
end saddled up anywhere other than together. Still, a girl needs to

protect herself in case the unimaginable does happen: and just as well I did, or so I thought at the time.

The call from the travel agent confirmed my fear (inkling?) that *his* plans did not include me and I was about to be cut loose. I felt confident, however, that the groundwork I had prepared with his wife would enable me to turn the tables, switch horses and still ride off into the sunset.

It didn't cross my mind for a second that *she* had another steed lined up and I might be left hung out to dry by her as well. Of course, once the penny started dropping it took less than a nanosecond to realise the recent chummy-chummy-pally interaction she'd developed between us during the build-up to this moment, had all been a show. And that her real focus had been on two things: to get her husband off her hands; and all the money into hers – and hers alone. I'm guessing she reasoned that if, along the way, she could also vent a touch of scorn in my direction, then all well and good.

So, she had undone the ties I'd thought we had in place between us and, in a slight of hand intended to sell me completely down the river, neatly attached the severed ends to the two guys who had just been escorted out of the room. She seemed to be sitting pretty. Smug and pretty.

The man in blue began to cross the floor towards me. I appeared to have very few things going my way, but felt there must still be something I could do about this - even if it was only to mitigate my own circumstances and drag *her* into the mire with me. She and I had joined forces. I may have been involved in all this much longer than her, but we had an arrangement; a plan. Surely it wouldn't take too much digging to find her paw marks over this entire mess just as much as mine were. Whatever she was doing to me, I should be able to return the favour. In any event, I had an arrangement with the Irish police in charge of this sting.

THE HUNTRODDS COINCIDENCES

After her husband's frantic call from *The Magpie*, I knew I couldn't rely on him to secure me a good deal, so I spoke with them direct. Actually, I felt girl to girl was my best bet, so gave just the gentler half of their duo a ring.

"As long as we get the drugs," she said in an accent quite some distance away from where anyone called Aisling O'Toole should hail from, "we'll see you right - or as right as we can." She explained, almost apologetically, that the Belgians were in control of the diamond side of this caper and, out of all the Europeans, they are the ones least likely to do anyone any favours. "But I'll do my best and make sure my partner will as well. Help us shut down this heroin racket and we'll see you right (she said, for a second time). You can trust us."

Well, not being blessed with a plethora of options, I went along with what they wanted. I got everyone together; made sure they were "invited" to the party; and.......talking of the Irish, where the hell are they? I still had a sense that they would be true to their word and, *see me right*, but, before they could do either the *seeing*, or the *righting*, they had to be here!

I scanned the room, as if hoping to find that the tall green hatted man and his short, blue eyed, platinum blonde sidekick had been standing in the corner all along. But of course they weren't; nor did it seem that they were about to appear anytime soon, let alone *see me right*. And as for *her* paws being all over everything; thinking back, I began to wonder if that was actually going to be the case.

What was her involvement with the car? She owned it, so her DNA will be all over it, but then, mine will be too. I'm the one who the police will have seen drive it here today. Also, now I come to think of it, she wasn't particularly *hands on* as far as any of the merchandise itself was concerned.

The smuggled diamonds in a golf bag in the boot. "Maybe you should just check the contents of the boot." she said. Everything's covered in my prints, not hers.

The heroin bricks in the tartan case I'd packed. "You sort out the transfer of the drugs from the boot into bag – I'll get us something to drink." she said. Everything's covered in my prints, not hers.

As to the case itself, the cops saw me drag it into the house. She had her driving gloves on when she brought it to me in the garage. Everything's covered in my prints, not hers.

The policeman who had begun unclipping the pair of handcuffs from his utility belt as he moved closer towards me had clearly been led by her. I started to imagine the tale of events she'd have given him along the way; about how the smuggled goods were arriving in Ireland – and how I was involved. How they made the journey across the Irish Sea – and how I was involved. How the transfer of goods and the subsequent payoffs were made – and how I was involved. How, once across the channel, the diamonds went south to Antwerp and the drugs north to Amsterdam – and how I was involved. How all this time, she'd had nothing to do with any of it other than being a woman scorned – and how I was certainly involved in that.

She was as clean as all the incriminating evidence was of her fingerprints. She would walk away from this with her finances as neatly separated from her husband as she herself would be, irrespective of whether or not he lived.

I felt the bitter touch of metal around my wrists and a slight pull on my arm. I realised, as I was being led along the hall and into the waiting van outside, that she had, just as neatly, separated herself from me as well.

Chapter 29

One blue hat, one brown coat, one green hat, one red car

VLAD

> Come freely, go safely and leave something
> of the happiness you bring (Bram Stoker)

The moment I had registered he'd turned left out of the restaurant towards the bridge, I instinctively went in the opposite direction. Equally instinctively, my faltering walk soon morphed into a full pelt sprint, the likes of which I hadn't done since my final term at Ramsden Comprehensive. Alan Llamas had just hospital passed me a ball in the traditional end-of-year School verses Masters rugby match, and Mr Griffiths had me in his sights. Our Welsh chemistry teacher had never really liked me: probably with some justification as my friend, Tim Fisher and I had spent most of the year in his class trying to sneak the largest item we could out of the lab undetected. I won with a three-foot burette stuffed down one of my trouser legs. I don't think Old Man Griffiths ever saw the funny side and in that spilt second I knew that unless I started going hell for leather, I'd be on the receiving end of 17 stones of pent up retribution.

Dismissing the Welsh Alfred Nobel from my mind, I concentrated on leaving Hadleys as far behind and as quickly as I could. After what seemed an age I saw a yellow light shining bright on top of an equally shiny and yellow vehicle travelling towards me: I'm not sure if I simply stuck out my arm, or actually jumped in the taxi's path but, either way, it stopped and I bundled myself in, crouching as low down on the floor as possible. I had dived into his cab with such drama I'm sure the driver must have been expecting me to shout something along the lines of, *follow that car*. I sensed his disappointment when instead I quietly asked to be taken to the Melrose Guest House. After a few hundred yards I risked raising my head and, Chad like, took a peep out of the window. I had a momentary seizure when I realised the route we were taking simply retraced the path I'd just run along, and we were now passing by Hadley's restaurant. I froze, but was shocked back to life by an enormous blast on the taxi's horn as my driver slammed on his breaks to avoid squashing a short blonde haired woman and young lad who'd walked out in front of us. He'd missed them, but clearly it had been a close call. He was shouting some abuse but, I suppose, seeing all was well, continued on over the bridge. As we left them behind, I watched as she grabbed the boy's shoulders and caught her piercing blue eyes staring straight at me, or at least the bit of me from the nose upwards that she could see.

When we reached my lodgings in Argyle Road, I dashed up to my room and bolted the door, leaning up against it for good measure. And there I stayed until the next morning.

Time, motion, breakfast and an absence of strange men or women following you into your chamber to shoot you are great healers. So, as I watched the sun rise and begin bouncing off the ripples on the North Sea, I felt composed enough to try to make a break for it out of town.

THE HUNTRODDS COINCIDENCES

I needed some flexibility for this next leg of my journey, so asked Reception to sort me out a hire car. I was a tad disappointed with the selection I was offered – if you can call just two options a selection, but she said given it was at such short notice, and for immediate departure, it was the best she could do. The American retro vehicle would have been some way from my first choice – and certainly not a red one – but it was preferable to the rather more cramped Fiat 500 alternative, so I went for the PT Cruiser.

Despite the annoying twang of the satnav's voice, I persevered and within a few hours it had navigated me successfully to a long planned highlight of my trip: the road in which stood the country retreat Abraham Stoker reputedly penned much of his work.

There were quite a few cars in the street causing a mini traffic jam, so I parked up and decided to have a wander round on foot. A sprinkling of rain had begun to fall on the windscreen and, momentarily forgetting I was in a leased vehicle, looked over my shoulder for the umbrella I kept in my own car for emergencies. Of course, it wasn't there, but in its stead, half tucked down between the squab and the door, was a blue baseball cap. I hadn't noticed it before but still, any port, or in this case, hat, in a storm so I pulled it on for some modest protection against the elements.

I sauntered up the street, sweeping the tail of my old sepia Inverness cape around in what I thought might look a dramatic, if not mysterious fashion, looking for AS's old abode at number sixteen. This had the feel of a somewhat pretentious estate where the residents obviously considered the time-honoured way of distinguishing one's house from every other just made things too simple for the humble mailman or milk-woman. Instead of any numerical distraction, they all had humorous names. I walked passed Susie's Bushygap, Sodom Hall, and Dicks Mount Cottage without so much as a titter and was trying to work out how Windy Bottom fitted into all this, when I was stopped in my tracks. An arm had appeared from nowhere and placed across my chest; a police officer was asking me to wait there for a moment.

I glanced up, but in doing so almost passed out. Not because I'd looked up too quickly, or had a rush of blood to the head; nor was there any queasiness prompted by the fact that someone with blood-stained clothes was being wheeled out in front of me by a couple of paramedics. No, my momentary seizure had come about as I stared down at the injured chap on the trolley. I recognised him immediately as the deranged stranger who, less than twenty-four hours ago, and from a distance of over two hundred and fifty miles from this spot, had all but threatened to kill me.

The medics were clearly keen to get him to their van so our eyes were only locked for a split second, although, just before the gurney was hoisted up and away from view, I'm sure I caught him mouthing something about dog shit.

The doors to the ambulance had barely been slammed shut when something else emerged from Windy Bottom: another man. While this one was upright and appeared more than able to walk under his own steam, he was, nevertheless being assisted by a couple of police women: one either side. As he climbed the steps and disappeared into the waiting White Maria, I turned, just in time to see yet another person being accompanied out of the house. She was slight, young and attractive and gave the air of someone not at all fazed by the fact that it seemed to have been deemed necessary for three burly policemen to all be involved in the accompanying.

The arm blocking my way was being lowered, although I felt no urge to move. After all these comings and goings, an odd sort of calm had filled the surrounding space. These last few minutes had offered up many things to ponder, but none of them seemed to have the strength to bounce the vision from my mind of the threatening man from Whitby, nor his bewildered stare as he was being transported away. Indeed, it took some rhythmic thudding somewhere in the distance to bring me back to the present. The ambulance and police van had left the scene and cleared my line of sight to the other side of the street. The sound seemed to be coming from a small, white caravan parked in a drive opposite, which was shaking as if in the middle of an earthquake. I wandered over towards it to investigate.

With the onset of dusk the dipping sun was reflecting on the oblong window, making it difficult to see, although I could just make out two figures inside shouting and banging their fists.

The one on the right was a gigantic man. He was so tall that I could only see him from his nose down: the top half of his head disappearing above the window and into the roof of the vehicle. He was obviously agitated about something but, while the caravan looked more like a purchase you'd make from B&M rather than Harrods, the manufacturers had clearly spared no expense on the double glazing because I couldn't make out a word that was being yelled. Even the man's ferocious attempts to bang on the pane sounded muffled, although that might in part be due to the green cloth wrapped around his fist. As my eyes began to get accustomed to the light, I could see the emerald material was actually a hat reminiscent of one I saw only yesterday, belonging to a dozing punter hunched down in the corner of a chip shop.

By contrast, the person next to him in the caravan was slight and small: so small, in fact, that only the top part of her blonde head, from her nose upwards, was visible. She also looked familiar, although I couldn't immediately work out where I might have seen her before. While I was wrestling with that vague memory, she must have registered someone was outside. The moment I caught those strong blue eyes as she turned to face me, I placed her instantly as the startled woman my taxi had nearly put an end to only the day before.

To the side of the vehicle, I noticed a couple of fence posts propped up against the door, jamming it shut.

I half moved towards it, glancing over my shoulder as I did so. At first I thought the boys and girls in blue milling around Windy Bottom's entrance seemed totally uninterested. I wasn't sure they were even aware I was here. Then one of them broke away and, looking over in my direction, motioned me away with one hand, while covering his lips with the index finger of the other.

I glanced at the officer's lapel and decided taking the hint from PC 42 might be a wise move. So, I returned to the hire car and drove off into the night, wondering if Mr Stoker would have sanctioned such an ending.

THE END

JP MAJOR

About the author

As a boy, JP Major appeared in Oliver! [2nd urchin and understudy to The Artful Dodger] at the Theatre Royal, Drury Lane; and two feature films, A Hard Day's Night [Boy in crowd] and Help! [High Priestess's train bearer]. Much in line with popular demand he turned his back on acting to pursue a career in sports, playing scrum half for England boys (under 18) at Twickenham against a side from Ko Samui; and cricket for Kent's second eleven. In later years he studied creative pottery; it has been said his work inspired Grayson Perry's Turner Prize success. He did a number of impromptu duets with Jake Thackray in the 1980s and could often be found busking in Covent Garden. On one occasion, he was recorded playing alongside Paul McCartney outside the tube station for a scene [edited out] for the ex-Beatles' rock film, *Give my regards to Broad Street*.

He dreams a lot.

- Not really my sense of humour. **Oliver Cromwell**
- The plot was a little bit too complex for me. **Joseph Heller**
- Much more sex than I was expecting. **Barbara Cartland**
- The twists in the tale were far from believable. **Agatha Christie**
- Once I'd started reading, I found it hard to put down. **Edward Scissorhands**

Printed in Great Britain
by Amazon